BROKEN PIECES OF GOD

DAVID B. SEABURN

Black Rose Writing | Texas

ISBN: 978-1-68433-764-4
PUBLISHED BY BLACK ROSE WRITING
www.blackrosewriting.com

Printed in the United States of America
Suggested Retail Price (SRP) $19.95

Broken Pieces of God is printed in Book Antiqua

*As a planet-friendly publisher, Black Rose Writing does its best to eliminate unnecessary waste to reduce paper usage and energy costs, while never compromising the reading experience. As a result, the final word count vs. page count may not meet common expectations.

For Our Grandchildren
Gianna, Makayla, Jude and Abel

BROKEN PIECES
OF GOD

CHAPTER 1

The first week off was fine. He fairly flew out of bed each morning, as if he were on vacation, eager to get at the day. He'd brew coffee, read the paper, check the weather forecast, shovel the snow, warm the cars, do the grocery shopping. But after ten days, his once scintillating routine had become drab and lifeless, mirroring his mood.

By then Eddy Kimes was struggling each morning to find an adequate reason to leave the shelter of his cocoon-ish bed. How deliciously soft the mattress was, how sauna-like the comforter. Was it possible that the sheets were lined with an invisible adhesive? So difficult it had become to throw them off, to sit on the edge of the bed and then stand on what felt like a ledge, to face a new day. Now Gayle was the first one up each morning, something that had never happened before. With all that was going on, bed was the last place she wanted to be.

Eddy's normal routine was to rise at 5:30am to be at work by 7:00am even though he didn't need to be there until nine. It was the best way to stay on top of things, to make sure his crew was ready to go. You could never tell what might happen and when. An outage somewhere. A storm coming. Pole down from a drunk driver. Always something.

Eddy sat on his bed for several minutes watching the curtains wave in the breeze. Spring was struggling to arrive; the air was still so cold it could have been the dead of winter. Eddy got up, made the bed, showered and finally started to wake up. The house was quiet. He wondered how, or if, Gayle had slept.

He looked in the mirror at his morning shadow and decided he didn't need to shave today. By dinner he'd look like a fading boxer — pug nose, square teeth, puffy eyes and a dark veil across his jaw. He'd like to grow a beard but Gayle thought it would make him look pudgier. Not pudgy, but pudgier. He leaned closer. He had extra face on every side.

Eddy got dressed, a pair of fire hose work pants, a black T and a flannel shirt.

He had forgotten that Gayle had early appointments. He didn't like having strangers in the house when he was still waking up, but like she said, "Tax season is tax season; we need every penny." Truer now than before. Gayle was a hard worker. And a good wife.

Coffee was brewed. He stood in the kitchen admiring March. There was snow in the far corner of the back yard where sunlight couldn't reach. The garden was thawing. No buds on the trees, but there were daffodils and tulips showing. A wedge of geese overhead, a reticulated woodpecker working the oak, some wrens at the feeder. The sky was blue. Nevertheless, they could easily get ten inches of snow that night. March in western New York.

The door to Gayle's office was closed. Eddy could hear murmurs inside so he knocked and stuck his head in. Jesse Gordon sat across the table from Gayle.

"Hey, Eddy, how's it going?" Jesse owned a string of gas stations.

"Good. You?"

"I'll know in about an hour." He smiled broadly. "I don't know what I'd do without Gayle here. And I'm not alone." He winked.

"C'mon now." Gayle was hunched over her computer, a legal pad beside her, tax forms stacked all around.

Jesse turned sideways in his chair. "Any final news on Universal and Scope?"

"Nothing," said Eddy.

"What a mess?"

"How's the gas business?"

"Prices are holding. Never can tell, though."

Gayle looked up from her work. Her face was sallow. She smiled. "Morning, honey. How's it going?"

Her back now to Jesse, her smile turned into a grimace. "Fine."

"Can I get you something? Tea, maybe?"

She stuck out her tongue. "No thanks."

"How about—"

"Nothing, really." Their eyes locked for a moment.

"Okay. I'm going for a walk. I've got my phone if you need anything. From the store or whatever."

Jesse shifted in his seat, eager to get back to his refunds.

Eddy stood on the front porch for several minutes. White clouds with smoky bottoms had arrived from the west. He breathed deep as a bellows. As the sun emerged from behind a cloud, he could feel a hint of warmth on his face. He unzipped his jacket. Another deep breath and he headed down the sidewalk.

Caroline Kerrigan was digging near her front porch. She wore baggy sweats and a hoody. And gardening knee pads. Her gray hair was tied in a red checked kerchief.

"Getting started already," said Eddy.

She got up on her hands and knees and then sat back on her heels. "You're still alive, I see. I don't think I've seen you since December."

"Decided to come out."

She got up and met him at the fence.

"We're like groundhogs, aren't we?"

"How was winter?"

"The kids came home for the holidays. Then they went back. We've been waiting for spring ever since."

"Yep."

"And you? How are you doing?" She leaned on the fence post. "How's Gayle?"

"Busy with taxes."

"Nothing stops that girl." Caroline leaned across the fence. "I think that's good."

Caroline's face had a pliable quality. Her smile could spread ear to ear, eyebrows up to her hairline. Or it could get small and closed down, eyes narrow and lips curled at the corners, held in place by her ample cheeks. That was the face she used now as she spoke; a face that was trying to say more than her words could tell. "It can be hard."

"This is true. See you."

"Okay. My best to your better half."

When Eddy was growing up, the Park Pharmacy was on the corner across from the village square. A few years ago, it was replaced with a Walgreen's so big that locals called it the battleship. Eddy wondered why they needed a drug store that sold groceries. The only smart thing they did in this transition was to keep Sam Cunningham as the pharmacist.

Sam was a classmate of Eddy's in high school. He was a star basketball player. Eddy wasn't. He had good grades. Eddy didn't. He went away to school. Eddy stayed home. Eddy was his best man when he married Marianne. And he held Sam's hand for months after Marianne died.

When you opened the door at Walgreen's, a tone sounded and someone would say, "Hi, how are you? Can I help you?"

Today, though, Nellie was behind the counter. She turned on her mic. "Oh no, is that Eddy Kimes; quick, tie everything down."

Eddy grinned and asked Nellie how she was doing.

"That son of mine is going to be the death of me. That's how I'm doing." She went on from there. It had taken many visits over an extended period of time before Eddy understood that Nellie didn't want any response, especially any suggestions; she mainly wanted an ear. He stood and nodded.

"Is the boss in?"

"Where else would he be?" She pointed toward the pharmacy.

Eddy passed row upon row of painkillers, sleep aids, nausea medicine, stool softeners and antacids before he found the condoms. He emptied five boxes into his jacket. He dinged the bell repeatedly when he reached the pharmacy counter.

Sam's white lab coat was pristine. He had four pens in his pocket protector. He took off his glasses, pulled a wipe from a nearby dispenser and rubbed his lenses with care. He held them up to the light and was dissatisfied, so he huffed on them and wiped again, this time with a tissue.

"And what can I do for you today? I can see you are experiencing great discomfort. If I were to guess, I'd say it was hemorrhoids. Wait, no, that's not it. Incontinence, right? I can see it in your eyes."

"Wow, and you didn't even go to medical school."

Sam pointed at Eddy's jacket. "What's going on there?"

Eddy unzipped his jacket, leaned over and the condoms filled the counter like so many shrink-wrapped checkers.

"An aspirational purchase. Always important to dream."

Eddy bowed slightly at the waist.

"You are becoming a degenerate old fool," said Sam.

"What do you mean, old?"

Another customer approached. Sam picked through the alphabetized prescription bins.

"There you go, Mrs. Hollings. Do you have any questions today?"

Mrs. Hollings shifted her cane from one hand to the other so she could manage the card reader better. She was breathing hard and found it difficult to speak. "No."

"Okay. Just click there… That's it… Now swipe. Let's try it again… The other way. No, the other other way… Okay, there you go. Just check the upper box. Now all you have to do is sign and you're free to go."

"Thank God." Mrs. Hollings's face was stern. She held up a crooked finger. "Didn't used to have to do all this. I don't like it."

"No one does. That's the beauty part." Sam folded the top of the bag and handed it to Mrs. Hollings. "There you go. See you next week, Nancy. Take care."

Mrs. Hollings inched away from the counter, her back arched.

"That's going to be us, Eddy."

"Come on."

"No, really." They both watched as Mrs. Hollings reached the front door, Nellie helping her out. "You sooner than me, but still." Sam swept the condoms into a box and put them under the counter.

The phone rang. Someone had questions about statins. Eddy was impressed with how much Sam knew about medicine. He should have been a doctor. But Sam told him it wasn't the life he wanted. Being on call all the time. Never turning off the light and calling it a day. Eddy didn't believe him.

Sam hung up and leaned on the counter. "So, have you heard anything yet?"

"Heard anything?"

"Yeah."

"About what?"

"Come on."

"Nothing really."

"Going to call them?"

"They'll call us, I'm sure."

Sam shook his head and looked at the register.

"What?"

"Don't wait too long."

Eddy nodded at the bins behind Sam. "I think you've got something back there for Gayle."

Sam retrieved a bag. "This should help some with the pain. At least for now."

"That's what we want."

"Yeah. Pain is, well, pain."

Sam's face got puffy and old right before Eddy's eyes, like he remembered everything in his life all at once and it wore him out.

"Look, Sam, thanks for—"

"It's nothing. Now go on before Gayley thinks you're lost."

Sam and Gayle had dated all through high school. They were lab partners in ninth grade biology. She was head of Debate Club. He was president of Key Club. They went to every dance and every sporting event together. If one was seen alone, someone always asked where the other one was. Sam and Eddy hung together on the weekends and some week nights, but Gayle always came first. Eddy and Gayle were friends by association.

Sam and Gayle double-dated to the prom with Eddy and Maggie Dunaway. Sam drove his uncle's white Caddy. The school had a tradition of couples switching partners for one dance, so Eddy danced with Gayle. He didn't think anything of it until she was pressed against his chest. Being face-to-face, her eyes so pale, so blue, was overwhelming. When she talked, her voice gently vibrating, she seemed so comfortable. Eddy's heart skipped beat after beat, though Gayle seemed not to notice. They clapped at the end and thanked each other. She smiled and pressed his arm with her left hand.

Sam left for college in early August. Gayle enrolled in community college near home and Eddy got a job with the cable company. Sam asked Eddy to check on his girl from time to time, which Eddy did, reluctantly at first. He'd call her on the phone or stop by if he saw her on the porch. Once they got together for lunch. Then they started seeing each other regularly.

When Sam came home at Christmas, they told him. He'd wondered why her letters had gotten shorter and shorter and less frequent. "You can punch me out if you want," Eddy had said. Sam laughed but stayed away until he went back to school in January. When Sam came home in the spring, he had a new girlfriend. He acted like nothing had ever happened. They never spoke of it again.

From time to time, though, he would still call Gayle "Gayley," his high school pet name for her.

"Will do," said Eddy. He turned to leave, then stopped. "How's Jamie?"

A frown crossed Sam's face. "Jamie is Jamie, you know."

"Has he come back from respite care yet?"

"Pick him up tomorrow."

"How did he do this time?"

"Pretty good, I guess. Less upset. At least that's what they said."

"It's hard. But sometimes you have to take a break."

"Yeah, well..." He pursed his lips and raised his eyebrows.

Both men shook their heads and looked at the floor. "If you need anything, Sam..."

Eddy stood at the corner of Park and Main. Grand elms, oaks and horse chestnuts filled the town square, their limbs still bare, some showing green tips. These trees, some over two hundred years old, were a source of pride for the town. Some had metal rods between their heavier, longer branches, and a few were rotting, but their resilience made everyone feel rooted, feel good.

The square had crisscrossing sidewalks that met in the middle at a white gazebo that was trimmed in navy; it had a vaulted roof and a flag on top that was so big you could hear it flapping from almost everywhere on the square. There were swings and slides and sandboxes in the southeast corner. A flower garden. A fountain that soon would be operational sat in the northwest corner. There were benches and picnic tables, all anchored in cement since several had been stolen a few years back. Great mounds of icy, blackened snow were piled in every corner, the only place the DPW could think to put it in the depths of winter. While most of the grass was brown, there were hopeful patches of green here and there.

Clevon Gaddis sat on a bench near the gazebo.

"How about this," said Eddy as he looked up at the trees. "Gives you a good feeling when you can sit on the square again."

"I suppose it does."

Eddy sat down and both men were quiet for a few moments. Clevon took off his gloves and laid them on the bench. His hands were chunky and raw, work hands.

"So," he said.

"Yeah, I know."

"What do you know?"

"I'm afraid not much more than you know. I am way outside the loop at this point."

"Damn." Clevon shook his head hard. "Not fair, not fair at all, plain and simple."

"Well—"

"What's going to happen to us?"

"Well, no one's closed the doors. Nothing like that. I've seen a lot of owners come and go. They all had 'new ideas'," he air-quoted. "And then they'd settle down or they'd sell out and we'd start over again. But the work still had to be done by someone. Cable doesn't lay itself. And that means they need people, people like you and me."

Clevon had been with Universal for seven years, which made him a newcomer. Eddy had been with the company when they were Minute Cable, Total Cable, Cable Quest, Cable 4U, Everlasting Cable, then Unlimited Cable and, nine years ago, Universal Cable. Every time there were changes, wages dropped, layoffs followed, some jobs were lost, then most people were hired back and, in the end, they went on.

"I still don't like it." Clevon's hands were fidgety and he looked back and forth like he was waiting for a train that was never going to come. "How many weeks you been off?"

"Eight."

"Eight. I'm ten. Driving me a little crazy. I don't want to sit; I want to work. That's what I do."

"Any hobbies?"

"You're looking at it."

"Well, I'm sure—"

"Of what? Did you hear about overtime?"

Eddy had heard rumors that he tried to ignore.

"I've heard a lot of stuff. Nothing certain."

"Well, this is certain. Ralph was at the meeting this morning and Danvers himself told everyone that unlimited overtime was a thing of the past. Do you believe that?"

Eddy unfolded his arms. "He said what?"

"What I said—no unlimited overtime. Period. End of sentence."

Now it was Eddy's hands that were fidgeting. The family room— overtime had helped buy that. The boat—overtime again. College for Rich and Sandy—if it weren't for overtime, they'd be working at Walmart, or worse, Universal.

"Are you sure about this? I mean, are you sure Danvers didn't say they were *thinking* about this or were just threatening to do it—"

"None of that. Done deal." Clevon was breathing hard.

Eddy rubbed his palms on his pant legs and leaned forward, his elbows on his knees.

"Look, Eddy, I know you been a company man for a long time; and the company's done good by you. You're a supervisor and all that. But times have changed. That don't matter anymore. Then was then. Now is now."

Clevon opened his mouth but closed it again. He patted Eddy on the back and stood. They shook hands. Then Clevon crossed the street and got into his gray Saturn.

Eddy didn't think he needed to tell Gayle any of this, at least not now. When you've been married as long as they'd been married, you learn when to say things and when to wait. Everyone says 'being honest' and 'always telling the truth' are what make for a good marriage. Eddy agreed. Up to a point. When it came to being honest, timing was everything. It's not what you say, but when you say it and how you say it. Or, whether you ever say it at all.

It takes a long time to figure this out, especially with someone you love. When Eddy was laid off the first time, Gayle was pregnant with Richie. It was a hard pregnancy. She was very sick. Eddy got up every morning and 'went to work' even though he didn't have a job, just to keep things normal. It was about three months before new owners settled in and he got his job back. In the end, he never told her. What did it matter? Sometimes you have to keep things to yourself; otherwise, everything might crash into a million pieces on the floor. Then what? Life only *seems* imperishable.

The park was getting busy. A half dozen squirrels on the run, moms and dads pushing strollers, kids on swings. Cardinals trilling and somewhere a woodpecker was pounding. When winter came, Eddy loved the silence. But he loved the sound of spring even more.

The chimes at the First Presbyterian Church marked the hour. Eddy stopped for a moment to watch city workers clean the fountain and then he headed for the church. A few tiles were missing from its slender spire. There were modest double doors at the entrance. There were stained glass windows on either side of the front door and three larger ones on both sides of the building. Above the entrance was a rose window depicting creation, modeled after the one at the National Cathedral. The sanctuary was lined with oak pews. Wood beams anchored the vaulted ceiling. On the altar there were a small lectern and a larger raised one where the preacher preached. The choir loft was behind the altar and above the loft was a gold cross, probably nine feet tall. At least that's how Eddy remembered it from when he and Gayle had gotten married.

Eddy headed round back to the meditation garden. It was sequestered behind dense holly bushes surrounding a twelve-foot-tall statue of Jesus. The bronze plaque said — Jesus the Consoler.

In the '50s, when the church was going great guns, a rich congregant died and left money for the church, stipulating that it had to be used for an "external adornment of a religious nature." Church folk say that the marble was quarried in Greece and sculpted in Italy. It arrived on a massive flatbed. Schools closed early so children could watch the fifty-foot crane hoist the gleaming white Jesus into place.

Some whispered that area Baptists, Methodists, Lutherans and Catholics smiled through thinly veiled covetousness when Rev. Cecil Upchurch discovered an imperfection—a chip the size of a man's thumb near Jesus's collarbone.

Stunned and embarrassed, church elders wanted to sue. But Rev. Upchurch saved the day. Kind of. He said the "notch," as it became known, was a sign of Jesus's identification with human imperfection and a reminder that Christ alone was perfect. Most members accepted this, though several members left for St. Paul's Episcopal Church, where money matters were handled more deftly.

This opened the door for every arm chair theologian in town to take shots at The Consoler. The biggest complaint was that Jesus's nose was too large; that it wasn't "Anglo-Saxon" enough; that it looked, well, "Jewy." Upchurch explained that Jesus was middle-eastern. And a Jew. Many congregants were aghast. Behind closed doors, some members suggested that it might be time for Rev. Upchurch to consider a new calling. Some even referred to him as "Rev. Upchuck." Others left to join the Chapel of the End Times out on Town Line Rd.

Finding no one in the garden, Eddy sat on the cool marble bench. He looked up at Jesus's face, which was tilted down as if looking back at him. "Howdy." Jesus looked a little sixties-ish, his hair long and his beard thick. There was a faint smile on his lips. His arms were outstretched, billowy sleeves hanging loose, palms up, fingers open and curled slightly. His feet were bare. The years and the winters had replaced his gleam with elephant gray grit.

Eddy came to the garden for the first time when he started getting bad news. He was out for a walk and passed the church. The bushes rustled in the wind and he looked up, noticing Jesus's face peering over the holly. At first, it seemed funny to Eddy. Notre Dame may have their Touchdown Jesus, but we have Jesus the Voyeur. He kept walking, but on the way back, he went through the opening in the bushes and sat down on the bench. There was nothing out of the ordinary about his visit, except that he enjoyed the aloneness of it. He went back from time to time after that.

When he first told Gayle, she stopped folding the laundry. Her expression said, 'I don't know who you are at all'. Not that she was anti-religion. It was more that they had never been church people. Neither of their families had been regular either. They went on holidays, but even then, it didn't matter which church they went to, just so it wasn't too far away. Eddy felt uncomfortable under Gayle's gaze. He tried to explain. "I, it's, I don't know what it is…it's just…"

Gayle seemed to accept his reasoning. "Do you pray or something?"

"I don't know."

"Okay."

He kept going. Touching the statue's feet or the robe made him feel different. He couldn't say why, except that he felt far away and nearby all at the same time. Other times, it felt worrisome to sit there staring at a giant slab of marble made to look like a famous man from old.

"Hey, Eddy." Peter Goff had been the minister for fifteen years. He was tall, slender, a little bent over, perhaps from the burdens of his calling; sinewy; a shock of white hair that made him look like an Old Testament prophet. Gray eyes. Peter was nearing his seventies. He wore black trousers, black shoes, and a long-sleeved white shirt buttoned to the neck.

"Mind if I join you?"

Rev. Goff often arrived shortly after Eddy sat down, his office window within sight on the second floor of the education wing.

"We could use a coffee machine out here." His eyes closed and his cheeks swelled when he smiled.

"You're the boss, aren't you?"

Peter eyed the statue. "Actually, he's the boss. From what I've read, he'd probably favor a wine rack to a coffee maker."

There was always patter at the beginning, usually about the weather or the need for repairs on the roof, sometimes sports. This was followed by quiet, adjustments to sitting on the stone bench, and then one of them would speak, if only to break the thunderous silence.

"You know, I've been studying that face for a long time. I think I've figured it out."

Rev. Goff liked to say things that invited a question. "What's that?"

He pointed up. "Who he looks like."

"Oh."

"I've only seen the painting in person once."

"Painting?"

"The Mona Lisa."

Eddy shook his head.

"I think his smile is Mona Lisa's smile." He waited for Eddy to respond, but he didn't. "You know, some researchers did a study of her smile. They had people rate whether she was happy or sad or what. And ninety-seven percent said she was happy." He rubbed his stubbled chin. "As far as I'm concerned, I don't know if it's that clear cut. Maybe all those people just wanted her to look happy." Eddy stole a glance at his watch. "The smile, if you want to call it that, seems more ambiguous, more mysterious to me."

There was eagerness on Peter's face. Eddy often didn't understand what Rev. Goff was talking about, but he liked him anyway. He liked that even though he was a minster, Rev. Goff insisted on being called Peter; he liked how curious he was about everything, like a child. And even though he usually came to the garden to be alone, he appreciated Rev. Goff showing up from time to time.

"I just think it's a nice statue."

The holly rustled and darker clouds began to assemble.

"So, Eddy, how are you doing?"

"I'm doing."

"I'm sure you are." Peter folded his hands in his lap and looked sideways at Eddy.

"You have a lot going on."

"Yes."

"Must be hard at times. Carrying so much."

"Well—"

"You've been coming here pretty often of late." He pointed to his office window. "I have an even better view of you than Jesus here."

"That you do."

Peter shifted and crossed his legs. He licked his lips and took a few breaths before he spoke again.

"You know, Eddy, this statue is called Jesus the Consoler for a reason. Everybody needs consolation, comfort, at one time or another."

Peter, his face aglow, looked up at the Consoler.

"Sometimes you need to lift up your burdens. You know, turn them over to a higher power."

This was the first time that Peter had ever gone religious on Eddy. Eddy understood, though, that Peter didn't show up so often just for sports talk and the weather. He knew Peter would love to bring him into the fold, to have him sit inside instead of out. Eddy wanted to say something, but he couldn't find words for the confusion inside.

"Well, I should go," said Rev. Goff. "Do you mind if I pray?"

He took Eddy's hands in his and bowed his head. His forehead was furrowed and his eyes fluttered, but he didn't say a thing for a minute or more, just "Amen."

Eddy stayed a few minutes longer after Rev. Goff had left. The brisk air made him stand. He looked at the stone face of Jesus towering over him. He started to walk away but stopped and turned back. Something was different. He stood on tiptoes to get a closer look. Then he turned away, blinked hard and looked at the face again. He did this several times.

It was the mouth. Something was different about the mouth. He stood back a few feet and squinted. He was sure that if a bunch of researchers asked a thousand people about this smile right now, ninety-seven percent would see sadness. He closed his eyes again and then took another look. Or was it puzzlement?

CHAPTER 2

"Do you have everything together that you want to take?"

"I think so." Gayle pulled open her backpack and peered inside.

"A good book?"

"Yes."

"Word search?"

She shook her head as her husband continued to chatter.

"Blanket in case you get chilled? You know what they said."

"Yes." Gayle piled a pillow on top of the backpack. Just as Eddy headed for the pantry, she said, "Let *me* get some snacks." She grabbed cheez-its, granola bars and three bottles of water. "Do you want anything?"

"Sure, add a couple more granola bars, the peanut butter ones."

Tax season was winding down. In recent years her business had exploded. Originally, she mainly did personal taxes. But then small business owners discovered her and began coming in droves, feeling in over their heads when it came to managing accounts. They entrusted their businesses to her, their lives to her, in fact, and she took their confidence seriously. "You're a life saver," was the consensus.

Sometimes it baffled her, how others, strangers really, could give her that amount of influence over their financial affairs. In twenty-eight years, she never had a single complaint and had cleared every audit. "Cross the t's and dot the i's," she'd say, whenever anyone asked her how she managed to have such a spotless record. She was relieved to have accumulated a large portfolio of loyal accounts. It was insurance against the ever-changing tides of Eddy's work.

She headed to the bathroom one last time. Eddy's time off had gone from eight to twelve weeks. No end in sight. Scope didn't dare use the L-word for what was going on. "No one is being laid off," they'd announce with every new round of layoffs. "We're just reshuffling the deck." She marveled at Eddy's patience and was infuriated by Scope's attempts at normalizing the abnormal: "In every transition there are rough spots before things not only smooth out but take off!" The latest move was a "re-examination of health insurance" which amounted to presenting graphs and papers arguing that the *company's* health was at risk. "We don't want to put local operations in jeopardy so we will be exploring insurance options. At every turn we will make the welfare of our corporate family JOB #1."

Eddy had been going to all the meetings. Except in the last few weeks. "I can find out what I need to know from the guys." He sat every morning staring at the newspaper, never turning the pages. "It's all going to work out."

Gayle felt cranky when she came back down the stairs; navigating her feelings was getting harder.

Eddy met her at the bottom. "How you doing?"

"I don't know. Let's just get going. The sooner we get there, the sooner we can come home."

She opened the front closet, searching for a hoodie.

"Wait a minute," said Eddy. "I got something." He went to the back closet by the kitchen to get a plastic bag. "Okay, close your eyes."

"Eddy—"

"No, really, just do it."

Gayle frowned but closed her eyes.

"Okay, open."

Gayle grinned, then smiled and laughed, her hands going up and then slapping her thighs. Eddy was holding up a pink T-shirt that said, 'Hey Cancer, Eat Chemo and Die!'

"That should do it, don't you think?" He pulled a second shirt from the bag. "I got one for both of us."

Gayle put her arms around Eddy and laid her head on his chest.

It was a large, rectangular room with scuffed linoleum floors and beige Naugahyde lounge chairs lining the walls and filling the corners. Each chair had monitors and IV poles. There were about seven people hooked up when they arrived. A nurse greeted Gayle. She was as welcoming as a hostess or a maître d'. She pointed to the room as if asking which table they would prefer; something near the window, perhaps? Eddy smiled sheepishly and Gayle didn't say much. The nurse nodded towards a station that was set apart from the others.

She couldn't recall what medicines they were giving her. The word that stuck in her mind was "cocktail." It would be a "cocktail" of "meds" designed to "aggressively attack" the cancer. She felt like a warrior going into battle against an enemy she couldn't see. They explained that the chemo would go to every nook and cranny of her body; searching out the enemy, she supposed. But it was less precise than that. Since the chemo went everywhere, it could wreak havoc everywhere, as well. This seemed odd to Gayle and Eddy, who looked at each other quizzically. To Gayle, it seemed like the plan was inefficient: We'll line up every organ in your body; then a firing squad will shoot them all, hoping they only kill the guilty one.

The oncologist, Dr. Chen, had been positive, hopeful. She never stopped smiling, no matter what horrendous things she was discussing. "And when the cancer swarms your ovaries…" But her overall optimism was comforting to Gayle. "I've treated this cancer hundreds of times" and "we will use the best available cancer technology." Gayle felt buoyed by this, even though later she realized Dr. Chen had never said anything specific about how things would go, or what the outcome might be. She was setting the table for Gayle, but there was no telling if the meal would be any good.

Gayle didn't share her anxiety with Eddy. She had committed to being confident about the treatment. It worked better for her and she didn't want Eddy to bear any more weight than necessary. Work was plenty enough.

She did ask Eddy to run interference with Rich and Sandy. Rich was in Columbus and was mostly focused on Rich. No one understood exactly what he did. "Sales consultant for a startup" was the closest they could get. But what would they see him doing if they watched him work each day? Who knew? He'd also recently gone through a messy break-up. Eddy explained to him that "Mom hasn't been feeling very well." Rich said, "That's not good."

On the other hand, Sandy worked for Facebook, or a subcontractor, or something like that; she spent her days staring at a screen. She diagnosed her mother's problem after hearing two symptoms. "Mom's got ovarian cancer." Eddy said "We don't know for sure" for as long as he could.

Sandy and Rich seldom came home, which was a source of consternation for both Gayle and Eddy. For now, though, she was glad they weren't there. The "kids" would make everything they were facing feel much bigger than it was. "I feel healthy. I am healthy. I just have this thing."

When the kids were young, the family vacationed on the southern coast of Maine. Gayle remembered standing on the beach each morning, cup of coffee in hand, cool sand at her feet. She'd study the sky, dark clouds on the horizon. Would they turn into a storm and ruin a beach day? Or would they dissipate, leaving nothing but sunshine behind. She could never predict which it would be. But she always tried.

That was how she felt about their lives now. There were clouds gathering, but what would come of them was hard to tell.

Everyone in the treatment room knew the routine. They seemed to know each other, too. Gayle felt like she needed to learn a secret handshake. If she had closed her eyes and listened, she might have thought everyone had gotten together to play cards. One woman gave Gayle and Eddy pink ribbon pins to wear. Eddy teared up. She looked away. Nurses came in with bottles of water. "Must stay hydrated," one called as she circled the room.

Two women shared pictures of their grandchildren. Another woman sat with her head in her hands. "You can do this, Alice," called a friend. Alice struggled to smile.

The woman closest to Gayle was breathing in and out slowly, her lips puckered. "I'm visualizing vicious little t-cells beating the shit out of the cancer cells. I like your t-shirt."

"Oh," said Gayle, who closed her eyes, pretending to rest.

"First day?" whispered her neighbor.

"Yes."

"It takes a couple of times."

"I'm sure."

"Most of us have been at this for a while. Cancer comes, cancer goes, cancer comes back. You keep fighting. That's the deal as far as I can tell." She wore a cap on her head that had a tiny propeller on top.

Eddy sat in a plastic chair beside Gayle. They both watched a steady flow of patients come and go. A few other late middle-aged men with their late middle-aged wives. One with his daughter. A teenaged girl with her mother and grandmother. They each had the same chin. She carried a stuffed dog; ear buds were wrapped around her neck. A pregnant woman and her husband holding hands.

Eddy nudged Gayle's arm. He nodded toward the corner of the room. "Look."

It was a man in a suit and tie. Bald head. Shined shoes. French cuffs and links. His nurse smiled and they spoke in soft tones, as if they'd known each other for a while. When the man sat down, he scanned the room.

"He had to have seen me," said Eddy.

The man seemed preoccupied with something in his lap, then his arm rests. His eyes settled on the floor while they hooked him up to an IV. He tipped his chair back and closed his eyes. It seemed apparent to Eddy, at least, that he wasn't resting. He was hiding, the creases in the corners of his eyes and the folds in his heavy lids were too taut.

"I'm going to talk to him." When Gayle didn't respond, he looked at her. Her mouth open, she was fast asleep.

Eddy walked across the room and stood in front of the man. When he didn't open his eyes, Eddy tapped his shoe with his foot.

"Eddy."

"Howard."

Howard sat up and crossed his legs. "Well."

"Sorry to see you…I mean under these circumstances."

"Yes, me too." Howard pursed his lips and looked back across the room at Gayle. "I didn't know."

"I guess everyone has something."

"I suppose."

"How's Frances?"

"Okay, I think." He titled his head back and made eye contact. "She's away somewhere."

Howard's cheeks sagged. He pulled himself up in his chair, trying to move without crimping the tubing. "Haven't seen you much lately, Eddy."

This was bullshit, thought Eddy. "I haven't worked in a few months."

Howard broke eye contact. "Of course, I knew that."

"I figured you did. You signed the letter."

Howard Engler was two years behind Eddy in high school. He was one of those guys who was always in your face, pestering you, jumping in front of you to get some attention. Every class had a Howard Engler.

Eddy ran across Howard in the high school parking lot one afternoon. He was crying and his nose was bloodied. He had knocked the books out of Mandy Shakespeare's arms and her boyfriend had settled things. Howard had asked Eddy why everyone hated him. Eddy gave him a tissue for his nose, but didn't answer the question. It was too easy.

Howard had only been with the company ten years when Universal sold out to Scope. He was a finance guy. He had refashioned his high school skills, no longer knocking books out of anyone's hands. Now he'd gladly carry anyone's books, or coffee, or briefcase as long as he might gain some advantage. He stopped asking people why everyone hated him. It was too easy.

"I'm really sorry, Eddy. It wasn't personal. It was personnel." He crossed his legs at the ankles. "When I saw your name on the list, I was shocked. It took several days before I could write the letter. But my hands were tied. If it were up to me—"

"How long have you been coming here?"

Howard took a deep breath, held it and then let it out. "I'm finishing my first cycle today. Then more tests. Started in my left kidney. It is what it is, I guess."

"I suppose you're right."

Howard laughed gruffly. "There's nowhere to hide when it comes to this stuff. Makes you wonder about everything."

Both were quiet in the way men grow quiet after they've talked about every imaginable home repair.

Gayle had opened her eyes by now and watched her husband walk slump-shouldered back across the room. He didn't say anything and she didn't ask.

When they got in the car, Gayle laid her head back on the rest and rubbed her eyes with the palms of her hands. "One down," she said.

"How about we run through McDonald's and get some fries."

She placed her hand on her husband's shoulder. "That sounds great, but I don't think so. Not this time, maybe next."

Eddy gripped the wheel tightly. "Well, at least the ball is rolling now. We're doing something."

"Yes, that's true." Gayle looked out the window at the houses passing by. "We should stop at Wegman's for a few things. We don't have anything for dinner."

"I'd be glad to go later."

"No, I'm fine."

In the end, the only thing that sounded good to Gayle was ice cream. They bought three different flavors of Perry's—Panda Paws, French Vanilla and Brownie Blitz. They sat together at the kitchen table, bowls full. Eddy finished in no time. Gayle's melted slowly as she skimmed cream from around the edge of her bowl.

"Not hungry?" asked Eddy.

"Not so much right now. Maybe later." She lay the spoon on her napkin, put the ice cream down the disposal, and then deposited the bowl and the spoon in the dishwasher. Everything was done just so. Dishes, ironed clothes, tax forms in neat piles, desk top clean at the end of the day.

There was an etched-in-granite quality about Gayle that Eddy loved. She was steady no matter what. When his parents divorced, Eddy was nine and life was a mess after that. Some weeks he didn't know where he'd be sleeping. He carried his clothes in his gym bag like he was on the run. His father had "lady friends" who tried to mother him, but couldn't. His mother was a turtle hidden in a shell of despair. That lasted until he was a teen; by the time his mother came out again, he didn't need her.

When he was still Sam's wingman, Eddy had told Gayle this story, and she said, "Oh no, that is just not acceptable." He fell in love.

"Nap time for me," called Gayle as she headed upstairs. She went into the bathroom, closed the door, turned the faucet on and threw up. She shut the door to their bedroom, pulled the curtains and curled up in bed.

Eddy needed some distance, so he went for a ride. Past Scope. Service trucks were lined up behind tall fences. Only a few of his drivers were left; the newer ones; the cheaper ones. The Universal sign was faintly visible under the red, white and blue Scope logo, which had wheels and dash lines off the 'S'. Clevon had kept him posted about the insurance discussions, the overtime discussions, everything. Until Clevon got his "permanent leave extension."

Only recently had the town taken notice of what was happening at Scope, but the city council trusted that things were being handled "with the best interests of the town" in mind. This, despite the dire reports of disgruntled ex-employees. As the number of complaints grew, though, the mayor and council held meetings with Scope execs, who bristled at the suggestion that they were letting people go.

They insisted that senior employees were only being encouraged to "take a career break"; others were being moved to "zero-time utilization"; one vice president said that employees were experiencing an "uptick in leisure time opportunities." Every few weeks a news release from corporate would hint at "re-integrating workers" even as they announced further "streamlining."

Eddy turned off the ignition and sat for several minutes, his headlights off. He grabbed the steering wheel in both fists and shook it as hard as he could, so hard that the car rocked back and forth, like an elephant having a seizure. Just as quickly as he had started, he stopped. Then he got out of the car and walked to the main entrance. He looked up at the logo, his hands on his hips.

He found a stone on the sidewalk and kneeled down on the cool cement. He scratched out a simple message. He stood and examined his handiwork, then tossed the stone to the street. He took several steps back and looked again, making sure that his message was visible. "GO TO HELL" it said.

CHAPTER 3

Sandy, wearing sweats and sneaks, her auburn hair in a high pony tail that waved from behind her Nike ballcap, stood in the security line which had come to a standstill. She heard laughter behind her and then felt a light tug on her hair. When she turned, the mother of a young girl, maybe ten, was yelling at her daughter for "bothering the lady." The mother insisted that the girl apologize, but she wouldn't. "I didn't do anything; I didn't hurt anyone." The girl crossed her arms in defiance. Her mother was mortified. "I am so sorry. Sometimes, she's just so, well, obstinate."

"That's okay, really," said Sandy. She looked at the girl and winked. The girl's face relaxed and she smiled.

The little girl's toughness reminded Sandy of her father's favorite story about her. Sandy was in fifth grade at the time. The principal had summoned her parents to school regarding an "incident with a classmate" that she didn't feel comfortable discussing over the phone. When they arrived at school, Sandy was helping the school secretary like a "little angel," as her father would always say. The principal, known to all as Mrs. H, stood smiling politely in the doorway to her office. "Please come in," she said with due solemnity.

Barely in their seats, Mrs. H told Sandy's parents she had "attacked" a "little boy" and "beaten him soundly." When the principal asked Sandy why she did it, Sandy shrugged and looked at her sneaks. Mrs. H persisted and finally Sandy said, "He called me a 'bitch'." Mrs. H sat back in her swivel chair. She took off her glasses and crossed her arms. "Sandy, I think you know we don't use the b-word here." She leaned forward to punctuate the point. "I think you know that, don't you, honey?"

Sandy shook her head and then added that Mrs. H had better tell Phillip because he was saying it to everyone. Mrs. H explained that they weren't talking about Phillip's behavior, they were talking about hers. Sandy was undeterred. "He also called me a 'fucking pussy'."

At this point in the story, Sandy's father usually broke into gales of laughter. He'd grab Sandy's arm and grin at her admiringly.

In the end, Sandy agreed to apologize for breaking the boy's nose only if he apologized for his words. The deal was struck. And a legend was born. Each time her father retold the tale, he had a look of bursting pride on his face. Sandy wished the story was a true depiction of who she was and who she had become; that it was a true measure of what her father called Sandy's "unrelenting inner strength," a quality that she feared had been replaced by unrelenting self-doubt.

She settled into her window seat and placed her bag on the floor in front of her. She watched baggage handlers in bright yellow jump suits toss suitcases and strollers and golf bags into the belly of the plane. No sooner had she crossed her fingers, hoping she would have no neighbors, than two business types, gray suits, loosened ties, delicate cologne, and finely coiffed hair, landed beside her. They ordered drinks and joked their inside jokes. Soon the one on the aisle opened his laptop and started to work, while the other one stretched out, sipped his vodka tonic and shifted slightly in Sandy's direction.

"Looks like a full house," he said, while taking possession of the arm rest and leaning his shoulder into hers.

Sandy started to belly breathe. She pursed her lips in a haphazard non-grin grin. She took another deep breath, but stopped as she was about to exhale, the aroma of her neighbor's taco breath invading her air space.

He checked her out. "You look comfortable. Must be going somewhere for some fun."

"Not really."

He let his arm unfold on the rest, his hand dangling over the end a few inches from her leg. He reached out with his index finger and tapped her thigh. "Hey, do you mind if I pull the arm rest up. We could both use a little more room." He gave her a pearly smile and raised his eyebrows as if to say, 'You can trust me'.

Her father always told her to "give people a chance." "If you don't trust people, you'll be sorrier than if you do." Then he would retell the story of being picked up by a "straggly bunch" of "Mexicans" when his car broke down —"Scared me to death, but what was I going to do in the middle of nowhere?" They took him home for dinner and went back to fix his car. Voila. Trust wins the day. She had always wanted to be as trusting as her dad.

Sandy looked at her neighbor's Rolex, which was as big as those ridiculous belts that boxers wear when they win championships. She thought of her father before she spoke. Her seatmate looked into her eyes, his hand now resting on her knee.

"Sure, no problem," she said. He started to raise the armrest and rearrange himself. She leaned toward him and whispered. "I shouldn't tell you this, but you seem like a nice guy."

He squeezed her knee, an eager grin on his face.

She giggled. "Oh, really, never mind, you'd think it was dumb."

"Oh, no you don't. Now you have to tell me."

Sandy rubbed her shoulder against his. "Do I, really?"

"Yes, really," he said, mimicking her.

"Okay, okay." She coaxed him closer with her index finger. Then she coughed hard twice. "Oh my, please excuse me."

"No problem, really."

"Okay, but you have to promise me you won't tell a soul."

He crossed his heart with his finger. "I promise."

Her forehead brushed his cheek. "Well, I'm just returning from a tour of Southeast Asia. Have you ever been?"

"No, I—"

"And I think I may have caught something. I have this rash and this morning I started coughing. I couldn't exactly tell security. I mean, I have to get home, you now?"

The armrest came back down. After that, all she saw was the back of his suit. She didn't like to lie, but sometimes she felt that was all they deserved.

When she deplaned in Rochester, she couldn't find her father anywhere. She stood in the corridor turning slowly in every direction until she noticed a man in baggy pants with a baggy face waving in her direction. Pulling her suitcase behind her, she had one hundred feet to gather herself and find something to say other than, 'What the hell happened to you?'.

They hugged. "It's so good to have you home, honey." He held on a fraction of a second longer than her.

As he paid the parking attendant and pulled into traffic, she watched his every move. Everything about him was gray. Not only his temples, but his skin, his sunken eyes, the air around him. He talked rapidly and in excruciating detail about the weather, the new lights on the gazebo in the park, the recent flooding along Lake Ontario. His voice was pressured, urgent; his laugh, forced. He looked at her, but not really. How was her flight, how was the layover in Philly, you never know what will happen there, glad it was smooth coming in, the weather is always a wild card.

She placed a hand on his arm. "Dad? How are you doing?"

He said, "Great!" so unconvincingly that even he had to pause and reconsider. "I mean, you know, your mom's going through this whole thing; don't get me wrong, she's doing well with it, but it's not easy." Things were never "hard," they were "not easy" or they "were what they were." "You know, she doesn't have hair at this point. It'll grow back, but not right now, and she's not interested in wigs; there are some beautiful ones, though, I've seen them at the hospital, but it's okay."

"I didn't know." His eyes began to well. "Dad?"

"It's just so good to see you. To have you home. It's been so long." He swiped his nose with his sleeve and forced a change in tone. "So, tell me, how's my girl doing? How's work been? Still fighting the good fight?"

Her dad had told everyone that she worked for Facebook. "Big time," he'd say. Technically, she worked for a subcontractor—

TrapperKeeper—that focused on cyber security, but that was close enough for him. Her assignment was to track Russian interference, fake posts, bots, outrageous stories believed by outrageous people.

"Yep. As best I can."

"And?"

She told him that her new assignment was "privacy," how to define it, how to protect it without destroying commerce. It was "fascinating work," trying to reconcile the first amendment with the 21st century explosion in interdependence. "No one seems to care about privacy. Everyone wants to be seen. The person with the most likes wins."

Her words came easily. Her father listened intently. What was she supposed to say—"I lost my job a year ago when the government's interest in Russia waned and Facebook decided they could talk a good game without playing a good game?" At least that's what she had said to her supervisor at TrapperKeeper, who then suggested she seek other employment. She noted that he never challenged her assessment.

She felt triumphant when she left, having taken a stand, believing that at twenty-eight, already with so much experience, she would be a great 'get' for some start up. But her triumph was short-lived. The word spread in the frat boy culture of high tech. It wasn't hard to get interviews. But interviews didn't pay the bills. She did some freelancing for small businesses trying to shore up their security, but it was a hard pull trying to compete with larger firms.

"Yeah, I'm chugging along."

"That's my girl."

He had a satisfied grin on his face and some color on his cheeks. She didn't need to tell him more. What would be the point? The only privacy that mattered now was her own.

"I have a surprise for you," her father said.

Her face turned quizzical. "Surprise?"

"Rich is already home."

"That's great. Can't wait to see him. Mom must be very pleased."

"Having both of you home at the same time, well, I can't tell you how much it means."

Sandy shook her head, although it wasn't like they were gathering around the Christmas tree, savoring mugs of hot chocolate.

"Anyway, he looks great. Seems, I don't know, like he's got his head on straight. He sounds content enough, I suppose."

Sandy and her brother texted every day. He hated Columbus. He was trying to catch on with a start-up of some sort but it was tough slogging. Evie had dumped him, which was bad enough, but not as bad as leaving him with the mortgage on a half million-dollar condo. "You can have custody of our 'child'," she had said. Good riddance, thought Sandy.

The expressway traffic was thin. The Rochester skyline rose before them, with Kodak, in all its faded glory, the first in line.

Eddy looked sideways at his daughter. In his eyes, she could have been thirteen years old, fifteen, with the same prominent nose and long lashes, the slight double chin that she had always hated, the loose auburn hair. She was right there beside him and yet he yearned to be closer, to be loved by her as much as he adored her. He reached across and placed his hand on her shoulder.

"It's so good to have you home, honey."

"Thank you, Dad."

He would savor this ten-minute drive home, this brief respite before they would all be together. His hands tightened a little on the steering wheel.

CHAPTER 4

Rich sat at the kitchen table while his mother poured water into the coffee maker and turned it on. She then reached for several mugs and arranged them on the counter. 'Why hadn't Dad told me how bad she was?' he thought.

It was all he could do to keep his jaw from dropping when she came to the door to greet him. He hugged her quickly so she couldn't see his face. He didn't know what to say. Her head was smooth as a billiard ball and she must have lost thirty pounds. Her speech was muffled from the blisters in her mouth.

He watched as she arranged Splenda and Equal in a tiny bowl, her fingers like brittle twigs on a dying tree. Her smile, as wide as a prairie, now made her face look skeletal. He felt nausea rise in his stomach. 'This can't be my mother'.

"Can I help you?"

"No, you just sit and relax, I'm fine. Your father and Sandy should be home soon."

They had given him the impression that she was doing well on the chemo. That she had finished a round and was waiting for test results so they'd know what to do next. A rest period, Dad had called it. His mother never complained, never let on that she was changing so drastically.

Had he known in advance, he would have prepared himself. He would have steeled himself, planned things to talk about, distracting things, light things that would make his mother laugh. He had always been adept at lifting her spirits. He just had a sixth sense about her needs. But this, this was different.

"So, Mom, what are they saying to you?"

"Nothing much."

"Well, aren't you seeing an oncologist?"

"I'll see the doctor again soon."

"Surely they've told you something."

His mother sat back in her chair, as if in surrender.

"Rich, it's nothing, really. I mean, yes, I'm having chemo, but you should see how many people are there. Much worse off than me. Do you remember Howard from your dad's work?"

"No."

"He's there. No one's immune. Everyone takes it in stride. It's just something that happens."

The gurgle of the coffee maker and the smell of fresh brew filled the room. To Gayle, Rich looked like a lost child, even though he was thirty. His face was gaunt and he looked unbearably thin. He'd gotten contacts for some reason and she almost didn't recognize him at the door. It was so hard to pin him down about anything. He tried to explain his new job but it sounded like gobble-de-gook, like he was talking with a mouth full of marbles. And Evie, so nice, what had really happened? When had he stopped telling his mother things?

She and Eddy used to laugh at how transparent he was. The first time he got an erection—"What's wrong with me, Mom?" The first, second, and third times he fell in love. When he was afraid that no one would ever love him back. Then nothing. For years. Is that what growing up means? Your kids stop talking to you?

Rich got up and went to the coffee maker for a second cup. He watched his mother from the corner of his eye as she shuffled across the floor, seeming unable to lift her feet. She opened the dishwasher and took dinner plates from the rack.

"Here, let me do that."

"Rich, really, I can do this. I do it every day."

He stepped in, nevertheless, and cleared both racks. She stood beside him, arms folded. It felt like there was a membrane between them, something that he didn't know how to penetrate. Had he stayed away too long? Or not long enough? This town, this reservoir of festering memories, had become gangrenous. He had surgically removed it from his thoughts, but phantom pain remained.

Gayle watched Rich hold his coffee cup with both hands, much as he had held his hot chocolate as a boy. She noticed that he had moved his part, that his hair was plastered with product, that his eyes were more vivid with the contacts. So handsome with his thick, dark brows, his light brown eyes. He still had a slight twitch in his cheek, just below his left eye. It had started during his senior year in high school. The doctor had shrugged when they asked what might have caused it. She watched and sighed. After all these years? She wished her cancer wasn't the reason he was sitting across from her again. She wished he'd come home because he'd wanted to, not because he was afraid. Not because he was, well, twitchy.

Rich was searching through the drawers by the fireplace for the Uno deck when they both heard the garage door opening.

Sandy looked as beautiful as ever; she could easily have passed for sixteen. The boys had always flocked to her girl-next-door good looks, always a smile, keen sense of humor, brightest in her class. Everything should have been easy for her, thought Rich.

Eddy's face was red with satisfaction as he watched his kids hug and laugh together in the kitchen, Gayle at their side looking almost energized. If there was only some holly, a wreath on the door maybe, or a turkey in the oven, or fireworks crackling in the distant night, any celebration would do. He dreaded the upcoming appointment with the oncologist and was secretly glad the doctor was on vacation. He could live for a while in a pocket of pretend, imagining that his children had come home on account of some happiness.

They both looked so good, so alive. He had always loved watching them, enjoyed their individuality, two human beings on their own, a part of him, yet doing well apart from him. When he told the good Rev. Goff that the kids were coming home, that it had been too long since the Kimes tribe had been assembled as one, Peter had asked, "What will it be like?" He had answered without thinking— "Wonderful"—but he realized he had no idea what it would be like.

He assumed that it would be wonderful, because, well, isn't that what happens when families get together?

From that point on, he had been a little apprehensive about the whole thing. What *would* it be like after all? Neither Sandy nor Rich had been the happiest pair in those final few years before they flew the coop. He felt like he lost them after that. There were Facebook posts and texts and the rare visits, but it was different in ways that he couldn't put into words. All he knew was that they had become warm, affable acquaintances, people you enjoyed but didn't know. He wished he hadn't been such a watcher when they were young. He wished he had held them closer during those years when they would have let him. Maybe all the overtime hadn't been worth it.

Pizza and wings arrived at the front door. Eddy searched for his wallet.

"You can put it away," said Rich. "This's on me."

They sat in a circle around the living room coffee table, a slice on every paper plate except Gayle's. Eddy had made her a peanut butter sandwich. Bottles of beer, glasses of wine, a pitcher of water. Gayle nibbled while everyone gobbled. Another slice and another.

"Krony's?" asked Sandy, wiping her mouth with a handful of napkins.

"Krony's is now DJ's," said Eddy.

Everyone took another bite.

"They deliver," said Eddy.

"Big changes and major innovations," said Rich. He never missed an opportunity to poke fun at western New York. He commented on the "terrible" schools in Rochester, the failed projects of the city's past. "Remember the fast ferry to Toronto? What a disaster."

Eddy chewed more intently. He took a longer gulp of his Genesee. There were things he wanted to say. Maybe if people hadn't moved away, maybe if they had committed to their home, maybe they would have come up with answers instead of easy criticisms. He swallowed his thoughts. "Yes, home sweet home."

Sandy glared at her brother. "How are the Red Wings doing, Dad?" she said.

"They're doing about as good as they ever do."

"Love that ballpark. Great food."

"Yeah."

Gayle took a full bite of her sandwich. Eddy's shoulders settled.

"Have you been to any games?"

"Not as often as in past seasons, but a few times."

"Visit Grandpa?"

She was referring to the brick on the walkway near the left field fence. When Eddy's dad died, his co-workers had bought it as a remembrance. Every time he and Sandy went to a game, their first stop was the brick, where they'd clean the lettering of his name and give it an affectionate pat.

"Always," he said with a smile.

Gayle chewed for a long time. Although the nausea had abated since her treatment cycle had ended, eating had lost its appeal. To satisfy Eddy she tried to eat, or ingest calories, which made him hopeful. It was hard to tell the difference between food and tin foil. Her oncologist explained that the chemo destroyed taste buds, which would, one day, return. Her doctor nodded her head, smiled encouragingly and suggested trying spicy foods. Perhaps that would awaken her dead cells.

Seizing on this advice, Eddy found a recipe called Death Wish Jambalaya. Gayle had never enjoyed jambalaya, death wish or not. But he convinced her to give it a go. He doubled the serrano and jalapeno peppers and added the coarsest Cajun seasoning. He then minced part of a ghost pepper and sprinkled it in, afterwards soaking his fingers in milk.

"What are you doing?" said Gayle.

"Nothing," said Eddy.

Eddy ladled the jambalaya into two deep bowls and dipped his spoon in. Gayle watched. As he slowly brought the steaming liquid to his lips, a drop fell, burning a hole through the table cloth. Gayle put her spoon back on her napkin.

Eating wasn't the worst of it, though. Gayle felt like she was trapped in a stranger's body, a body over which she had no control. She noticed bruises on her legs and arms that came from nowhere. She always hurt, but when Eddy asked where, she couldn't say. A walk up the stairs was a breathless climb up a forbidding mountain. Vomiting, of course, and diarrhea and bleeding. Oh, and headaches, can't forget the slamming headaches.

Her body had become a cranky, rusted-out old jalopy, suitable only for the junk yard. When Eddy said, "You're doing great, honey" she wanted to say, 'Go fuck yourself'.

Sometimes if she sat still and did nothing, she felt almost like herself. So that is what she did. Watching her children made sitting almost pleasurable. Here they were, full grown people living in the world, making their own decisions, when once they were just cell clusters nestled in her womb.

Sandy was such a remarkable young woman; she strode through her life, it seemed, confident of her ideas, protective of her feelings. She never doubted that Sandy would succeed, but she always worried that she might never find someone, that she would end up alone, the worst of life's possible outcomes.

Richie—she could never call him that, not since he was thirteen and had taken her to task for using "a baby name" in front of his friends—Richie was a different matter. Their bond was easy from the beginning. But as he neared adulthood, he stumbled often for reasons she couldn't understand. It was like he'd fallen off a cliff right before he left for college. And it seemed Sandy had followed close behind.

She took another bite of her Jiffy peanut butter sandwich and then put it back on her plate. She chewed slowly until she could barely recognize what was in her mouth.

"Wasn't it Aunt Ruth who, on Thanksgiving, always said—'If you had a million dollars, you couldn't eat any better than this'?" Rich licked the chicken wing sauce off his fingers. "At least, that's what she always said until Sandy got up in her face." Everyone laughed.

"What? I was eight. You have to admit it didn't make any sense," said Sandy. "I mean, really."

"So, Sandy says, she says, 'Aunt Ruth, you gotta be kidding, right? I mean, if we had a million dollars, we could eat like Kings and Queens, not like us, not like Kimes's'."

"Wow, I was a little bitch," said Sandy.

"No, no, you were adorable. You were very serious about it, like maybe Aunt Ruth didn't realize that she was mistaken," said Eddy.

"You're right, Sandy, you were a little bitch." Rich pushed her over on the couch.

Everyone ate some more pizza and wings, and drank some beer, perhaps too much, as the conversation began to falter. Eddy tried bringing up more reminiscences, like the time their dog pushed over the Christmas tree, but these stories were met only with politeness.

"It is so good to have everyone together, isn't it?" Gayle leaned forward in her chair and looked at each one in turn, her eyes dreary, her mouth a wan smile. "You father and I appreciate you coming home very much, don't we?"

"Yes, we do," said Eddy.

"It just feels good, doesn't it, being together like this, just the four of us, like old times."

The room fell silent as Gayle started coughing. When she began to choke, Eddy stood, but she waved him off. She struggled for another minute. She took a deep breath and appeared to clench again, but managed not to cough. He handed her a glass of water. She put it on the table.

"Are you—"

"There, that's better." She struggled to catch her breath.

"Mom, what's going on? I mean, really," said Sandy.

Gayle remembered the incident with Aunt Ruth differently than Eddy. She didn't remember Sandy being concerned; instead, her voice had a tone to it, an edge that could make anyone on the receiving end feel small, stupid. The same tone, perhaps unintended, that was in her voice now.

"You're not telling us something. What is it?"

"Sandy, come on," said Rich. "Mom's sick."

"Of course, I can see that. But that's not the whole story."

"What's that supposed to mean?"

"It means what it means."

"Jesus Christ—"

"Please, stop," said Eddy. He bowed his head and grabbed at each breath before any words could escape. "Stop it. Please."

"I'm sure everyone is getting tired," said Gayle. "Maybe it would be best if—"

Eddy held his palm up. He turned to face Sandy directly.

"Do you want to know why we asked you to come home? Something we should never have had to ask. I'll tell you why." Eddy gulped and his face blanched. He looked at Gayle, who averted her eyes. "Your mother has been fighting, actually, your mother and I together have been fighting a battle with everything we've got. Your mother's allowed the doctors to put poison after poison into her body, without a hint of complaint and with every reason to hope it was the right thing to do. And I have tried to support her, to be there, to hold her up when necessary. We are fighting a battle that should be fought. Life is that precious."

He could feel emotion bleeding into his voice. Sandy and Rich looked at each other but didn't speak.

"But we are fighting a battle that, in all likelihood, we're going to lose."

Gayle's mouth fell open.

CHAPTER 5

Rich and Sandy wheeled their bags up to the bar and sat on the stools. Through the window opposite them, they could see a plane taxiing onto the tarmac. A moment later it roared down the runway and disappeared into the pale evening light. There was a stocky man at the far corner of the bar, navy suit bulging, open shirt, computer bag on his lap, phone in his hand. Two flight attendants sat directly across from Rich and Sandy, early fifties, also in blue with white blouses and knotted scarves, martinis in front of them, four glasses empty, two glasses full. The bartender washed and rinsed several pilsner glasses and put them on a towel to drip dry.

Rich caught his eye. "A Guinness and..." he turned to Sandy.

"Pinot Grigio."

"...and a pinot for the lady."

Rich leaned his elbows on the bar and raised his eyebrows at his sister. Sandy raised hers in return and shrugged one shoulder.

•　•　•

Gayle swished the bathwater with her finger tips. For years she and Eddy had intended on insulating the pipes because they were embarrassingly loud whenever they turned on any faucet. Never got done. If she closed her eyes, she could imagine a freight train roaring into her bathtub.

She swished the water again and then turned off the faucet. She hung her robe on the hook behind the door and put one foot in. Once her foot adjusted, she put in the other. She lowered herself slowly as the initial burn faded into blessed warmth. She closed her eyes and sighed.

Eddy sat on the toilet in the guest bathroom. He noticed that the corner tile near the bathtub was loose. And the grout along the base of the tub was cracked and crumbling. It had been months since he had worked and yet these simple jobs weren't getting done. He and Gayle had made a list and, at first, he dove into the chores with enthusiasm. But soon lethargy set in. He spent time in the basement at his workbench and in the garage, but had nothing to show for it.

He flicked the exhaust fan on. When he was done, he washed his hands, dried them and tossed the hand towel onto the toilet seat. He frowned into the mirror and then left the room.

He knocked gently on the door.

"What?"

"Can I come in?"

Eddy opened the door. Gayle's collar bone was what he saw first, jutting, skin taut and white.

"Well." Gayle didn't look at him.

"Yeah, I know."

.   .   .

Rich placed his beer back on the bar and turned it slowly with his fingertips. He looked up as another plane roared down the runway. Sandy crossed her legs and tried again.

"So — thoughts? Like, what in the world is going on?"

"It was strange, wasn't it?"

"Strange? 'Strange' doesn't come close to describing it."

"Is Mom dying? Or not? Is the chemo working?"

"Or not?"

"Yeah."

"It was like they hadn't cleared their stories with each other. They hadn't exchanged notes."

Eddy's little speech and dire pronouncement not only caught Sandy and Rich by surprise, it stunned their mother, as well. She gasped and covered her mouth with her hand. "What are you talking about?" she said. Their father stumbled— "Well, it's, well, like I said" —which spiked the confusion by a factor of ten. Sandy and Rich's heads, as if balanced on fulcrums, turned back and forth between mother and father, as their parents' improvisation catapulted forward.

Their father tried to throw everything into reverse when he saw the consternation in his wife's eyes. Gayle insisted that they didn't know anything yet, that they were comfortable with where things were at, how the chemo was going, and that they had confidence in the "team." Their father agreed with everything she said, his head shaking so briskly that he looked like a bobble head doll mounted on the handle of a jack hammer.

Mom glared at Dad. The room grew silent.

"So," said Eddy, wiping his palms on his pants and then clapping his hands once, as if to announce the show was over.

"When I talked to Mom alone, I didn't get much," said Rich. "It was so odd. She said she was fine and when I asked about what Dad had said, she said, 'We'll see', like I'd asked if I could stay out past curfew."

Sandy gave the stink eye to the stubby man across the bar, who ordered a drink and waved at her, as if to say, 'Wanna join me?'. "Dad's scared. That's clear. He's always a little jumpy, but he seemed..." She raised her hands, making them quiver and shake. "I don't think I've ever seen him like that."

• • •

"I don't know what I was thinking. Maybe I wasn't thinking. Maybe I..." A pout was perched in one corner of Eddy's mouth.

"'Maybe I' what?"

"I don't know."

Gayle squeezed the hot wash cloth onto her shoulder, water sluicing her back. She closed her eyes, not wanting to be distracted from the feeling.

"They need to know what's going on," Eddy said in a single slow breath.

"They do?"

"They're not kids."

"They aren't?"

"Come on."

Gayle turned the hot water on again and paddled it with her hands until she was enveloped once more.

"What do we actually know?"

"Well…" Eddy pulled a towel from the rack and laid it on the floor near the bathtub. Then he sat on the toilet seat beside her.

"I mean, definitively." When faced with uncertainty, Gayle demanded as much precision, as much exactitude as possible. This was no different. "When we met with the oncologist last week, did she say I was going to die?"

"No, not exactly."

"I think the answer is 'no'."

Eddy placed one hand on the side of the bathtub. "I have not given up hope, if that's what you're thinking. But did you see the oncologist's face when you asked about the prognosis?"

"Did she say, 'Gayle, you are going to die?'"

"Did you hear what she said about the rate of success for this new trial?" Eddy's head fell forward into his hands. He reached for a roll of toilet paper and wiped his eyes.

"Stop it."

Eddy's breathing hiccupped one last time and then he was clear-eyed. He put the toilet paper back. "I'm sorry. I just felt like…like I wanted them to pay attention, pay attention to us, to you, for a change, I wanted them to know…so they'd come home again before…"

"Before what?"

Eddy turned away. "Before it's too late to do whatever we need to do, say whatever we need to say. No matter what happens."

Gayle watched her skin go goose flesh in the steamy water. She hated that Eddy was speaking this truth, was saying it out loud, which only made it truer.

• • •

Rich waved to the bartender, pointed at his sister, then at himself. Sandy sipped the last of her pinot just as the bartender placed another napkin and glass in front of her. She checked her phone; her flight to Chicago was on time. They would be calling her to board soon. Rich took a third of his beer in one gulp. He hadn't shaved and he looked tired. He had two more hours to wait for his flight.

"How did Dad put it?" said Rich. "He'd like us to come home 'regularly', to 'make the effort'." He held his glass up and shook his head.

Sandy looked out the window at yet another plane. "I think he's right."

He looked at her to see if she was joking. But her face was stony. "I don't know if I can," he said.

"Not enough time, really?"

"No, it's not that; I mean, time is always…whatever…it's just…did you take a good long look at Mom?"

"I did."

"Jesus."

"Uh huh."

"It will be worse each time we come."

"It's hard, I get it. Tell me something that isn't hard." Sandy chewed the inside of her cheeks.

"Fuck, Sandy. I don't expect it to be easy."

Sandy shook her head. "I know, I know, I didn't mean…it's just…I don't know…"

The boarding call came. Sandy stood beside her brother who sat slumped over his beer. She rubbed his back and then poked him in the ribs.

"I gotta go."

He stood and took her in his arms. "I love you."

"Of course, you do; how could you feel otherwise?" She held on an extra beat, then let go. "Next time."

"Next time."

•   •   •

Gayle wrapped herself in a blue terry-cloth robe. She put on wool socks and quietly went downstairs. Eddy was gone. She entered her office and locked the door behind her. She studied the stacks of 1040-ESs that she needed to sign. She divided the forms into stacks of ten. There were forty-two stacks lying about the floor.

After two hours, her face had gone slack, her hands shook, her back ached. She dumped the completed forms into boxes for Eddy to mail. She folded her hands on the desk and listened to the fluorescent light buzz above her and the furnace hum below. Since everything had erupted, her only survival strategy had been to keep moving, believing that a moving target, a body in motion, was hard to thwart.

Even though Eddy wasn't there, she called for him. In the echoing silence that followed, she felt her aloneness like a cold hand clutching her heart. She gulped air and tried to stand, but couldn't. Fear coursed through her legs. She laid her head on the desk and closed her eyes.

•   •   •

Eddy stood at the corner looking at the pharmacy. He could see Sam at the back counter, a few customers in line. He debated about visiting his friend, but decided to walk on instead. It was a crisp evening; there was a new moon. He held his phone to the sky and tapped the SkyView app. In a line across the southern horizon, he spied Jupiter, Saturn and Mars. He lowered the phone and squinted up at the tiny dots. 'Is anyone looking back?' he wondered. 'Are we the only ones?'

Why was everything falling apart? Could he have done something differently, made better choices along the way? He thought about all those months he had remained hopeful about Scope. It will work out, he had insisted. Had he been foolish? Had he been willfully blind? Gayle had always had reservations, doubts about his work, his future, their future. It drove Gayle crazy, the uncertainty, the unpredictable changes, the lack of control. She felt like they were indentured to executives who didn't even know who worked for them or what their lives were like.

This made him feel small, helpless, inconsequential. He'd defend the company: "It's just the nature of the business." "They know a lot more about how to run things than we do." "Don't worry, we'll land on our feet."

"You're a good man, Eddy," she'd say. "You don't deserve this."

She was right, but what was he to do? Where could he make comparable money with no education? No other experience? So, he stayed, weathering the storms at work and at home. Gayle didn't complain nearly as much as she did in those early years. But even her silence was pointed.

He should have taken Sandy and Rich to the airport, even though they had declined his offer, preferring Uber. How were they handling the news? What he had told them wasn't completely true, it was true enough. Sometimes you have to punch up the truth a little before anyone will pay attention. Gayle would have waited to the very end if she were left to make her own decision on this. He didn't feel it was her decision to make alone. Sandy and Rich needed to step up, get involved. He shook his head, hating the tone of his own thoughts.

The light shining through the trees cast dancing shadows on the square. He stood near the gazebo. It was his senior class that had proposed the project to the town council. He and Sam and others from the Shop Club had worked on it for several months under the diligent tutelage of their teacher, Mr. Hammer, who deserved all the jokes his name inspired. They finished just weeks before graduation.

Graduation was scheduled at the gazebo, but rain changed the plans and also revealed more work that had to be done over the summer. He resented it at the time, but now felt warmly about it as he remembered the planks piled on the grass as the boys waited for their primitive carpentry skills to kick in. They were eighteen that summer and snuck beer into their lunch pails. Hammer never understood why they laughed so much and for so long.

There wasn't anyone at the meditation garden when Eddy sat down on the cold granite bench and looked up at the Consoler. Soon, though, he heard someone else rustling through the bushes.

CHAPTER 6

"And you don't have any insurance?"

"Well, not exactly. Part of the severance was six months of insurance."

"Okay," said Rev. Goff, encouraged.

"But, you know, a five-thousand-dollar deductible makes it almost useless, plus the medicine is all out of pocket."

"Jesus."

"I guess."

Eddy studied the palms of his hands. Talking to Peter made him feel foolish.

"How much does Gayle know?"

"Most of it."

"And?"

"And she's too sick to even think much about it. And she shouldn't. I made the mess."

"What do you mean? It's not like you planned it, Eddy."

But Eddy felt that if he had been a better planner all along, they wouldn't be in this sinkhole. He fumbled with his hands and bowed his head, not in prayer, but humiliation. "I think we're fucked."

"That's an awfully strong word—"

"Yes, it is. A perfect word."

Rev. Goff's brow furrowed.

"I'm unemployed. No insurance, really. Gayle has cancer. It's not going so well." His shoulders fell. "Fucked, that's what we are." He looked at Peter. "I'm sorry."

"You don't need to apologize to me. I'm sure you feel...effed. I've felt that way too, maybe not exactly in those words, but bad, really bad. At my last church, my wife left me for our organist...Janet. But that's me..."

They both looked up at the Big Guy, the Consoler of all who needed consolation. Peter cleared his throat and stood in front of Jesus, his arms out, as if shadow dancing with his Savior. Then he turned to Eddy. "I think it's time for you to start praying. I mean earnest prayer, prayer like you've never prayed before."

Eddy waggled his head neither up nor down.

"Look, you come here so often, I know it's not just for the quiet. If it were, you could go for a ride in the country and not have to face me all the time. I think you're looking for something. I *know* you're looking for something."

"I don't know."

"Now's as good a time as any. Your life reminds me a little of Job. From the Bible. He lost everything for no good reason at all. His life was effed, too."

Eddy stood. He looked at Jesus's face, trying again to decide how he'd vote about the smile. He didn't know what to do. He didn't want to offend his friend. Or the statue, for that matter.

"I'm not sure about the prayer thing."

"What do you mean?" said Peter, hoping he was gaining an advantage.

"I don't know."

"If you don't know how to do it..."

"That's not it."

"What is it then?"

"No offense, but I don't think it works."

Advantage, Eddy.

Peter took a deep breath, held it for two counts and exhaled. "I understand. I do. Lots of people are skeptical at first. They feel uncomfortable, they can't find the words, they're not sure why they're doing it. I get it. But you have to understand that millions upon millions of people believe otherwise. Billions. Probably." He was building up a head of steam. "The faithful, and the unfaithful, have been praying for millennia; it's a vital part of every culture since the beginning of recorded time."

Eddy brought one thumb to his mouth and started to bite his nail. "I know it's got a long track record. And that's impressive." He raised his eyebrows at Peter for punctuation. "But just because people have always done it, doesn't mean it works, does it? I mean, have you ever had one of those treadmills? For exercise? Millions of people use treadmills. Does it really work? Have you noticed how fat everyone is? And how many treadmills end up on the curb for trash pickup?"

"Eddy," said Peter, a little too loudly. "Eddy, Eddy, we're not talking about treadmills here, we're talking about people who pray because it makes a world of difference. It's a matter of faith, Eddy."

"You have to believe."

"You've got it."

"No offense, but that's not good enough."

"Not good enough?" Peter laughed bitterly.

"You're saying that I have to believe that God is up there listening and that he will do something about what he hears?"

"Well, I suppose—"

"I mean, the evidence that God is doing anything about anything is, well, thin at best."

"What do you mean, 'thin'?"

Eddy pulled his phone from his pocket and opened a news app. "Okay, let's just look at what we got here." Peter leaned in. "Listen to this. Here's an eighteen-year-old girl with a two-year-old son. Her boyfriend took her into a field and strangled her to death. And a month later, they found the remains of her little boy. And listen to what her mother says: 'I never trusted him. I prayed she would be safe, but...' and she goes on."

"Well—"

"And here, the floods down south, devastation, homelessness; and here, two mass shootings yesterday; twenty people dead; thoughts and prayers, thoughts and prayers. What does it matter, thoughts and prayers?"

"I don't—"

Eddy's shoulders jerked. "I'm sorry, I don't mean to be disrespectful, but why believe that God is going to help me with my job, or more importantly, with Gayle's cancer, when he hasn't done anything about all this other stuff?"

"It's—"

"In fact, with all these terrible things going on, what sense would it make for God to do something for me? I mean, really, how fair would that be? Don't get me wrong, but my problems are nothing compared to..." Eddy held up his phone.

He wiped spittle from the corner of his mouth. "Look, Peter, I've got a lot of respect for you, I do. I know you believe, I know you're sincere, and you know a lot more about this than I do; and maybe it works for you, but as far as I'm concerned there's nothing to warrant praying for anything, except maybe praying that you have the strength to bear all the stuff that God doesn't seem to give a fu...an eff about."

Peter looked at the statue of Jesus. He raised his hands to his face.

"I'm sorry, I shouldn't have said all this, especially in front of him." Eddy pointed at Jesus and then dropped his hand quickly, remembering that his mother had taught him it was rude to point.

Peter stepped toward Eddy, who took one step back. Peter put his arms around Eddy and held him gently for a long moment.

"I'm just saying give it a try."

CHAPTER 7

When the flight attendant came around, Rich ordered two martinis. He unbuckled his seat belt and tipped his seat back the maximum three inches.

"Leaving home or going home?" said the woman beside him. She wore wire-rimmed glasses and had long gray hair pulled back in a pony tail. No makeup. Startling blue eyes. Rich thought about her question.

"I don't know."

The woman held up her glass of merlot and said with a chuckle, "Good luck deciding."

He looked out the window, the wing glimmering in the sunset. The plane banked over the southern shore of Lake Ontario and then leveled out, heading southeast toward Columbus and the broad midsection of America.

Monday morning threatened from a distance. A sales meeting, or as his boss liked to call it, a "pep rally," was scheduled for 7:30am. Staff would leave their boxy, plexiglass offices and gather around a massive granite and mahogany conference table; they were a mix of late millennials and early gen-Zers, all males, all white except for the obligatory Asian, all surfing their hand-held tablets for big ideas.

To the casual observer, the eager confidence of the group might suggest a design team for space exploration or urban development.

Instead, they would be gathering to pitch ideas about how to sell a new app—Humpr.

The founder, Felix Thunderstone, a university dropout with "genius ideas," who demanded his employees call him "Doc," framed his invention as a "healthcare innovation." "There are apps that track your blood pressure, your exercise, your calorie intake, your heart rate, your almost everything, except," said Thunderstone, "your need for sex."

"Yes, *need*! Not just want. Need! It's a scientific fact! Humpr will revolutionize how we think about and address our insatiable biological need for sex."

During Rich's Skype interview for the job, Felix went on to explain: "The Humpr app will take your sexual temperature and notify you when you need to have sex, when it is crucial for your well-being to have sex, when sex matters more than food or water for your overall health." The app worked "optimally" if the user carried their phone in a pocket near the "area from which your sexual heat emanates, admittedly more difficult for women, though we're working on that."

Rich stared at the screen. He realized that he hadn't needed to wear a tie for this interview. Felix wore a purple t-shirt that read, 'Keep on Humpin'. He couldn't stop talking. "When your temperature reaches 'HumpNow', your phone vibrates and profiles of would-be HumpMates, male and female, who are also at 'HumpNow' appear in sequence on your screen from 'great match' to 'perfect match'. You scroll through and double-tap the one you want." He then leaned back, a broad grin on his face, "The rest is bliss, man."

"This isn't for real, is it?" said Rich.

Felix almost toppled his mink ergo-chair. "What did you say, man?"

Rich did a quick calculation: Evie's departure (including her ample income) plus mounting bills plus no other job options in the queue plus desperation equaled—"I said, this is so for real, isn't it?" Felix howled and Rich signed his name on the screen.

When his parents asked about his new job, he said he was doing marketing development for a new startup. He knew their eyes would glaze over and they wouldn't know what else to ask. "That's nice," they said. It was easier that way. How could he tell them he hustled big and little pharma, sex toy manufacturers, prophylactic producers, sex tourism agents, anyone that dwelled in the smarmy underbelly of society's hook-up culture, hoping to sell them ad space on Humpr. "It's a living," he said, matter-of-factly.

His traveling neighbor was asleep and Rich's martinis were gone. He closed his eyes. His mother's withering frame appeared. He opened his eyes and leaned against the window to watch the electric stars dotting the landscape below. She's dying. Moisture formed in his palms. He wiped them on his pant leg and shook his head, hoping to toss his thoughts out the window.

He pulled the tray down in front of him and laid his head on it. He closed his eyes and listened to the deep whir of the engines, his body vibrating. He felt pulsing below his left eye again. He pressed it with his finger. He could hear his sister's voice:

"Before I forget, I saw Mr. Cunningham at the pharmacy. He asked about you. I told him you were in Columbus now. He asked me if you were coming by to see Jamie. It's been so long, he said, that it would be a lift if you did." She paused here, tilted her head and pursed her lips in mock scold. "I told him I didn't know what your plans were, but that you might not have time. You know, with Mom and everything. He said he understood. I guess everyone knows."

Rich was surprised how calm Sandy's demeanor was, how nonchalantly she spoke of Jamie, how easily she seemed to compartmentalize the past, as if there was nothing there.

"Small town."

"For sure."

"How's Jamie doing, did he say?"

"Mostly good, he said. Although it sounded to me like he's the same." Sandy's mouth folded into a soft frown.

Rich balled his jacket on the tray and laid his head down again. When they were in high school, he and Jamie had been tight. They went everywhere together. They were co-captains of the Ranger football team their senior year. They worked at the Garden Factory every summer. They went to Bills games in the fall and Red Wings in the spring.

Jamie had planned on becoming a pharmacist like his father. Not because he wanted to, but because he couldn't think of anything else to do. His father happily urged him to follow in his footsteps. In fact, when Jamie was eleven years old, his father dressed him like a pharmacist for Halloween. White coat, plastic nametag, soft-soled shoes, and a caduceus on a long stick, two snakes wound around a winged staff. "It stands for medicine," Jamie explained while Rich rolled on the ground laughing.

Jamie had applied to the University of Buffalo, while Rich planned on attending community college because, as his father put it, he "didn't have a clue" and "needed time to mature." Eventually, Rich would transfer to RPI. But Jamie never went anywhere. His future came to an end on a high school football field. It wasn't even a game. It was the last full-on contact practice before their contest against rivals, Hilton.

Jamie, a running back, got the ball and hit the middle of the line. Rich remembers it clearly, because he was playing middle linebacker and watched the play unfold. Jamie got hit hard at the line, twisted forward and was hit again and again, Rich among them.

Everyone got off the pile except Jamie. He lay still, his fingertips shaking. There was panic on the field as their coach and the trainer descended on Jamie. Everyone on the team took a knee except Rich, who stood over his friend as Coach kept calling Jamie's name. "Come on, son, come on!" Rich held his breath. "C'mon, Jamie, it's me."

Jamie started to move his head and bend his legs. The whole team applauded as he was helped to his feet. His eyes didn't seem to focus on anything, though. Coach took one arm and Rich took the other. He hobbled to the bench and fell back when he sat. They pulled his helmet off. Jamie's breathing was shallow and his face was snow white. He groaned and leaned over. Then he toppled to the ground.

"Are you okay?" said the merlot-lady seated beside Rich.

"What?" Rich sat up.

"You don't look...is everything..."

"Excuse me," Rich slid past the woman and headed down the aisle.

One rest room was occupied but the other was vacant. His locked the door behind him and slid to the floor. He circled his arms around the toilet and vomited. Then he sat back, his legs straddling the commode, his face dripping perspiration.

CHAPTER 8

"Kathleen!" Sam Cunningham said as he came through the back door into the laundry room.

"In here." Kathleen's hair was in a soft bun, strands falling around her ears. She wore a flannel shirt, tight jeans and nursing clogs. She smiled under gray-blue eyes, the only expression he had ever seen on her face.

Sam rifled through the mail on the kitchen counter, then took his coat off and hung it on the back of a chair. He looked in the refrigerator for something to drink. Opened the freezer and took out some beef patties and tater tots to thaw. Then he went into the living room.

"How's he doing today?"

Kathleen beamed. "He's doing so well. I got him up and he sat in the front room by the window for the longest time. I kept telling him everything that we could see, like the trees and leaves, the dog across the street, and he, like, made a high sound, a happy sound, it seemed. It's been a good day. He smiled a lot."

"That's good." Sam's face looked as empty as a promise unmet. "I don't know what I'd do without you, Kathleen."

"It's nothing, really."

"No, it's everything. Really." He smiled sheepishly, looking at her sideways.

"Hi, Jamie." He rocked in a wing-backed chair facing the TV beside his bed. It was too risky for him to navigate the stairs, so Sam and his wife had converted the dining room into what they called his apartment. They added a full bath where a half bath had once been.

He didn't look up. "Jamie! It's Dad, how are you doing?" Was he watching the TV? Was he staring at nothing? Sam had decided long ago that Jamie watched TV and that he knew he watched TV, and that when he made any noise, it was in response to the TV. The TV had become another family member, someone that interacted with Jamie more consistently than anyone else.

"Jamie, how's it going?" Sam's smile looked super-glued to his face. "Kathleen said you've had a good day, a very good day." Over the years, Sam had adjusted to Jamie never responding, at least in the way most people responded. He sat beside his son and placed his hand on Jamie's knee. Jamie's long brown hair had grown into tangles. His eyes, brown as hen's eggs, were busy, but with what? His stubbled chin, his glasses, always sliding down his nose, his limp hands, his feet, resting on their sides, his once washboard belly overflowing his stretchy pants.

"Do you know where Papa is?" Jamie turned his head sharply, noticing his father for the first time. He reached out and patted Sam's face awkwardly. "There you are," said Sam. He took Jamie's hand in his, fingers weaved together. He kissed his forehead. Jamie smiled. "You know who I am, don't you?" Jamie opened his mouth wide, his eyes dancing, his tongue darting in and out. "Paaaaa." He patted his father's face again.

"That's right. It's Pa." He hugged his son and pulled his head close so it rested on his chest. He closed his eyes, drawing comfort from the steady beat of Jamie's heart. "That's my boy."

When Jamie was growing up, Sam understood that one day he would no longer be able to call his son "boy." Sam remembered chastising his own father when he had had the temerity to call him "boy" in front of some friends. Sam, nineteen at the time, was so offended that he pointed a finger at his father and told him in no uncertain terms that he was to never call him "boy" again. Only later did he realize that his behavior was the reason his father declined to call him the one thing he wanted — "man."

There would be no such battle between father and son this time. Jamie was still his "boy" and always would be.

"He didn't have a bath yesterday?" Sam raised his eyebrows questioningly.

"No, he didn't." Kathleen had let her hair down and put her coat on. Sam didn't say anything. "I can stay to help you, if you'd like."

"I hate to—"

"That's fine." She took her coat off and got a basin from the bathroom.

Sam watched her, how she moved quietly, delicately; how she swept her hair over to one side when she bent. He looked away, embarrassed. Jamie was rocking back and forth to the music from the *Ellen* show. His jaw jutted and drool ran down his cheek. Sam wiped it away with his hand. "Rock on, Jamie."

Kathleen filled the basin with soapy water and carried it back into the living room, placing it on the coffee table. She gathered some wash cloths and towels. She never minded washing Jamie on her own, but it was awkward doing it with Mr. Cunningham there.

They pulled Jamie's pajama bottoms off and washed his legs, the warm water calming him.

"You were made for this work," said Sam. "I mean, you could do anything, but you're so good…"

"Thank you, Mr. Cunningham."

He had stopped asking her to call him Sam.

"And I can tell that he loves you."

Kathleen didn't respond, her attention focused on Jamie. She rinsed her washcloth and then pulled Jamie's shirt up, exposing his belly, a professional half-grin on her face.

"At least that's what it seems like to me; he always responds so well to you."

"We get along," she said, matter-of-factly.

"Yes, that's it. You two get along."

Sam tried to wash his son's arms, but soon let Kathleen take over. She was efficient, thorough. Bath over, she put her coat on again and headed for the door.

"Sure you wouldn't like to stay for dinner?"

"No thank you, Mr. Cunningham."

"It's no problem, believe me."

"That's okay."

"I grill a mean burger."

Kathleen forced breath through her nose, the closest thing to a laugh she could muster.

"I'm sure you do."

He held his arms out wide as if to say, 'Why not?'.

She tried to grin.

"Okay, then, Kathleen."

"Have a nice evening, Mr. Cunningham. I'll see Jamie tomorrow. Bye Jamie," she said with a brisk wave.

All the oxygen, all the life, seemed to be sucked from the room when Kathleen closed the door. Sam sat beside Jamie until his show was over and then he turned the channel to Nickelodeon. Jamie's eyes fixed on the flashing lights and colors while Sam slipped quietly out of the room.

He put the burger in the broiler and the taters in the toaster oven. Took a Peroni from the fridge and sat down at the kitchen table. He could hear brisk wind tossing the maple that brushed the porch roof. He closed his eyes for a few minutes and massaged his temple. He opened his laptop, checked the tots and burger again, pulled another beer from the fridge, and then went to Facebook. Kittens, kittens, kittens, babies, babies, babies, angry politics, angry politics, angry politics, birthdays, friends with news of note — "My foot is getting better" "I'm tired today" "I have lost one of my shoes. How is that possible?"

Then he went to the search option and typed in Kathleen Aggerwall. Her profile picture was backlit by a setting sun so her face was partially shaded, but you could see her rounded cheeks and her long neck. She was wearing a straw sunhat and smokey, round shades. She looked mysterious in the shadows, so different than her daily conservative, formal presentation.

He would never have thought to search for her except that a few months earlier she had come up as a 'friend suggestion'. Sam was flattered. He thought the friend suggestion came directly from

Kathleen. Like 'Hey, we know each other pretty well, let's be friends!'. When he realized that he had been selected by an algorithm, he felt too embarrassed to click 'add friend'. What would she think?

The first thing he found out was that Kathleen was forty-one, which was a shock. Her skin looked so soft, her face unwrinkled. He assumed she was thirtyish. Her status was "single" and, while there were pictures that included men, there were never pictures of the same man over and over, or someone side-by-side with her. She appeared to love pigmy goats, Starbucks, Billie Eilish (whoever that was), *This Is Us*, Thai food, and the Hallmark Channel. She got her RN fifteen years ago and had worked for VNS ever since. And there were many pictures of a little girl with curly blonde hair. Kathleen had three hundred thirty-six friends and went to Las Vegas at least twice a year.

Each time Sam went to her page, he felt like he was opening a jewelry box full of shiny, delicate objects, each more fascinating than the one before. Sometimes he scrolled through her photos, studying the variety of expressions on her face, expressions he had never seen before. She looked like a happy person. A happy person who took care of Jamie; a happy person that he saw every day, talked with every day, shared time with every day. It made him feel like he could be a happy person, too.

Sam found Jamie asleep in front of the TV. He touched his arm and whispered, "Let's go, buddy." As Jamie's eyes opened, his mouth tore back in a grimace. He started flailing. "You're okay, son. You're okay." Sam rubbed the back of Jamie's head gently, slowly. He calmed down. He looked at his father and smiled. He said, "Paaa?" with a rising intonation, an upspeak, a plaintive questioning, as if to say, 'What happened?'. Sam helped his son to his feet and guided him to his bedroom. Jamie curled into a fetal position, his favorite stuffed bear clutched to his chest. Sam stopped at the doorway to watch his son, to listen to his snore.

He turned off the TV. Shut off the lights in the kitchen and family room. Checked the front door to make sure it was locked. Before going upstairs, he reluctantly closed his laptop.

"Good night, Kathleen."

CHAPTER 9

Over the ensuing months, Rich and Sandy kept their promise. They came home a second time and called almost every week. Often Gayle was too tired to talk on the phone but she listened. Eddy talked about the weather, happenings in town, the weather, stories from the local paper, and the weather. When they asked about the treatment, Eddy always said "smooth as silk." He made sure that Rich and Sandy knew little more when they hung up than when they first called. Too many things were in flux.

Gayle went into her office every day. She tried to manage client questions and problems via email or text. Sometimes when the phone rang, she let it go to message; talking was too labor intensive.

"Gayle, please, don't work so long on that stuff. It's not even tax season. Take a break." For years, this had been Eddy's mantra. He understood little about her work, about what it took to keep her clients happy year-round—state and federal filings and audits were just the tip of the iceberg. In the early days most of her clients were individuals, usually friends, or mom and pop operations with few needs except in late winter and early spring. But over the years she lured a larger firm here, a growing business there, and soon she could pick and choose who she wanted in her portfolio.

She could have expanded her business more quickly if she had been willing to hire some junior accountants and tax geeks. But she didn't want to. She liked keeping her eye on everything, having control over what came into her office and what went out. The less anyone else knew about her work, the better.

The oncologists were encouraging her to enter yet another experimental trial. This only served to punctuate the failure of her multiple rounds of chemotherapy. "There are always new treatments," her doctor said with a confident smile. "Immunotherapy is making strides every day."

The equation they presented was simple: more time is better than less time. The complicated math of quality vs. quantity had not yet been addressed. "No need for that at this point," her nurse said.

There was more to be done to fight this disease. The doctors said this. Eddy said this. There were always reasons to keep going. There were always reasons for hope. And even if there weren't reasons for it, hope remained. Right?

Gayle ate most things. She walked short distances. She was often sick, though; often in pain. She wasn't strong, not like she used to be, but if she worked hard, she could do most things. She was always tired. She went to a movie now and then, if only for a nap. She sat with Eddy watching TV and holding hands. She loved this, but didn't dare tell him not to lean against her, despite her aching arms. She lay awake at night for hours trying to find a comfortable position or warding off unwanted thoughts and inescapable fears. Often when she closed her eyes, she hoped she'd never open them again.

When she first started treatment, she thought progress would include going back to the way things were. It wasn't long before she understood that going back wasn't an option. She felt like she was on a train in a darkened tunnel and no matter how tightly she squinted her eyes, there was no sign of light at the end. She stopped looking.

•   •   •

Eddy played the "one day at a time" game as best he could. But panic was always hunched over his shoulder. Universal was no more. Scope had erased any semblance of what had been before. Weaker contracts. No overtime. Healthcare options that left many employees out in the cold.

"How did it go this week?"

Eddy had met with this woman before, but he couldn't remember her name. In the beginning, he tried to make a connection, but soon it didn't seem to matter. Everyone at the unemployment office was interchangeable, their faces numb with boredom, their eyes vacant as they processed a never-ending parade of discouraged and often angry people who hated being there as much as the workers did.

"Well, there wasn't anything available, really."

"Didn't I give you a list?" she said, fingers skating across her keyboard.

"Yes, you did, but like I've said before, Taco Bell, McDonald's, and Pizza Joe's aren't real options." He placed his hands on her desk and held his breath. When Eddy exhaled, it wasn't carbon dioxide that came out of his mouth, it was his soul. "You know as well as I do that I make more money not working. I know it doesn't make sense, but..."

"You remember what it says, don't you, Mr. uh..." she looked at her computer screen, "...Kimes. I mean, we gave you the paper work long time ago, didn't we?"

"Yeah, somebody did, but—"

"Do you remember what it says?"

"Not word for word—"

"Let me remind you; it says that every recipient of unemployment benefits must make at least three work search activities per week to keep their benefits." She turned her face to him but didn't make eye contact.

"But, like I said—"

"Mr. Kimes, I'm sorry, but those are the rules."

Eddy sat up in his chair, back straight. "I'll bet I hooked you up."

"Excuse me."

"Telephone, cable, the whole deal. I bet that I, actually my team, hooked you up; and I bet that when a snow storm knocked you out, you called and it was me that responded."

"Mr. Kimes—"

"I have worked all my life and I've never needed anyone to remind me to work hard, or to keep trying. I wanted to work. I wanted to pay my way. I wanted to make a life for my family. I have a home, two grown, successful children, and a wife with cancer. And no job. And no health insurance."

"Mr. Kimes, I'm sorry, but—"

"I know you see dozens of people like me every day, and after a while they all kind of run together like so many random parts on an assembly line." Eddy wanted to say: *I want you to know that this is what makes a person go insane. This is exactly what makes someone get a gun and wave it around, just to get somebody to pay attention. It's fucking crazy, isn't it, but over here on this side of your desk where I'm sitting, it makes sense. It's the only way out when there's no way forward.* But he didn't.

"Here's what I want; I want you to remember me tonight when you go home, when you sit down for dinner. Remember Eddy Kimes, who had a job, a good job with good pay, a job that he lost, excuse me, a job that was taken away from him for no good reason. Remember that."

Each day Eddy watched for the mail through the living room window. He'd shuffle through it quickly, surreptitiously, before turning back to the house. Once he got to the garage, he slid the worst of it into his pocket. In the beginning, the mortgage and the car payments and the utilities worried him most. But once the hospital bills started rolling in, the others seemed inconsequential. The numbers were laughable. Immunotherapy would be even more expensive. The only way they could pay for Gayle's healthcare would be if one of them died, preferably two months ago. Then life insurance would have kicked in, saving the day.

Lucky for him, Gayle was too weak to care much about any of this. He didn't open the envelopes from the hospital any more. Instead, he put them all in an accordion folder that he kept in the bottom drawer of his dresser.

•   •   •

Eddy stood for a moment looking through the window at Walgreen's until Sam noticed him. He waved for Eddy to come in, but Eddy shook his head, gave him a thumbs up and walked on.

The sky looked like the inside of a gray, metal dome. His shoulders curled in the wind, just as they had a year before when he had come upon Clevon in the square and spring was rehearsing its return. Clevon had been desperate about what was going to happen at Scope.

At the time, Eddy still felt hopeful about Scope, about Gayle, about almost everything; a run-of-the-mill hope that everyone must be born with, hope that is confident, though untested and, perhaps, ill-informed. Things had changed over the spring, summer and now the deep fall. Clevon was long gone. He had moved his family to Nashville where they lived with his cousin. Things had not worked out with Scope. Things had not worked out with Gayle. Things had not worked out, period. Eddy's hope was on the wane, like a breathless sprinter thrust into a marathon, fist planted deep in his side, legs limp as dish rags.

He looked across the square at the church spire. He hadn't been to the statue in weeks. The bushes surrounding the Consoler looked unkempt. Eddy swept leaves off the marble bench and then sat. He looked at Rev. Goff's office window, but the room was dark. The expression on Jesus's weathered face was as inscrutable as ever. He stood again, this time on tiptoes, trying to see more clearly the famous notch in Jesus's collarbone. He touched the graying folds of his robe and studied the exacting detail of his feet. He felt ridiculous being there. He looked again at the darkened window of Goff's office. He pulled his collar up and tucked his hands into his pockets before sitting back down.

"Just speak from your heart," Rev. Goff had told him. "God will incline his ear."

"Do what with his ear?"

"God will listen."

"And then what?"

Peter had shrugged his shoulders. "It's hard to tell."

"Hard to tell," he said to himself now as he looked vacantly at the statue. He bowed his head and folded his hands. He opened one eye to make sure no one was looking. He opened his mouth and closed it. He relaxed his hands and unbowed his head. He stretched out his legs and leaned forward to ease the tension in his back. How to start? Rev.

Goff prayed silently, so that wasn't any help. Channel surfing on Sunday mornings, though, Eddy had seen snippets of many televangelists, their arms outstretched, their faces looking painfully constipated.

He raised his arms and lowered his head. "Dearest Jesus and Thou Father God of all and writer of the Bible, I have never done-est this, which Thou must surely know-est." He shifted his weight on the slab. "Actually, I...lie-est. As a child my mother always made-est me say my prayers before I went-est to bed at night. 'Now I lay me...' you know the rest. But as an adult, I have not prayed. I know-est that Thou dost not know-est me well at all." 'Jesus', he thought. "I'm Eddy. Rev. Goff, Peter, said I should pray because I have so much in common with Job." His lips flapped as he exhaled hard. "I am, or amst, sitting before Thee here on this marble bench in a beseeching frame of mind." He lowered his arms and raised his head.

Eddy knew he couldn't do it like the big time pray-ers on TV. "Look, I can't pray, so I'm just going to talk; I'm going to speak my mind, if that's okay."

Eddy could feel the statue engulfing him, swallowing him. He steadied his hands by pressing them against his thighs. "Let's see, I made some notes." Eddy opened his wallet and unfolded a sheet of paper. "Okay, so, number one..." but he choked.

He put the list and wallet back in his pocket and shifted his weight yet again, trying to avoid his sciatic nerve. His eyes narrowed, his chin jutted and a glowering shadow crossed his bulky face. "Okay, so here's my question: What the hell, excuse my language, but what the hell kind of God are you, anyway?" It was quiet except for the wind rustling the bushes. Jesus the Consoler's expression remained unchanged. Nothing bad happened, so he went on.

"Gayle and me may not be church-goers, but we are good people, especially Gayle. We raised two great kids. We're hard workers; we pay our taxes; we're good friends to everyone we know. We vote. We give to some charities when we can. We don't hurt anyone. We don't complain. We ask for almost nothing in return, just a house and enough money to pay the bills. We like to go on vacation every year, too. We do have a flat screen TV, big, but not ridiculous; and two cars, nothing extravagant, although we do have an SUV, which isn't so good on your creation. But it's just an Equinox. Anyway, I'm off topic.

"The point is, we are living our lives as best we can, so why mess with it? Why cancer? Let me amend that. Cancer is cancer, I get that, but why a cancer that you can't do anything about? And my job? Okay, Gayle has been warning me for years, but, really, why now, why the exquisitely poor timing? Actually, cruel timing?

"Even if we had to face these things one at a time, it would be better than this. But all at once? You don't know anything about health insurance, do you? You don't know anything about what it's like down here, do you? A lot has changed in the last two thousand years."

Eddy's cell phone buzzed in his pocket. He looked at Jesus, then looked at the phone.

"Hi honey…Yeah, heading home…Sure, what do we need?…Just milk?…How about some ice cream or pudding? How's that sound?…Yeah…A milkshake, sure, I'll make you one when I get home…Okay…No problem…Love you, too."

Eddy slipped his phone back into his pocket and stood in front of the statue.

"I guess, for now, I'll have to put an amen on this."

He stopped briefly at the opening to the garden, pulled his jacket collar up again and turned back to Jesus the Consoler, whose eyes appeared to be averted.

CHAPTER 10

The parking lot had thinned out by the time Eddy and Gayle arrived at Blue Ridge. He pulled into a perfect spot directly in front of the entrance. It had been several weeks since they'd been there.

"Lucky day," said Gayle.

"Skill, not luck." Eddy backed up and eased forward twice, trying not to block the parking space beside him. "There we go."

Gayle opened her door and turned sideways to get out of the car. By then Eddy was holding the door open.

"Can I..."

Gayle elbowed the seat and leaned forward until her feet were settled on the pavement. She hoisted herself up to a standing position. Then paused, finding her balance. Eddy looked across the parking lot and did not speak while she completed the process. Gayle looked around the lot, relieved that no one was watching. She was glad that Eddy hadn't said anything encouraging, hadn't tried to lift her spirits.

The girl at the counter greeted them with a broad smile. "There you are!" She grabbed two menus and led them to 'their' booth by a window. Before Gayle sat, the young woman hugged her and whispered, "I love your hair; looks wonderful." Gayle blushed and thanked her. For a time, her scalp had been too sore to put anything on her head, but recently, she had decided to "do something" despite the discomfort. Natural hair was too much bother, so she bought a synthetic wig that was almost the color of her own hair. Except it was shorter and curlier.

"I love it," Eddy had said.

"It doesn't make me look like Pat from *Saturday Night Live*?"

"No." Eddy managed a convincing incredulity, even though Gayle was right, she looked like Pat.

"So good to see you. Coffee?" Gayle and Eddy shook their heads. The waitress patted Gayle on the shoulder.

"I'm a cancer celebrity," said Gayle.

Eddy looked up from his menu and smiled faintly. He ordered an omelet, hash browns and French toast. Gayle got two eggs scrambled and a dry English muffin.

They sat with hands folded, studying the diners around them, hoping there wasn't anyone they knew. Gayle pushed her eggs around the plate with pieces of muffin while Eddy went at his meal in earnest. The waitress topped off their coffee a second and then a third time. Both checked email and Facebook. Soon Gayle pushed her plate to the side, still full; Eddy pushed his to the side, empty. Coffee cups, cooler now, sat in front of them.

"So." Eddy raised his eyebrows.

"I don't want to talk about this."

Eddy slid his hand across the table. "Honey, we have to talk."

"Is there really anything more to say?"

Eddy didn't want to talk the about cancer any more than Gayle did. They'd talked about it continuously in the beginning. But as treatment wore on, they went days without even saying the word. They were pulled along by the inertia of routine.

In recent weeks, though, with treatment at a crossroads, it was impossible to avoid it. Nothing else mattered. The only time they didn't discuss it was when they were with others or when they talked to Rich or Sandy. They had become over-protective parents since Eddy's disastrous attempt at divulging what was going on.

"There are decisions —"

"Really? Decisions imply options." Gayle looked at her coffee cup.

"Look —"

"I'm too tired."

"I know you are."

"And you are, too."

"Yes, we're both tired. But we have to—"

"We don't 'have to' anything."

Their waitress came for their plates and they fell silent.

"Can I get you anything else? More coffee?" They declined. "Okay, hope you have a great day." They wished her the same, then waited a beat or two.

"I don't know if I want to do anything more."

"You can't mean that."

"Why can't I?"

"You're, well, you're young for one thing. You have so much life ahead of you."

Gayle looked away.

Eddy was undeterred. "You *are* young. And there's the kids and maybe grandkids one day. And your business, where would they go?"

"The kids, they'll be fine."

"Come on, that's not true."

"Not at first. But eventually."

"Jesus…"

"And the business, let H&R Bloch take care of them all."

Eddy leaned back and folded his arms. "What about me, Gayle? What about me and you? Can H&R Bloch take care of that, too?"

"Well—"

"Gayle, really, why are you being so, I don't know, so obstinate about this? It's not like you."

Gayle folded her hands on the table and looked into her husband's all too familiar eyes, framed as they were in dark circles.

"Eddy." She reached for his hands. "You are going through this with me, but not really. Just like you went through the birth of our kids with me, but not really. I had the babies inside me. And I have the cancer inside me. You are my witness, the one who loves me and suffers alongside me, but you can't be me; and you can't know what is best for me."

"But Gayle—"

"I hate saying it, but it's true. You're there for me every day, you talk to me, you hold me, you do things for me, but what you can't possibly understand is that I'm gone. I don't know exactly when it happened, but I'm gone. There's nothing left of me and I'm tired."

Eddy looked down at their hands resting on top of each other.

"When I first got the news, I was scared. I was afraid I'd die. Made me feel sicker than the chemo."

Eddy squeezed her hand tighter. He felt icy fear on the back of his neck.

"I'm still afraid, Eddy. But it's different. It's more like I'm scared I won't ever be done with this."

"Gayle, I don't know what...Gayle, look, I'm here, I am, I'll always be here for you no matter what happens."

Gayle leaned forward and kissed the back of his hand.

"I'm so sorry...for all of this, for you feeling so...lost...I can't imagine..." When he swallowed, there was a fist in his throat.

"Eddy, honey—"

"Look, the chemo didn't do what it was supposed to do, I know that. But that's not the end of the line, not really. I still have hope, I do, I have enough for both of us. And the doctor said this new thing, the immune thing, whatever it's called—"

"Eddy—"

"She said they take some stuff from you and from the cancer, or something, like it's designed just for you, and it makes your body fight harder. Look, there's more time out there for you, honey, there is. We just have to—"

"Eddy, please. I love you."

"I love you too, that's why—"

She put her fingers to his lips. "I don't want to do this anymore. I can't."

CHAPTER 11

Once Humpr started getting some traction, Felix Thunderstone encouraged all of his employees to take the app "out for a spin," dangling bonuses over their heads. Rich, and a plurality of the married staff, had been holdouts. He explained that he had broken up with his girlfriend recently and wasn't feeling much like, well, humping. Thunderstone laughed at this. "It isn't love, my friend, it's sex; it's health maintenance, pure and simple."

Rich explained that he hadn't felt sexually aroused in months. Thunderstone: "Does a major league baseball player *feel* like grabbing his bat in December or January?" Rich said he didn't know. "Of course, he doesn't! At least not until he *does* grab his bat, then the heat comes back and he wants to hit that thing as hard and as often as he can."

"Are we still talking about baseball?"

"Your problem *isn't* that you don't *WANT* to do it; the problem *is* that you're *NOT* doing it. Simple. Trust me on this, bro."

Speechless at this rationale, Rich reluctantly agreed to "go for a ride," which got his boss off his back for a few weeks.

"This guy's not for real, is he? I mean, what's he thinking?" was Sandy's response when he called her.

"Well, he thinks we'll do a better job selling this thing, if we've had the…experience. Kind of, can you sell a car if you've never driven one? Would you sleep on a mattress if you never tried it out?"

"I do that every time I stay at a motel. And I sleep fine."

"You get what I mean. He's convinced this is a health thing, not an intimacy or even a sexual thing. It's just good for you, period. And so, if a customer says, 'Have you tried this?' he wants everyone to be, how do I put it, familiar with the product and its benefits. I mean, several of my colleagues, even a few who are married, have tried it and rave about it. Sleeping better. Calmer. Blood pressure improvements. Self-confidence boost."

"Look, Richie, I am not living under the Humpr spell so I think I can say this with confidence: This is bullshit."

At their monthly "confab," even before Rich got seated, Thunderstone asked how it had gone.

"I've tried, I have, but I haven't gotten any responses."

Thunderstone laughed and then frowned. "C'mon, bro, that's not possible. All you have to do is push start and someone will come up."

"But I thought you had to have a HumpNow match?"

"Rich, let's not be naïve. How would we make any money if even once you pushed start and nothing came up? People would dump the app immediately. We have to satisfy our customers, right? So, there's no way that someone doesn't come up. I can guarantee that."

Thunderstone went on to explain that he'd recruited 'app adjuncts', male and female, from all around the country, every market, who were always available. For an additional fee. "Would you try Uber a second time if you were left standing in the rain the first time?"

"Wait, what?"

"I've brought on attractive men and women who are struggling to make ends meet, who need a break in their lives, who can't survive on what they're making at McDonald's; single moms; college grads who need to pay off loans; middle-aged guys and gals who are bored and want to, want to make a contribution to the betterment of people's lives."

"Really?"

"Really."

Rich's mouth fell open, like his jaw had become unhinged.

"So, you're paying—"

"They're paying me, us, Humpr."

"What?"

"For the opportunity. Then they charge whatever fee seems reasonable for their prompt availability."

"But mainly we have real members, I mean people who have paid to join, right?"

"We're getting there."

"We're getting there?"

"The demand for services is currently greater than our available resources."

"You mean, people aren't signing up—"

"Look, Rich, sometimes a business grows faster than expected, and you have to do whatever is necessary—"

"What percentage of our 'resources' are people who have actually signed on as members?"

"About twenty percent."

"So, eighty percent are—"

"Adjuncts."

Rich fell silent after this. Again, he swore he'd take the app out for a spin before their next meeting, which would be more of a 'deadline' than a friendly 'confab'. He waited several days before he called Sandy, hoping to find the right way to frame things.

"Well, Humpr is exploding. The requests for services are enormous, so things are going well. The struggle is with membership. We are growing steadily, but not fast enough to meet demand. So, we're, we're bringing on, like, placeholder members."

"Placeholder members?"

"Yeah, you know, until the membership can meet the demand. Thunderstone came up with the idea of adjunct members."

"I have no idea what you're talking about. You sound positively corporate."

Sandy listened, her stomach slowly balling into a knot.

"Rich, do you have your computer there?"

"Yeah, why?"

"Okay, Google 'escort services Columbus'."

She listened patiently to Rich's busy keys. When he stopped, she asked, "Did you find Humpr?"

"Uh huh."

"Okay, use your app and search for a match."

Rich clicked on and a dozen names came up. He clicked on the first one, swallowed and leaned back in his chair.

"Rich?"

"Yeah."

"What did you get?"

"I got a young woman who is in desperate need of clothing."

"Is she a member?"

"She's an...'available option'."

"How much does the 'available option' cost?"

"Depends on the amount of time I want...and what I'd like to do..."

Sandy's voice was smooth and calm, like she was talking someone off the ledge of a building. "So, Rich, do you understand now? If it looks like a duck and walks like a duck..."

"Uh huh."

Sandy could hear Rich mouth-breathing.

"Are you there?"

"Uh huh."

"Look, Rich, Humpr is an upscale escort service parading as something else."

"Uh huh."

"Listen to me. I am not judging anyone who is doing sex work. I'm not. The reasons are complex, believe me. My concern is that you're working for a scumbag who is masquerading as some kind of altruistic-healthcare-I-don't-know-what. I'm telling you, it may not happen soon, but he's going to fall. I just don't want you to fall with him."

Rich was curled in a fetal position on his bed.

"Sandy, do you have any idea how far in debt I am? I mean, after Evie left...I can't even tell you how much. I'm trying to catch up on the fucking mortgage. If I lose a paycheck, even for a month, I'll be out on the street. Do you know how much he's giving us if we try out the app? Ten thousand dollars. 10K! The money is going to be enormous."

Now Sandy was curled in a fetal position on *her* bed. She wanted to say: It's simple; do the right thing. Ever since high school, she'd tried to make choices that would move her closer to that 'right thing', whatever it was. She tried to ignore the noise, the false persuasions, the manipulations designed to make her do what someone else wanted her to do.

"Sandy?"

"Yeah."

"I can't crash. I just can't. With everything that's going on right now. I don't know what's going to happen with Mom. Dad's seems like a hapless mess. And then I come along, 'Hey, guess what, I can't keep a job; I'm broke; Can I come home?'"

"Yeah, I get it."

"I just can't fail again. Not now."

"Richie, you're not a failure."

"It's like I'm always in survival mode, like I'm crawling along and every time I try to get up, my feet slip out from under me."

Was there ever a 'right thing'? Sandy wondered. Or was it just something you believed in when you were small, when right was right and wrong was wrong? Was all that meant to help you get started in life, but not meant to sustain you? It had been a long time since the 'right thing' test applied. Mostly, she felt like she was on a rock wall reaching for what she hoped would be a good grip. Was survival life's default mode?

"Richie, I love you. You know, no matter what you do, I'll always support you."

When she hung up, Sandy went to her work desk and picked up a neatly stacked pile of bills. But she couldn't bring herself to open them. Instead, she went online, Googling 'job opportunities'.

CHAPTER 12

"What are we doing here?"

"I don't know, Sam, it's just…isn't it relaxing to sit here, I mean you got the bushes around you so nobody can bother you. It's quiet." Eddy took a seat on the marble bench. "Trust me, it's a good place." He patted the bench. Sam sat.

"I've never been this close to…" He pointed at the statue.

"Something, huh."

"It's Jesus with his arms out."

"Amazing, really."

"What's that by his shoulder blade?"

"It's called The Notch, capital T, capital N."

"The Notch, capital T, capital N. Okay."

"When they first put the statue up, way back in the fifties, they discovered an imperfection. It was a big deal, but then someone decided it was a sign of Jesus's humanity, you know, like us, a little bit broken, and it was okay. So, they just left it the way it was. It's kind of—"

"Are you alright, Eddy?" Sam felt a frown crossing his face.

"What do you mean?"

"Just what I said—Are you alright?"

"No, I'm *not* alright. My wife's got cancer, I lost my job—"

"I didn't mean that. That's awful, I know. But this…" He nodded at the statue. "What's with this? You haven't gotten, you know…"

"Religion?"

"Bingo."

"No, I don't think so anyway."

"Praying to the statue, are you?"

"Well—"

"That's what happens, you know. Someone has a string of bad luck and all of a sudden they're religious and the blinders go on."

Eddy took a deep breath and spoke in a whisper. "I don't have blinders on. Wish I did. If religion gave you blinders, I'd sign up in a minute."

Sam pointed at Jesus the Consoler. "Why are we here?"

Eddy looked away and sighed deeply before speaking. "I don't know why we're here. Who does?"

"No, I meant, why are we *here* in this garden in front of this statue?"

"I can't answer that either." Both men fell silent.

Thin clouds crossed the full moon. In the distance, there was laughter and talking, then car doors closing and engines revving. A small-town hum filled the air.

"How's Gayley doing?"

Eddy shook his head and swayed from one side to the other.

"Where to start. She's gone through round after round of these different chemos. She's felt like shit for a year. And, as far as they can tell, it hasn't worked."

"What?"

"Just what I said. Looks like it's spreading."

"Jesus."

"Yeah. And that's not even the worst of it."

Sam scratched his temple and then drummed his fingers on his leg. "There's something worse?"

"It's Gayle. She's changed."

"I'm sure…"

"She isn't herself anymore."

"Well…"

"You know how Gayle is. She's organized, she's a clock watcher, always planning, getting things done; even while she's been sick, she's kept working and staying on top of everything."

"Yeah."

"Now, it's like she turned all of that off." He snapped his fingers. "Just like that. Gone."

"Is she depressed? I mean, she's got to be depressed."

"You'd think. But, no, she's not depressed. If anything, her mood seems better. She seems calm. She doesn't get upset: she doesn't seem worried about anything." Eddy's face winced. "I feel terrible saying this, but sometimes she's just plain odd or goofy."

"Goofy?"

"I'm sure that's not the right word, but it's the only one I got. The other day, I'm standing by the sink, drinking my morning coffee, and it's quiet as anything, and all of a sudden she comes out of nowhere, pokes me in the ribs and says, 'Boo'."

"Boo?"

"She's buying these wigs and new clothes, stuff she'd never wear, and sometimes I find her by herself, just smiling. For no reason. I don't get it."

"Maybe she's trying to distract—"

"When I came home the other day, she was upstairs in the bathroom. She didn't hear me, so I watched from the hall for a moment. And she was taking one of those wigs out of a box."

"She probably wants—"

"It was bright red. I mean, like a clown might wear."

"Well—"

"She looked in the mirror and laughed." One corner of Eddy's mouth pulled up, then the other. He raised his arms and then let them fall. "Do you know how long it's been since I've heard her laugh?"

Sam held his breath, unsure of what to say.

"Well, that's a good thing, right, I mean maybe she's getting her strength back…"

Both men heard a siren in the distance but said nothing.

"She listens to rap music."

"Rap music?"

"I think that's what it is. And like I said, she's wearing all these bright colors. No more beige. It's insane." Eddy shook his head slowly. "And she seems happy."

"Happy?"

"Yeah."

"Well, that's good, right? Happy is good."

"I suppose." Eddy couldn't put his finger on it, but Gayle's happiness didn't seem to have anything to do with anything. Nothing. It was happiness from out of the blue. While it was good to see her smile, it was puzzling, as well, even strange.

Sam's hand went to his chin, a finger lay across his lips. He looked down at his legs, crossed at the ankles.

"When did all this start, Eddy?"

"Right after our last meeting with the oncologists. They were straight about what was going on, that the chemo, how did they say it, 'wasn't bringing the progress they had hoped for'. That's when they brought up this other thing, the immune something."

"Immunotherapy." Sam sat up straight and unfolded his legs.

"Yeah, I guess."

"So, that sounds good. I mean it opens another door."

"That's what I thought. But Gayle wasn't that interested. I could see the doctors were surprised, or confused, I don't know, but it wasn't what they expected. All she said was she'd think about it. I was dumbfounded."

Eddy pulled the collar up on his coat and rubbed his hands together.

"And."

"And so, we went to Blue Ridge for breakfast, like we always do, and I asked her what was going on. And she said she was done."

"Done?"

"Yeah, just like that—'I'm done'," he said with a jerk of one wrist. "She was too tired to go on with the treatments. She didn't see the point. They were killing her, that's what she said, 'They're killing me'."

"Jesus, Eddy."

Eddy wiped his nose with his coat sleeve. He sniffed, then coughed.

Sam's neck felt stiff. He rubbed it as he spoke. "That doesn't sound like Gayle at all. I mean she's always been a fighter. I mean, I've seen her get frustrated, but I've never seen her give up on anything. She's just not made that way, you know?"

"I'm telling you, she's different."

"Maybe she just needed to take a break and this was the only way she could think to do it. Don't worry, she'll turn around."

Eddy wiped his eyes again.

"I don't know, Sam. It's almost like she's ready."

"Ready? Ready for what?"

"I'm not sure. Ready for whatever is going to happen. Ready to fucking die, for all I know."

"No, that's not —"

"We been together all these years. I'm telling you, I never loved anyone else. It's been side-by-side the whole way. We've faced everything life has thrown at us; we've done it all. Together. And here we are, the biggest thing ever in our lives, and all of a sudden, she makes this decision without even telling me. Like I'm some stranger or something."

"Eddy —"

"Maybe she's ready, but I'm not. I'm telling you, I'm not ready and I never will be."

Sam gulped his next breath. "No one ever is."

They both looked at the statue. Eddy reached for his friend's forearm. Sam's voice went raspy, like his words were crawling across gravel.

"I'm still not ready... and it *already* happened. I wish to Christ Marianne hadn't...I wish I could have done something..."

"Yeah, I'm sure —"

"We had Jamie, you know, and it was hard, but he was alive and at least he wasn't getting worse."

"I know..."

"And then she was gone. Just like that. No warning."

Eddy felt his Adam's apple swell.

"Good weather. Straight road. No skid marks." Sam shrugged.

Eddy squeezed Sam's forearm harder. "Sam."

"I know, I know. Been a long time. You know, you can't help but wish things were different."

"No, you can't. You were a good husband. She was a good wife. And you both were good parents. You hope that's enough."

Sam turned sideways, straddling the bench. He was pointing now.

"Look, Eddy, I'm telling you, Gayle's still here. She. Is. Still. Here. You've got to get her to fight. You've come too far together. You don't want to end up alone, if you don't have to."

Eddy took a deep breath and let it out by inches. He took another and his heart found its rhythm. He patted Sam's back firmly.

They could hear the footsteps and the light conversation of a couple walking by. The church steeple, with its stiletto spire, stood firm against the wind that tilted the trees across the street. Jesus the Consoler, arms in far-flung pantomime, robe draped in immoveable folds, and face in permanent gaze, seemed impervious to the men that sat chilled on the tiny bench before him. Sam looked at the statue, trying to understand its frowning smile.

CHAPTER 13

Gayle hadn't driven in months, but the thought of sitting at home another minute was about to crush her. She sat sideways on the edge of the driver's seat and then, one at a time, she gingerly lifted her legs into the car. She reached for the door handle, her face wincing at the strain. She sat back in the driver's seat for a long moment, out of breath. Gayle had asked her doctor whether she could drive. A crumpled look had crossed her face, as if Gayle had asked her if she was healthy enough to go over Niagara Falls in a barrel.

"Well," was her first answer. Concise, to the point. She went on: "I don't know if it's a good idea." Her mouth was a straight line as she leaned her head to one side, perhaps an attempt at empathy. 'I don't know if it's a good idea' did not sound like a 'No' to Gayle.

There was a box beside her on the passenger seat, a new wig. Vibrant, wavy, red. Almost the same shade of red as the dress she was wearing, which was sequined. When she put it on, it reminded her of Ann Margaret, or at least a hint of Ann Margaret. Beside the wig was a pair of rhinestone sunglasses with pointy tips. Why not? She hadn't told Eddy about her purchases. He would only have worried that the cancer had finally reached her brain. For all Gayle knew, it had. If that were the case, she was enjoying it. She felt oddly free in recent weeks. She hadn't seen her doctors in a couple of months.

Tax season had returned. And although she had promised Eddy that she would refer her clients elsewhere, she kept them all, picking away at their returns at odd hours of the day (and night) when Eddy was less likely to notice. It wasn't out of the goodness of her heart. There was money to be made, needed more now than ever.

There were two boxes of tax returns on her back seat. Her first stop was the post office.

"Excuse me," she said, waving to a man who was about to get in his car. "Would you be so kind as to help me carry these in?"

"Sure." As he came closer, she recognized him as an old neighbor. "Well, hi, how have you been?" she said brightly.

"Fine," he said, his tone formal, polite.

Her smiling face turned grim. He doesn't recognize me. She decided not to explain who she was. It would have led to a discussion of why she looked so different, so not-herself. What had happened? Oh, my. How are you doing? So sorry, etc., etc., etc. She had lived well over a half century and yet there was only one remaining story to tell. And she was sick of it.

"Good morning, Arthur." Arthur had been their mail carrier for years until a bum hip forced him indoors.

"Hi, Gayle, good to see you." Gayle could have hugged him for not asking how she was doing, a question he had posed to the three previous customers. They covered the weather, a little news about the price of stamps going up and whether Gayle needed any before the increase.

"Do you need any forever stamps?"

Their eyes met as he blushed.

"Yes, I'll take a book. It is encouraging to know that something lasts forever." She laughed a breathy laugh, but he was unsure how to respond. She leaned across the desk.

"A joke is still a joke, Arthur."

He reached under the counter for the stamps.

"Looky here, I found some with your picture on them." He winked.

She sat in her car for a moment. Where to next? Her arms were shaking. Her legs ached. She took a deep breath, exhaling through her teeth. She closed her eyes tight and then opened them wide. She arched her back to rearrange the pain. "Okay, Gayle, let's go."

She turned right onto 104 east, passing dealership after dealership, plaza after plaza, then the mall and eventually the massive campus that once was Kodak Park. She waved in honor of her father, a Kodaker for thirty-five years until the crane accident. "He could have taken a retirement package last year," her mother had said. "But he wouldn't." Within a year, she was gone, as well.

The highway cut through Irondequoit Bay, it's heavily wooded hills plunging into the frozen surface, ice fishing tents by the score; Lake Ontario, a ribbon of blue on the northern horizon. Soon the country opened up, small towns and apple orchards. Gayle felt a comforting numbness settling into her body. It felt good to be going, even if she was going nowhere.

Richie had mentioned a new craft brewery near Oswego called The Broken Spine.

"Mom, you love IPAs. Gotta go sometime, you and Dad."

Eddy would have thought it foolish to go, given what was going on. But Gayle felt different.

It was 3pm by the time she reached The Broken Spine, which sat on the shore of Lake Ontario, a mile or so from the state college. The western sky was white wash gray; there was ice on the shore. A jagged line separated 'Broken' and 'Spine' on the sign that hung over the rustic front porch; plastic tables and chairs were stacked in corners, awaiting spring. There were two cars in the lot.

Gayle tucked her hair under the new wig. She brushed it briskly, looked in the mirror and laughed. She reached into her purse for the shades and put them on. She looked into the rearview mirror for several minutes, happy that she didn't recognize herself, happy to be going somewhere she'd never been before, happy that no one would know her, that no one would look at her with pity.

There were two men sitting on stools at the rugged mahogany bar. They chomped pretzel pieces and popcorn, several glasses in front of them. Behind the bar was a beveled mirror with a buck carved delicately into the middle. Windows opened onto the lake on the far side of the bar and there were ten to twelve tables scattered throughout. It smelled like burning wood but there was no fireplace to be seen. In the back was another window; behind it, two copper brew kettles and a mash tun.

"Can I help you?" The bartender rolled up to Gayle in a wheel chair. That answered that.

Gayle stood on tiptoes to get on the stool. "Yes, you can." She looked at the chalked menu on the wall. "I'll have your...hm, let me see...I'll have your Hop-To-It."

"Good choice. It's our best seller. Twelve, sixteen, twenty-four or thirty-ounce?"

"Decisions, decisions."

"Might be the most important decision you make today."

"Let's do a sixteen."

"Sixteen it is."

Both of her bar mates, hands wrapped around their thirties, stared at Gayle from under the brims of their Harvester ball caps. The bartender returned with her beer and a basket of fish crackers.

"You're not from around here, are you?"

"No, I'm not. How'd you guess?"

"I know everyone from around here and I'm sure I'd remember you." He checked out her wig and sunglasses as he spoke. Gayle laughed and he chuckled. "It's a look, that's for sure."

"Thank you. I've never had a 'look' before."

"First time, as they say. Everyone calls me Boxer."

"Everyone calls me...Danger."

Boxer extended his hand. "Is that right?" His leathery face stretched into a grin; his mouth framed by wrinkled parentheses. "I better be careful, then."

Gayle shook his hand and tipped her head so she could look at him over her sunglasses.

Boxer wore a Dead T-shirt. He had Betty Boop holding a snake tattooed on his forearm; a barbed wire choker tattoo around his neck; and a sleeve of gargoyles. He wore a Greek fisherman's cap and a floppy gray Fu Manchu moustache. His forearms rippled as he headed down the bar to his other customers. His legs were strapped together and looked toothpick thin.

Gayle took a sip of her beer and closed her eyes, letting the chill warm her the whole way down. Here's to you, Richie, she thought, raising her glass slightly before putting it back down on the bar. She popped one fish cracker into her mouth and let her tongue savor the salt. She swiveled once and then rested her elbows on the bar. She took a deep breath, enjoying the feel of her ribs expanding.

She nodded at the voyeurs at the other end of the bar. They nodded back.

The day Gayle passed her driver's test, she asked her mother if she could take the family car out on her own. She drove to town and, somewhere along the way, realized that at that very moment no one knew where she was; it felt like freedom in its purest form.

It was happening again—no one knew where she was. It felt just as good now as it had then.

"So, Danger, what's your story." Boxer drew another beer, this time for himself.

"My story?"

"Yes, your story. Look at you," he growled. "This has to come with a story."

"I'm sure *your* story is much more interesting than mine."

"Born with a broken spine. End of story."

"That sounds like the beginning of the story—"

"No, no, no you don't. Come on. I've never seen you in here before in my life. You just show up in the middle of a dreary afternoon looking like I don't know what, a cross between Harpo Marx and, well, Elton John, only more feminine. There must be a story."

Gayle felt her insides tingle, as if she were about to dive off a cliff into a shot glass.

"I don't know if I can trust you with something as intriguing as my story."

"Have I ever betrayed you before?"

Boxer took Gayle's empty glass and replaced it with a full one. The sun shone across the wood plank floor, launching dust particles into flight. Gayle looked this way and then that.

"I am a person who has access to vast amounts of money."

"Oh, you're an heiress?"

"No, let's just say that other people entrust their money to me. And I make it grow."

"Stock market?"

"Among other things."

Boxer picked his legs up with his massive arms and shifted them slightly.

"Go on."

"I move money from here to there, one place to another, and back again. My clients like what I do for them. And I like what I do for me. It's mostly on the up and up."

"Mostly?"

"Yeah, mostly."

"Uh huh." His face turned mischievous.

"I take little bits and pieces of money when no one's looking."

"And how do you do that?"

"Hypothetically?"

"Sure."

"Hypothetically speaking, let's just say that when I move their money, there may be a couple of stops they don't know about. You might say that at each of these stops, a little bit falls off the truck, so to speak."

"It does, huh?"

"For example, let's say…I offer a tax service as part of my financial management package." Gayle stared at the ceiling, trying to think of what to say next.

"And?"

"And…we do their taxes, they sign their returns, I give them their copies, and… and then I go back to the originals and make a few changes before I send them off to the IRS."

"Hm. You *adjust* them?"

"I guess you could say that. Maybe I change the math here and there, inflate things a little, not much."

"How much is a little?"

"I bump the refund…maybe a couple hundred dollars, who knows for sure."

"Uh huh."

"The original full refund goes to my client and the loose change comes to me. No one's the wiser."

"So, you make a little walking around money on the deal," said Boxer, unimpressed.

Gayle gauged the disappointment on Boxer's worn face. She decided to amp things up.

"Let's say, hypothetically, of course, that I have...let's say, a thousand clients. And, I've been doing their taxes for years and years."

"Okay. Wait a minute." He opened the calculator on his phone. "Okay, let's see...Jesus, that's $200,000 in one year...How about we look at twenty years?"

"If you want."

He crunched the numbers. "Four million. C'mon."

Gayle tossed her head back and guffawed. "My God, that is a lot, isn't it?"

"Impossible. The IRS would have been all over you."

"I know, I know," she said with a goodhearted wave of her hand that landed on the bar — smack! "Hey, you asked for it."

"Yes, I did! You are a wild woman, Danger," he said with a gleam in his eye. "What does your husband think about this, this fantastical scheme? Is he worried about the feds?"

Gayle took a sip of her beer and wiped her mouth with a cocktail napkin.

"Who said anything about a husband?"

"Never was?"

"Yes, once upon a time. But he died."

"Sorry."

"Mountain climbing in the Alps."

"Oh!" He shook his head, appreciating the exotic detail.

Boxer pushed up on his arm rests again. There was a fourth customer at the bar now. He took his order, but looked back over his shoulder as if to say, 'Don't leave'.

Gayle's beer had completed its journey to her bladder and was ready for a quick exit. She went to the 'Gals' room, wiped off the toilet seat and took a rest. She looked at the stall door in front of her. Someone had drawn a perfect little Christmas tree on it. She grinned.

The beer made her feel like an astronaut, weightless and afloat. She giggled and played with the tips of her synthetic hair. When she was done, she added ruby red lipstick to her 'look'.

"Wondered where you went," said Boxer.

"Duty called. I better get going."

"Not so fast. So why the get up?"

"Well—"

"You on the *lam* so you don't end up in the *hoosegow*?" Boxer was broadcasting to his disinterested audience as they looked on blankly.

Gayle leaned over the bar and gestured with one finger for Boxer to come closer.

"Yes, I am. I'm heading to New York. From there I'll catch a Lufthansa flight to Zurich where I'll be reunited with my money. And my lover." Boxer closed one eye and aimed the other one at her, laser-like. Before he could speak, Gayle concluded: "You wanted a tale, didn't you? I guess I wanted to make it as tall as I could."

Boxer hooted and pounded the bar. "My God, lady, you can come back anytime you want." Gayle, feeling triumphant, raised her hands over her head, flashing two victory signs.

Once in the car, something began to surge in Gayle, something drawn from a deep inner well. She felt it filling her core, seeping into the cracks and crevices of who she was. She erupted into shoulder rattling laughter. She held the steering wheel until it subsided, leaving behind a warm flow of cleansing tears.

Gayle could see Eddy's silhouette at the front door as she pulled into the garage. He was at the back door when she opened it.

"Where have you been?" His hands were on his hips.

"How are you, Eddy?" She walked past him, took off her coat and hung it in the closet. When she turned around, Eddy was in the middle of the kitchen, same pose.

"Honey, really, where have you been?"

"If you must know, I drove to the Broken Spine saloon in Oswego. I met a paraplegic bartender whose name was Boxer, and I told him how I got rich by stealing from the IRS."

Eddy's face showed nothing. His hands were still on his hips.

"And then I told him I was heading to Switzerland to get my money."

With each deep breath, Eddy's chest labored to lift his ample midsection. His lips sucked against his teeth.

"Okay, if you don't want to tell me where you were, what you were doing, that's your business. But you don't seem to understand that there's someone back home who doesn't have a clue what's going on. I called the police; I called every hospital I could think of." He was blinking and clearing his throat. "Don't you get it? I'm worried to death about you. I care, even though you don't. Why are you doing this? Why are you giving up?"

"Eddy, I'm sorry that you were worried. But I don't want that poison in my body anymore." She crossed her arms and clenched her shoulders. "I don't."

"Do you want to die? Is that what you're saying?"

"I want to live, Eddy. And I haven't been alive since this whole thing started. You know what was different about today, Eddy?"

Eddy shifted his weight; his arms fell to his side as he leaned against the refrigerator.

"What?"

"I felt happy, that's what was different."

"Gayle, I don't want to lose you."

"Did you hear me, Eddy. I felt happy today."

Gayle put her hands on Eddy's chest and patted him softly.

"Look, I know this is confusing to you. It's confusing to me. And I know it looks like I've given up. But I haven't. I'm trying to go forward." She laid her head on his chest. "Just in a different direction."

CHAPTER 14

Rich sat on the couch, folded arms and shined shoes at attention. He looked at the clock. On the table before him were two glasses and a bottle of Malbec. He'd ironed his tan Dockers and put on his best cashmere sweater, V-necked. He got up and walked to the dining area window. Then back to the couch where he crossed and uncrossed his legs twice. He got up again to check the artichoke dip. He emptied a sleeve of crackers into a slender wicker serving basket. He took one cracker and raised it to his mouth.

There was a knock at the door. "Dammit." He shattered the cracker in the palm of his hand.

"That's it, bro," Thunderstone had said. "I mean, I don't get it. Are you a fucking monk or something? What's wrong with you?"

"I just—"

"No more 'I justs', bro. I told you, what was it, three, four times, to get this done. To do this one thing for me if you wanted to stay in the game. And I like you. I mean, I've dumped five guys who are better at their jobs than you, but I like you, so I figured I'd give you a little more rope than the others. And this is the thanks I get. I've been loyal to you, bro, but you…well, there's no need to fucking belabor this—"

"Wait, wait…look I'll do it. I will."

"Oh my." Thunderstone clapped both hands against his cheeks. "Gosh and gee whiz."

"No, really, I will. I don't want to lose this job."

"Uh huh." Thunderstone circled Rich, like a spider ready to wrap up his prey for a late-night snack.

"This weekend. I promise."

Thunderstone completed another circle as he headed for the door. "Full report Monday morning, bro. Otherwise, your last day."

·   ·   ·

Saturday, he went on Humpr. Twenty matches came up immediately. Twelve included selfies, all in cutesy poses. (He was surprised that three were men. They posted intimate pics, too, just not of their faces.) He scrolled through and picked one at random. Shannon posted a head shot, a hesitant half grin on her face. She had short cropped brown hair, glasses; who knew what color her eyes were. He looked at the background, but could only make out a wall mirror and a closet door handle. It didn't appear to be a motel room. Her face was full, round, her neck thick. She didn't look like what he thought a drug addict would look like — emaciated, gaunt, hollow cheeked, stringy hair. (He turned on a rerun of *Law and Order* to make sure.) Her profile was a little on the bland side. Most said things like, "Come and get it!" or "Ooo, baby, come to Momma!" or, more to the point, "Let's F*#k all night long!" Shannon's said, "Hi, I'm Shannon."

She sounded low risk, almost safe. They texted back and forth. He was impressed that she didn't use any abbreviations, didn't use LOL for punctuation, and didn't use exclamation points at the end of every sentence. She was either a normal person, or a serial killer masquerading as a normal person, or a normal person who was so embarrassed by being on Humpr that she'd have to kill him after they met, just to hide the evidence.

He texted: *Well, should we meet?*

Sure.

'Sure', hm, he thought. Hard to read her mood, her intentions. Was she curling her lip in disgust? Was she bug-eyed, like a sociopath, screeching with laughter? Was she sharpening her machete? Was she showing this to her boyfriend, driving him into a jealous rage? Would he show up? With the machete?

An exclamation point would have been comforting.

Great!! Two are even better than one, he thought. Maybe this would help her open up. *Where would you like to meet? Coffee shop? Restaurant? A walk in the park?*

I'll come to your place. Address?

OMGF! he thought. What have I gotten myself into? He looked at Shannon's picture again. Why was she hiding her surroundings? Could she be in jail? Is she just getting out and wants to punish some poor schlub for how her loser husband had screwed her over? F*#k!

For two hours, Rich had been sitting on his couch opposite the wall clock Edie had bought. It had long wing-tipped hands, gold no less, but no numbers. "Why no numbers?" he'd asked her. "Jesus Christ," she had responded. Maybe the no-numbers clock was her way of saying, 'Time's up, buster'. They had reached the end of the end.

Shannon's knock came exactly on time—7pm. At first, he pretended that the knock was next door. He didn't move a muscle. He didn't make a sound. Shit, another knock, this one a little more insistent, like she was saying, 'I know you're in there! Man up!'

Rich pasted a smile on his face and opened the door. Shannon, wearing a purple PINK sweat suit and gray Reebok's, blurted, "Where's your bathroom?"

Before he could answer, she flew past him, half bent, her hand clutching her mouth. She slammed the bathroom door behind her and clicked the lock. From behind the door, Rich heard sounds that made him shudder. There was moaning and growling and heaving and crying.

Rich shook his head, embarrassed that he had never considered that Shannon would be possessed by the devil. Would he have to hire someone to clean the walls? Just when he started to Google 'exorcists for hire' the bathroom fell silent. The toilet flushed. The water in the sink ran. Deep sighs were followed by deeper sighs.

Then the lock clicked again and the door opened. There stood Shannon, her face pale as a porcelain toilet bowl. He hadn't noticed the freckles on her selfie. She wiped her face with a tissue.

She held her hand out. "Very sorry. I'm Janet."

Janet? "You mean Shannon?"

She frowned. "No one posts their real name. For safety sake."

"Safety?"

"Serial killers. Pervs."

Rich felt offended that his picture had given off a pervy vibe. "Oh."

"You don't seem like either. Your name is actually Rich, isn't it?"

"Yeah."

"You used your real name. That's different."

"I didn't know…"

"So you're a virgin at this."

"I was going to use 'Ramone', but it seemed…"

"Pervy?"

"Well, I wouldn't…"

Janet sat on Edie's white leather sofa. "Do you mind?"

"No, no, make yourself comfortable." She kicked her sneakers off and curled into the corner. "Are you okay? I mean, it sounded…"

"I'm fine. Although, I may have to use the bathroom again."

"Okay. So, this is a regular thing?"

"You mean going to a stranger's apartment…"

"Condo, actually."

"…and puking my guts out."

"Well…"

Janet leaned forward and wobbled her head in a circle for emphasis. "First trimester's a bitch."

Rich schlumped into Edie's white leather chaise. "First trimester? So, you're…uh?"

"I won't take offense; you can say it."

"Pregnant?"

Janet stretched her legs out and wiggled her toes.

"You didn't expect a prego? Is that what you're saying? You expected, like, a sweet little nymphet, an over-sexed playmate?"

"No, no…I don't know what I expected." Janet pulled a pack of gum from her pocket and opened a stick. She reached out to Rich. "No thanks. I mean, I know I didn't expect someone who was pregnant, but that's okay, I mean…I don't know…"

Janet slid across Edie's white leather sofa, nearer to Rich. "I know you." She squinted her whole face at him. "You don't know who I am, do you?"

Rich leaned back on the chaise. 'Fuck me', he thought. "Should I?"

"Figures. You're one of the higher-ups. One of the 'bros'."

Rich had never used that word in his life. And was proud of it. His vote against misogyny.

"One of the bros?"

"I'm just a lowly secretary, barely a synapse in the massive corporate shit machine."

Who the hell is this? Rich looked at the clock. They had been together for ten whole minutes. He wondered if this was representative of hook-up culture. Angry pregnant women who throw up in your apartment. Condo, actually. What had he gotten himself into and how was he going to get out?

"Can I get you something to drink?"

She sneered at the wine glasses. "I'm pregnant."

"I meant water. Would you like some water?"

Janet sat up and put her feet on Edie's glass coffee table. Edie would have been enraged by this affront. Rich smiled, if only with his eyes.

"Bottled? Tap?"

"Tap, of course."

Rich took a glass from the cupboard, held it under the water dispenser on the fridge and added a few ice cubes. Janet was rubbing her stomach.

"Are you okay?"

"For now, yes."

"How pregnant are you?"

"One hundred percent."

"I mean, like…"

"Ten weeks."

"Okay. Congratulations. Is your husband excited?"

"Wife."

"What?"

"Is my wife excited?"

"Oh." It got very quiet.

"We've spoken before."

Rich was back on his heels again.

"We've what?"

"I said, 'Good morning, Mr. Kimes' and you said, 'Okay'. Not 'Good morning' or even 'Hi' but 'Okay'. You didn't look at me, but you said, 'Okay'."

She was giving him her best Cheshire cat face now. She knew who he was. What exactly was the deal?

"You know me?"

"And you don't know me?"

Rich felt nauseous. Could he also be pregnant?

"I'm…I don't know…"

"We both work for the same asshole."

Rich's mouth fell open. He sat up and slid forward on the chaise. He gestured at her with one hand but didn't have words to accompany it.

"Are you okay?" said Janet.

"Am I okay?"

"You look…I don't know, you look kind of —"

"Just what exactly are you trying to do? I mean, did someone send you here? To see if I was doing what I've been told to do? I said I'd do it and now I'm doing it, so what's this about?" Rich was clapping his knees together. "Who are you, really? Who sent you? What's the meaning of this?" A vein on his neck surfaced like a python rising out of the Everglades. All of his blood rushed to his cheeks and neck, leaving his extremities in a deep chill. The twitch below his eye was break dancing.

"Okay. Take a breath."

"What do you mean, 'take a breath'?"

Janet held both hands in front of her chest. "Like this." She took a deep breath, straightening her back for emphasis.

"I know how to take a breath," he said, gasping.

"That's good. So, do it."

Rich swallowed, then drew air through his nose, collapsing his nostrils.

"Slowly."

He tried again, his chest heaving.

"Belly, through your belly." She held his wrists and breathed with him. "That's better. Jesus. Have you always been so—"?

"I'm breathing, I'm breathing." Rich retrieved his arms and sat down on the chaise again. Color returned to his face, reluctantly.

"You work for Thunderstone?"

"Uh huh." She sat down on the sofa again.

"Did he send you?"

"What?"

"Did he send you to, to spy on me?"

"To spy on you?"

"He's been on me for weeks to take the app out 'for a spin' and I've been avoiding it. But he said I'd lose my job if I didn't do it by Monday. So, are you checking on me?"

"No. Absolutely not."

He met her eyes.

"Okay, okay, that's good. So, you're just, you're trying it out?"

"Ew. Fuck no."

Rich's body folded.

"So, I don't get it. Why'd you take my request?"

Janet sat up straight, ran her fingers through her hair, then placed her hands in her lap. No more puking-Janet. Her jaw looked set.

"Okay, I'm going to trust you. But if it turns out I can't, you will have to do a lot of explaining about this whole thing." Her hand, one finger in the air, went round in a circle. "Several of us on the front end have gone on Humpr trolling for co-workers who are looking for hook-ups. Men and women, doesn't matter. We use aliases and post fuzzy, blurry pictures and we wait. If someone HumpNow's us, we go for it. But not for the reasons you'd think."

Rich's knees were rubbing together so hard that he could have started a fire. He listened but he wasn't sure he wanted to hear.

"Pay attention, okay." Rich nodded. "We are recruiting other employees to join our class-action suit against Thunderstone for fostering an abusive, hostile work environment, including coercing employees to engage in sexual acts against their will."

Rich made a guttural sound, like an animal that was a few seconds away from meeting the fender of an oncoming car.

Janet kept talking. "We have to act. We have to put an end to this fraudulent bullshit."

He had been a frog on Thunderstone's skillet all along; and each time the heat was turned up, he made the necessary adjustments, rationalizations, justifications, until he didn't even notice that he was being cooked to a crisp.

"That's our goal, plain and simple — bring the motherfucker down. We've got twenty employees joining the suit, so far. You'd be twenty-one. Our attorneys say that may be enough." Janet looked pale again. "Sorry." She headed for the bathroom.

Rich didn't move. He looked at his quivering hands. He closed his eyes and took another deep breath, hoping to keep the vertigo at bay. He looked at the bathroom door. What should I do?

The toilet flushed and the sink faucet was running again. Janet opened the door and walked slowly back to the sofa. "So. Are you with us?"

Rich didn't answer. He stared at the floor, one finger pressed against his cheek, just below his eye.

"Rich. Are you with us?"

He shook his head.

CHAPTER 15

Eddy stood just inside the door, a long line ahead of him. Soft music, the smell of flowers, murmured conversations. He tried to button his sports jacket, but his belly wouldn't allow it. He wished he had shined his shoes.

He saw Benny Stapleton and Marty Stanford and a few other Universal guys ahead of him. He didn't bother to get their attention as they chatted with their wives. They held hands or entwined their arms. He didn't ask Gayle to come with him. It would have felt too much like a rehearsal.

Eddy had noticed that Howard Engler stopped coming to chemo. Someone else was at his station, a boy in his late teens. At first, he thought Howard was between rounds or that his schedule had changed; he asked one of the NPs but she couldn't divulge any patient information. Maybe Howard was in remission. He felt ashamed that he resented that possibility. Once again, Howard gets by. After a time, Eddy forgot about Howard. Until he saw the obituary.

There he was, a dazzling smile on his face. Howard had gone to Nazareth College, gotten his MBA from the Simon School; he had worked in advertising and marketing at Kodak; then Universal (Scope) where he rose to the position of Vice President for Employee Affairs; he'd retired recently, but remained an active Rotarian and member of St. Paul's Episcopal Church where he taught Sunday

School and was a lay leader. He loved to golf, garden and spend time with his four grandchildren.

Eddy looked for more. That he was a weasel; that he was disliked by almost everyone that knew him well; that he had always looked out for himself first and foremost; that he had betrayed his friends and colleagues. Eddy folded the paper and put it in the recycling bin.

"Remember how we wondered what happened to Howard Engler?"

Gayle, wearing a Hawaiian moomoo, featuring a humpback whale breaching, poured herself a cup of coffee, then added chocolate mocha creamer and a squirt of Ready Whip. "Uh huh."

"He died."

"He did?"

"In the paper this morning."

"Poor man."

"I suppose."

"Eddy, really."

He blew ripples across the surface of his coffee and then slurped.

"Are you going to calling hours?"

"I suppose."

"Do you want me to come with you?" She said this as she walked away.

"Not necessary."

They had all been kids together once upon a time. Back when no one was going to die. The only things that mattered then were whether you could get the car for Friday night, or find a part-time job so you could buy your own car, or whether so-and-so was really doing it with so-and-so. Tomorrow meant the next day, not the future. But the future was coming like a bullet train, whether they recognized it or not.

There was a tap on Eddy's shoulder.

"Jesus, Gunner," said Eddy, as Gunner wrapped his arms around him.

"How's it going, boss?" Gunner pushed his glasses back up his nose. He was a head shorter than Eddy, which made him seem younger, even though they were roughly the same age.

"Well..." Eddy's eyes widened as he looked at the surroundings.

"I know. It's not the old break room, is it?"

They both grinned and shifted their weight back and forth.

"So, how you been, Gunner?"

"A little better than Howard."

Eddy stood on tiptoes to see how much closer they were getting to the receiving line.

"Didn't have the balls to call me into his office. You know how I found out?"

Eddy shook his head.

"His fucking secretary left me a message on my cell." Gunner leaned his head back, as if waiting for Eddy to explode.

"Jesus..."

"Fucking Christ, for sure. Asshole."

"What are you doing here, Gunner? I mean..."

"This is as close to justice as I'm gonna get, you know what I mean?"

There's no justice here, thought Eddy. Universal sold out. Howard had to fire us. He got cancer and died.

Howard was in viewing distance now. Three little boys in black slacks, red sweaters, white shirts and striped ties, and one little girl, in a white dress with a lace collar and a red satin bow in her hair, sat in high-backed chairs, paper plates covered with cookies balanced precariously on their laps. One boy nudged the other and some of his cookies fell to the floor. The others put hands over their mouths as their shoulders quaked.

Eddy shook hands with two young men who looked like Howard and one young woman, who looked like Howard's wife. He said, "You have my condolences" three times before reaching Frances. Downcast eyes, tear tracks, quivering chin, tissue in one hand. Her daughter held her arm. She looked like she hoped someone would explain why she was there, what it all meant, how it had come to be.

He took her hand in both of his. "I'm so sorry, Frances."

She looked through him, though she smiled. "And you are?"

"It's me, Frances; Eddy, Eddy Kimes."

She looked at him. "Oh, my goodness, yes." She embraced him. "Eddy Kimes, of course." She held his hand. "I wish Howard could be here, you know. I mean, so many people. Such thoughtfulness. He'd be pleased to think so many people cared. He truly would. And his 'tribe'." She glanced at the grandkids. "That's what he called them. They were his world, his whole world. It was their idea for us to wear red, their Grandpa's favorite color. He'd take them out for breakfast on Saturdays, you know, and then to the Play Museum or somewhere, I don't know. Their special thing. No Grandma." She took a sudden breath. "They are so young. What will they remember? You know? Of any of this."

She tightened her grip. He felt perspiration between his fingers.

"He thought so much of you, Eddy. He's smiling somewhere."

Eddy stood over the mahogany casket, which was lined in red velvet. Howard wore a navy pinstriped suit and red tie. There was an American flag pin on one lapel and a Scope logo on the other. His plaster hands gripped a cluster of red roses and baby's breath; a flowing, cream colored ribbon with "Grandchildren" embossed in script adorned the bouquet.

Howard's eyes were sunken, his lids sewn shut, his mouth stretched and pressed, accenting his triple chin. His pale, pie dough face was drawn and flat. His hair was parted on the wrong side. His leftover self looked like him, but not really.

Eddy crouched on the kneeler and folded his hands. He searched for a positive memory, but could think of none. He was glad that there were others who could. He closed his eyes for what he thought was an appropriate length of time. When he opened them, there were three others in line behind him. "Goodbye, Howard," he whispered.

He perused the pictures mounted on sheets of oak tag. Howard as a baby; Howard with his siblings; Howard playing baseball; Howard and his clarinet; Howard graduating high school (Eddy was surprised to see himself in the background, looking so young, so full of hope). Howard getting married, on vacation, holding his newborn grandchildren, sitting at his desk at work, etc., etc., etc.

Gayle was *their* picture person. No matter where they went, she made sure that they stopped briefly for a smile and a snap. There was a wall of albums in the basement that no one ever looked at. In the back of each album were negatives, just in case someone wanted duplicates. No one ever did. Eddy assumed the digital pictures were filed away on Gayle's computer.

There were decades of tax returns locked in her office and a metal filing cabinet filled with receipts for everything they'd ever bought, including their wedding bands ($226.49) and first baby crib ($22.13). It wasn't that Gayle was nostalgic. She believed that every life should have a well-organized paper trail that explained things to anyone who might need to know. The world, it seemed, was divided into the auditors and the audited. She believed that everyone would be visited by an auditor at some point in their lives, so you'd better be prepared to give a full account of yourself, much like arriving at the pearly gates, except the IRS was much less forgiving. What was Eddy going to do with all those files?

Eddy erased his grim thoughts with recent good news. Richie had found an apartment and would be moving back soon. Both he and Gayle were excited, although they didn't understand why he was making such a change. Did living in Columbus make it too painful to deal with the loss of Edie? Was he fearful about his mother?

Gayle had burst into laughter, then tears when Richie had called.

"Well, I've got some news," he'd said.

With Richie coming home, Eddy and Gayle discussed her current situation and how to explain what was going on. Eddy urged Gayle to say she was "on a break" from treatment. She was inclined to say she had stopped. Eddy felt that was too negative, too hopeless, and that it would upset Rich and Sandy, as well as their friends, unnecessarily.

Gayle's face had turned crimson. "We can't avoid the truth. Do you think that something or someone is going to save the day? That all of this is going to go away? Poof." She splayed her fingers into the air.

Eddy tapped his leg with one hand, his mouth open.

"Honey, really, what do you think is going to happen?" she said.

Eddy didn't answer.

"I'm sure you understand that every road, no matter where we think it's going, is a dead end. My road is just going to be a little shorter than we thought."

Eddy had taken her in his arms. "Please don't."

As Eddy headed toward the funeral home exit, he could hear Frances speaking to another mourner: "He thought so much of you... He's smiling somewhere."

Eddy's car sat in the lot while he walked down West Ave. and then Amity St. and finally Church St., passing the Baptists and Methodists before arriving at the rear of the Presbyterian Church, the chimes marking the hour. Mounds of dirty, frozen snow filled the corners of the town square again. He gingerly crossed the soggy church yard and entered his quiet place.

It was hard to remember how he'd felt a year or so ago when he'd come here for the first time. Now his job was long gone; Gayle's treatment was long gone, as well. Had he been hopeful when he first sat on this bench? He remembered telling Gayle that things would work out at Scope. She had been so tired at the time. So weak. Successful treatment was going to be their safety net, catching them both before they hit bottom. Lifting them up, in fact; possibly setting things right. Now Gayle was no longer tired, no longer weak. But closer to dying. How odd.

They'd been living off what were supposed to be their retirement accounts, which he suspected, were nearly bone dry. Gayle had found the accordion folder of unopened bills which was full to overflowing. They didn't talk about options anymore. They didn't talk about their situation much at all; instead, they went from one day to the next, like they were leaping from one tiny island to another, each time breathing a sigh of relief that they hadn't fallen into shark infested reality.

Eddy stared at the Consoler's face. "So." He shook his head and looked around, hoping no one was listening. Hoping that Peter wasn't there to encourage him. "You may know by now that Gayle has stopped her treatment. I don't understand what's gotten into her. It's almost like she's lost her mind. She acts happy, sometimes giddy. It's like, I don't know, like she has no idea that her life could end at any time. She says she's living 'in the moment'. I can't stand that stuff. For every person that's living in the moment, there's someone else who's worried sick about tomorrow, you know what I mean?" Eddy sighed.

His arms dropped to his side. "I've lost my job. And we are running out of money fast. We're just here, waiting. We're waiting and hoping that whatever's coming doesn't get here. That it gets waylaid or derailed or whatever the fuck. I hate this goddam waiting, but I'll tell you, I'd rather keep waiting, it doesn't matter how long, just so...just so *it* doesn't arrive."

Eddy startled when the wind shook the bushes and leaves whirled around him like a nest of hornets. He looked up at the statue and then down at his hands. What was he doing? He was a little man with a little life facing a big problem that the world wouldn't remember for more than a split second.

He thought of those astronauts who saw the earth from outer space, how seeing that blue ball hanging so peacefully in the firmament had changed them. When Eddy saw those pictures, he thought how small and vulnerable the earth looked, like a cracked egg hanging in a sea of darkness, and how infinitesimally small were its inhabitants, busy ants on a hill. It didn't make him feel humble; it made him feel invisible, inconsequential.

Eddy slumped forward, his elbows on his knees, his hands holding his face. He rubbed his eyes and stared again at his unsteady hands. He looked up at Jesus's face, covered as it was in winter mire, the smile that wasn't a smile at all, just the product of a hammer and chisel on stone. Eddy stood, reached out with his fingertips and removed some of the grime from Jesus's foot.

When he turned to leave, Peter was standing at the entrance, his arms clasped tight across his chest, his head bowed. Eddy passed without a word.

CHAPTER 16

"Have you lost your mind?" Sandy wanted to say something more supportive, more encouraging, but instead, her true feelings leap-frogged everything else.

"Jesus, Sandy."

"What are you going to do? Move back in with mommy and daddy? I mean, really?"

"Back off."

Sandy sat on the floor of her bedroom clutching a soup spoon, a half-gallon of Bittersweet Sinphony between her legs. She dug in.

"What else am I supposed to do? Once I signed on to this, this legal thing, I couldn't in good conscience go to work every day, pretending I was one of Thunderstone's 'bros'."

"I get that. Totally. But among all the options available to you, including getting another job in Columbus, why would you go back to western New York? There's nothing there for you, except Mom and Dad. I don't mean that's a bad thing, but...it's Mom and Dad. And everything."

The phone went silent.

"Richie? You still there?"

"Yeah, I'm here." More silence.

"And?"

"Sandy, look, I am fucking lost. I'm going home because...because it's home. I don't have anything here, not since the break-up. I convinced myself that work would make the difference, that my job would keep me afloat, not only financially, but socially, the whole thing. But that was bullshit. You know what I'm talking about."

Now Sandy was silent.

"I didn't even know the last names of anyone I worked with. What's that?"

A spoonful of ice cream was numbing Sandy's brain. She got into bed, leaned back against the headboard and stretched her legs, trying to avoid a cramp. She couldn't think of what to say. She wanted to convince him that moving back home was a mistake, but how? Nothing came to mind. She thought of home. If she could erase one year from all her growing up years, like sliding a Jenga block skillfully from the tower, she, too, would be tempted to go home. The pull was always there. Especially now. But she never gave in. Thinking of Richie living on his own in Columbus was often enough to convince her to stay in Chicago. If he could do it…

"Sandy? Are you listening to me?"

"Yeah. I'm here."

"Look, I know this isn't ideal. I know that it's, like, a big step backwards or something, but I can't stay here. I can't."

"Come to Chicago. You could live with me." Sandy closed her eyes, wincing as she said this. She loved her brother more than anyone in the world, but the thought of living together, well, it just wouldn't work. His neat freakiness alone was a deal breaker.

"I thought of that, I did. But I don't want to live with anyone. I'm not going to live with Mom and Dad either. I'm not. No matter what I do, I have to live on my own. I have to feel like I'm standing on my own two feet. At least a little. And there's no way I could afford to do that in Chicago."

Sandy opened her eyes and spooned some more ice cream. Richie had a line on an apartment in Spencerport, about twenty minutes from home. Close, but not too close. Jobs were scarce, but he had some feelers out. Hoped to move in a month or so.

"I figure it will give me a chance to check things out, you know?"

"Yeah."

"Have you talked to them recently?"

"Yeah, actually, I talked to Mom a couple days ago. She sounded great. Her voice was all kinds of excited and she'd been doing things and going places. She's happy to be off chemo for a while and she thinks she's doing better."

"What?"

"Those were her words—'doing better'. I didn't question it. I was just happy she sounded like her old self, you know?"

Richie heaved a sigh.

"What is it?"

"Jesus. When I talked to Dad last week, he was, like, all gloom and doom. I thought he talked to you. He's going crazy because she's not on chemo right now; he's afraid that things are getting worse. I thought he was calling to tell me Mom died, that's how bad he sounded."

Sandy dropped her spoon into the ice cream and pushed it aside with her foot. She got up and sat on the edge of her bed.

"Sandy?"

"No, I didn't know any of this." Her dad had called, maybe a week ago, but she was working and didn't answer. He didn't leave a message and she forgot about it. "Who do you believe?"

"Well, that's the thing. I don't know."

When they finished talking, Sandy felt a chill cross her back and neck. Her arms fell limp at her side and her chest felt like an empty balloon.

When she was a young girl, she always hated New Year's Day. That's when they undecorated the Christmas tree. That's when the tinsel was balled and tossed into the wastebasket and the colorful ornaments were wrapped and put away in a giant Tupperware tub and the lights—green and red and yellow and blue—were turned off for another year. That's when her father dragged the needleless tree to the curb. Today it felt like it was her life that was being undecorated.

Hard to admit, but, like her brother, she was racing down the track to nowhere. Freelancing hadn't been the romantic path to wealth and independence she had hoped it would be. In the last month, she had worked forty hours. Ten setting up a website for a writer whose books wouldn't sell. Twenty-two revamping a site for a day care center. They were able to pay for ten. And eight for Carmine's Auto Body Shop. She'd done piddling hours at Carmine's for about six months. Carmine had ideas that he shared freely about what Sandy should do next.

A cigar hanging from the corner of his mouth, yellowed fingers, grease under his nails, Carmine stood six two, two hundred eighty pounds, at least. Every time she came into his shop, he greeted her with a bear hug and a ready smile. "How's it goin' today, darlin'?" Then he'd say, "What the fuck are you doin' still working junk hours for a guy like me, beautiful girl like you could be making real money, I'm tellin' you." He'd shake his head and point at her. "Take my advice."

His advice: Carmine's daughter, Lilly, was paying her way through Northwestern by working at "one of those, you know, gentleman's clubs." He'd lower his voice each time he said the name — "Venice's Flytrap." "Don't get the wrong idea, or nothin', she's a good girl, savin' it for the wedding night and all that." He explained that she didn't work on stage, "none of that crap with the poles and shit. No, she's a server, that's all, serves drinks to these executive types who come in lookin' for a good time."

The what-kind-of-person-do-you-think-I-am look on her face the first time he mentioned the gentleman's club idea, made him back off. "Okay, okay, I didn't mean nothin'. Just tryin' to help, that's all."

'Who's kidding who', she thought, 'Lilly isn't saving anything for anybody'.

Then she met Lilly.

"I haven't worked for a few weeks. Studying for the LSATs. It's all day, all night prep. My professors are giving me some slack, so I'm hitting it as hard as I can."

"Oh." Lilly had raven hair, gorgeous brows, moony eyes and a platinum smile. "Sounds hard," said Sandy, feeling out of her league.

"Very. But U of Chicago is Everest, so whatever it takes."

"What kind of law do you want to…do?"

"Constitutional. I'd like to clerk for the Court, if possible. Then, who knows."

"Okay." Sandy's smile substituted for anything else she might have to say about "the law."

"Dad said you were interested in Venus's Flytrap." She looked Sandy up and down. "You've got the right look. Pretty. Good physique." Sandy looked down at herself. "Do you dance?"

"No, no," the words coming out on a laugh. "No poles, none of that."

Lilly remained dead sober. "Okay. Waitstaff, then?"

"Yeah, I guess, I'm not sure." Sandy explained her ambivalence — drugs, pimps, pervs, prostitution.

"Oh my." Lilly must have been all of twenty, yet she seemed so street wise. "My father doesn't know this, but I dance every once in a while, when someone bails. It isn't a big deal. You smile, make some eye contact, never more than a few seconds, pick up your money and get off the stage. I did lounges every once in a while, but didn't like it. That's where the guys get a little too disinhibited for me, no matter the tips. I won't bullshit you, some of the girls are strung out and they've got 'managers'." She air quoted this. "Some are into doing extras, which is basically, anything goes if you've got the money. No doubt, that's where the real money is. And parties, that sort of thing. That wasn't me and that was fine. Not everyone does it. No pressure, really. You choose. There are some great girls, a couple of med students, a law student, that sorta thing."

"What about the guys?"

"Guys *and* girls, you'd be surprised. Mostly middle-aged, married executive types. Guys on their way home. Some conventioneers. Married women, experimenting. Most important, though, they all drink. Three drink minimum. And they tip. They're not gonna fuck you over."

"Is it safe?"

Lilly frowned and shrugged one shoulder. "What's safe, you know? I've run into more trouble dating college guys than I've had at the club."

"How's the money?"

Eyes wide, she said, "Yep, there's money galore. On a weekend night, I've made nine-hundred on tips. Three, four-hundred on weeknights."

"Really?"

"No shit." She got her phone out and started texting. "You'll do fine. Look, I'm letting Ronnie know about you, that you're the shits."

Lilly said Ronnie had some rules. All the girls had to wear tight, black, off-the-shoulder bodysuits—"Check Lululemon"—with black mesh back-seamed stockings; black skirts, no longer than ten inches from the waist to the hem; and plexiglass heels, four inches or six. "Six inches is best if you can handle it. Lengthens your legs, tightens your ass, increases your tips."

Sandy felt a nervous tingle run through her body after talking to Lilly. Lilly was so cool about the whole thing, like it was all just part of The Plan. Working in a strip club was the most viable option, the most flexible, the most lucrative. It was a stepping stone to something better. Risky business? "No, I'm not worried about it fucking up my future. Everyone's got something. I've got an Instagram page up about it. Hundred thousand followers." She was on the upward slope, the summit in view.

Sandy wanted to believe it was the same for her. That this was a well-considered decision woven into a grand design. But was paying rent and buying groceries considered a road map to anything? Could well-considered choices be made out of desperation? What were LSATs anyway?

"Are you sure you don't wanna dance?" was Ronnie's first comment when she arrived for her face-to-face. "I mean, Jesus Christ, guys would pay a lot to watch a girl with a body like yours dance...and stuff."

Sandy, in her six-inch heels, towered over the five-foot-five Ronnie. He leaned over his desk, lighted a cigar and sat back, his chubby ankles bulging between his socks and trousers, his feet unable to reach the floor.

"So, what's your story?"

Sandy's skirt barely reached her thighs. She stood knee-to-knee, covering herself as best she could. "No story. Just need to make some money."

"You never done this before, have you?"

Sandy smiled.

"Lemme tell you, this ain't no walk in the park, you should know that right from the get go. You may not wanna strip or go into the back rooms, but these guys are looking for more than a few drinks. Not that you can't make a buck waitressing. But, really. Between you and me, Lilly made a mint. And trust me, it wasn't from just serving drinks."

"Well..."

"Com'ere." Sandy took two wobbly steps forward and looked down at Ronnie's comb-over. Ronnie's chair squeaked as he leaned forward. He stuck his cigar in the corner of his mouth, his nose now an exhaust pipe. "'Hey honey' the guy says, and you go to the table, right." He coaxed her forward with his pointer. "So, he says, 'I'd like a martini and my pal here would like a vodka tonic'. And all the while he's ordering and smiling, he's doing like..." Ronnie places one hand on the back of Sandy's thigh, caressing it. "And, so, you say what?"

"Get your fucking hand off me?"

Ronnie laughs. "No, that's what you think, but what you say is, 'Whatever you want, sir'. And then you smile." Ronnie removes his hand. Sandy's breath is caught high in her chest. "You see, the guy's thinkin' 'Maybe I got a chance' and so he orders drink after drink until he's so drunk, it's don't matter anymore. He leaves the rest of his cash on the table, just hopin'."

'This asshole just sexually assaulted me', thinks Sandy. "Why did you touch me like that? I didn't say you could do that?"

"Trust me, honey, that won't work either. You say that to these guys and, well, goodbye bucks cause you're done."

"I mean you. What made you think you could put your hand on me?"

"Oh, Jesus, here we go. Look, it's a job interview and it's job training. A two-fer. These guys are going to give you a fucking lot of money and all they're gonna get in return is a little leg, a little grab ass, what's the harm. If ten, twelve guys touch your ass and at the end of your shift you go home with like a thousand bucks, who's the fool, huh?"

Sandy's face looked rock hard.

"You gotta park that MeToo stuff at the curb, that's all I'm saying. Look, these guys ain't a bunch of Harvey Weinsteins. Jesus Christ, I hate that fucker. These guys aren't like that. They're just guys."

Despite her heels, Sandy could feel herself shrinking. She could feel her skin crawling, her insides drying up, her eyes glazing over.

"Look, you got great stems, you're a gorgeous girl. You'd do very well, believe me. But you gotta hold your tongue, you know what I mean? There's a time and a place for that stuff, but not here."

She looked past Ronnie. There was a family photo on his desk; smiling wife, smiling Ronnie and two smiling daughters, one with braces, neither yet teens. Ronnie would go home late that night and maybe he'd get up in the morning and wish his daughters well before they got on the bus for school. Maybe he was protective of them and, as they got older, would become a glaring, threatening father trying to intimidate any boys who came around the house. But in his heart, he'd know that there was a good chance those boys were going to become 'guys being guys', which his daughters would learn, perhaps the hard way, much as Sandy had.

Ronnie stood, his cigar between his finger like a pool cue. "So, whadaya think? Start tonight?"

CHAPTER 17

Gayle stood on the front porch for several minutes. An armada of chubby dark clouds were rolling east. She breathed deep as a bellows. She looked straight at the sun as it sprayed light from behind a cloud; she hoped for warmth. Gayle unbuttoned the neck on the Seneca Indian poncho she had recently bought at a reservation. There was a soaring eagle against a brilliant red sun with delicate beading and buckskin fringe. She had almost bought the buckskin leggings and footwear, but figured that would have sent Eddy over the edge.

Another deep breath and she headed down the sidewalk. Caroline Kerrigan was digging near her front porch. She wore baggy sweats and a hoody. And gardening knee pads. Her gray hair was tied in a red checked kerchief.

"Getting started already," said Gayle.

Caroline, startled, got up on her hands and knees and then sat back on her heels. "You're still alive, I see." Then her face freeze-dried.

Gayle looked herself up and down. "Yes, I think I am."

"Jesus, Gayle, I'm so sorry. Wasn't thinking. I guess I mean I haven't seen you since last December." Caroline, her face now matching her kerchief, got up and met Gayle at the fence by the sidewalk. She reached for Gayle and pulled her close. "How are you? How are the treatments going?"

"Remarkably well, Caroline." Gayle didn't have the energy to explain what was really going on. Caroline, God love her, was the town crier. While Eddy disputed this, Gayle knew it to be true. Why else had Gayle received dozens of supportive emails and Facebook messages from Caroline's closest friends. And relatives. "C'mon, honey, she just cares and doesn't know how else to show it," Eddy would say. Caroline was a good person. And a good neighbor. And Gayle loved her. But, really. All the attention made her feel like she was a cancer patient rather than a person.

"That's wonderful. You know, I see Eddy now and then and he keeps me posted, but it's so good to see you out and about." Caroline, like a human MRI, scanned Gayle top to bottom. "You look different."

Gayle stood there, not saying anything, waiting to see how Caroline would approach this.

"I like it. Very much. Where would someone get something like that?"

Gayle pulled her poncho up, revealing a gray buckskin skirt and an orange tunic top with a herd of buffalo stampeding across it.

"Oh, my," said Caroline with a concerned whisper.

Gayle let the poncho fall. "I know. Really."

Caroline clutched Gayle's hand. Her eyebrows met in the middle. "Gayle, honey, is everything, you know, you can tell me anything, you know that, don't you?"

The touch of Caroline's hands warmed Gayle all over. She saw in her friend's worried eyes both fear and love.

When she stopped treatment, Gayle had also cut the cord connected to her feelings about dying. She left it all behind and was now tramping through a forest where every path led to something new, or at least that's how it felt. Freedom, freedom everywhere. Farewell to the chaos her body wrought. Dressing up helped her forget.

Caroline's warm hands, though, so present, so real, awakened in Gayle the melancholia that was driving her journey, her escape. She looked past Caroline to the trowel stuck in the muddy earth and couldn't imagine not being in this world, not touching and being touched by its muddiness, its everything. Caroline squeezed her hand gently. Their eyes met.

"I don't want to die."

"I know."

"I'm trying as hard as I can—not to die. The thought of it; the thought of not being here…"

"Come here." Caroline pulled her closer.

"All of this, everything you see, it's just me pretending."

"And that's fine."

"Is it?"

"That's what we do when we can't think of any other way to keep going."

Gayle stepped back and wiped her eyes with the palm of one hand. Why hadn't she talked with Caroline more often? Only three houses separated them, yet months would pass without a word between them for no good reason at all.

"Thank you, Caroline."

Caroline kissed Gayle's hand.

Gayle continued on her way. At the corner near the square, she pressed the walk button and waited. She watched the activity across the street in the pharmacy. She could see Sam behind the counter laughing with a customer. Looked to her like he had lost some weight. She closed her eyes, trying to remember what the two of them looked like when they dated in high school, but she couldn't. All she knew was that, for a time, they had been each other's world. Had he not left for college while she stayed home, would they have married? She had been married to Eddy for such a long time, that it was hard to imagine someone else in his place. But, once upon a time, Eddy was merely background to the relationship she had with Sam.

She didn't miss Sam as much as she thought she would when he left for college, but she did feel lonely. She got asked out a lot, but the yoke of loyalty to Sam prevented her from accepting any invitation. Eddy was there as Sam's stand-in, so to speak, there supposedly to take care of her. Only later had she understood that, in all likelihood, Sam had been worried he'd lose her if no one was there to keep an eye on things. She was so young. It was hard to discern the difference between love and control.

Sam was a high school prize, much sought after by all the girls. She fell in love immediately. Not so, with Eddy. At least not with the eyes-meeting-across-the-room electricity one hopes for. Eddy was more like a warm blanket at a time when she felt alone and cold. He wasn't tall and handsome like Sam, but, unlike Sam, he listened to her and tried to understand her and when he smiled at her, she felt loved. She loved the way he looked, loving her. Slowly she started to have feelings for him. She missed him if he didn't stop by when she expected he would. She found herself waiting by the phone, just in case. And she started smiling back when he smiled.

Eddy often said, "No, Gayle never fell in love with me. It was more like she lost her balance and I caught her." Gayle always laughed at this. She never admitted that it might have been true. Can you lose your balance and find yourself in love?

It seemed like forever before Eddy finally kissed her. She had assumed his loyalty to Sam was the problem. It was okay, though, because she was afraid of how she'd feel when he did. More to the point, she was afraid she wouldn't feel anything. When he took her in his arms and kissed her long and soft, though, she was surprised that she felt exactly like she hoped she'd feel, and more.

As the crosswalk light flashed on, she found herself smiling as she stepped off the curb. She stood at the entrance to the pharmacy, but decided not to go in. She could get her ibuprofen another day. She crossed back and headed down the sidewalk, passing Caroline quietly as she worked diligently clearing her garden of winter detritus.

Gayle stood on the sidewalk looking at the Cape Cod home where they'd lived all their married life. Two white dormers, four front windows with black shudders, gray clapboard shingles and a center white brick chimney. The shudders were graying and some of the shingles were frayed. There were hydrangeas on either side of the stoop and clusters of green shoots fronting the edge of the yard. Overgrown spiraea hid the front windows.

They had had a plan when they married almost thirty-two years before. This would be their starter home, an affordable purchase when Eddy was first hired in the cable business. In those days, everything was a step toward something else. They hoped for a colonial in a new development outside of town. And Eddy wanted to start a business, any business, anything where he would be his own boss. Gayle would manage the books once she'd gotten her associates in accounting. And babies, of course. Maybe four.

Gayle looked at the maple they had planted when they moved in. Gone were the sticks and ropes holding that young twig straight. She leaned back to see the top, now fifty feet above her.

There are plans and there is life. Life always wins.

She smiled at the portrait before her and walked up the sidewalk to the front door.

"Eddy!" She tossed her coat on the hallway bench and looked into the living room. She heard the toilet flush upstairs and footsteps in their bedroom, then the hall. "Eddy?"

"Is everything okay?" he called.

He had been on high alert for over a year. She could see it in the circles under his eyes, his stubbly face, his ever-expanding waistline. She was always encouraging him to take better care of himself. She almost laughed to think of it given her stance about treating her cancer.

"Fine, everything's fine, honey." She could hear him stumbling around their room. Perhaps he'd been napping. No amount of sleep was enough.

She hadn't expected a surge of energy when she stopped chemo. The heaviness in her eyes waned. Her arms and legs, though weak, worked more efficiently than they had. And she ate. Even with pain, she ate. She had nearly an inch of hair, which she still hid under a variety of colorful wigs. "Really, honey? Are you sure about that one?" Eddy was concerned at first about the wigs and the clothes, but then let go of the issue.

In the beginning, the pain had been unrelenting. Her back, her pelvis, her stomach. Sometimes the bloating was so pronounced that she looked nine months pregnant. Ten months. It came and it went and after a time, stayed. She took meds that made her feel like she was living in a fog, made the pain seem distant, but never so far away that she didn't feel it. She was nauseous so often that eventually she didn't think of it as nausea. It was how she felt, that's all.

Once she stopped chemo, it wasn't like a light came on and she felt better. It took weeks, but as she redirected her energies to other things, she noticed that she felt good, not only emotionally, but physically. At first, she maintained her pain meds regimen, but started weaning herself off after a month or so. When she told Eddy this, he was skeptical. He had an almost religious faith in chemo, believing that blind acceptance of everything that came with it was a test of one's devotion and a sign of one's commitment. She wondered if his sacred trust in chemo came from his frequent visits to that statue and his frequent conversations with that minister.

Dropping chemo, though, hadn't been an act of blind counter-faith on Gayle's part. She wasn't naïve. She worried that her improvement might be a lie. She worried that soon the tide would turn and she would be caught in cancer's relentless grip again. She had told herself it didn't matter, that she'd prefer to live her life on her own terms even if death was the outcome, but now she wasn't so sure. Maybe quantity of life, newly appreciated, was a path to quality. She would love to see their maple bloom and then watch the leaves turn and fall and bloom again and again and again. She would love to grow old.

Eddy came down the stairs slowly. He smiled at the sight of her. He hugged her, something he did every time he saw her, even if it had been a matter of minutes.

"Eddy, we need to talk."

"Sure, what's up? Are you sure you're okay?"

"I want to talk to you about this whole treatment thing."

CHAPTER 18

Sam Cunningham watched Gayle standing at the corner cross walk. He took a deep breath, noted that she didn't have a prescription in the bin, hadn't in a while, and waited on another customer. When he looked out the window again, she was still standing there, the light having changed at least twice.

What was she wearing today? he wondered. It looked Native American but he couldn't tell for sure. She looked like she was deep in thought, or confused, or both. Not Gayle at all. He put both palms on the counter and shook his head.

Sam reached for the pill tray and spatula. He emptied white pills into the receiver, took the spatula in hand and counted five pills, swept them into a receiving tube and counted five more, and five more and so on. Little had Sam known when he graduated pharmacy school that he would spend most of his life counting to five and flicking his wrist, counting to five and flicking his wrist. He knew that some of his colleagues still counted by threes and one colleague on the southern tier reportedly counted pills one at a time. Sam had settled on five after his first year in practice.

He closed the tube, tipped the contents into a prescription bottle and sealed the cap. He started again. Blue pills this time. Followed by yellow, pink, green. Some round. Others oblong. Footballs, rectangles, pentagons, middle creased, initialed. Each perfect in its way. Even beautiful.

When it was late in the day and the pharmacy was closed, he would stand over his tray counting for hours, deep in something that looked like thought, but wasn't; it was more like watching, or trance, or away-ness.

When he wasn't dreaming of Marianne or Jamie, he was counting in his sleep, sometimes awakened by his twitching right hand. One, two, three, four five. Five fingers, five toes, five appendages, five senses, five, his rudder.

He glanced up and she was gone. He stepped to the window and saw Gayle walking down the street. He bit the inside of his cheek and went back to his counting, then stopped, put the spatula down and studied the pills in the tube. He tipped them out again and recounted. Nineteen. He added one and then set the tray aside.

He called Nellie overhead to come back to the pharmacy so he could take his dinner break. He retreated to a back closet crowded with mops and buckets and a small desk and chair. He took his lunch bag from a small refrigerator that doubled as a desk leg. He unwrapped his tuna fish sandwich on white and took out the apple, Honey Crisp, and set it aside. He tore open a bag of Sun Chips and put several in his mouth. He reopened the fridge and grabbed a can of A&W from the rack.

Sam looked at his watch. Kathleen would be feeding Jamie. He had his home phone number on speed dial.

"Hi, Mr. Cunningham."

No, she would never call him Sam. "Hi Kathleen, how you doing today?" He didn't need to call her every day. He knew it. She knew it. But he enjoyed the sound of her voice, like soft wind blowing through chimes. After the debacle of inviting her to dinner, it took weeks before she appeared to relax around him. He shook his head to think that she was the only woman, the only woman aside from Nellie, that is, that he interacted with on a daily basis.

"I'm doing fine, Mr. Cunningham. And you?"

"I'm doing well, too, thanks." Usually, he had other questions to ask. 'Did you have a nice weekend?' was always a good Monday question. 'Do you have plans for the weekend?' was reserved for Fridays. In the middle, it was hard to know what to ask. And if he didn't ask a question, there wasn't anything to talk about except Jamie, of course. Weather was always an option.

"Sure is a beautiful day, isn't it? I mean, you can feel spring coming, you know what I mean?"

"Yes, it is a nice day. I hope there's more on the way."

"Me, too!"

The pause that followed went on a beat too long. The conversation was over.

"How's my boy today?"

"He's doing great, Mr. Cunningham. He's watching Elmo right now. He ate some oatmeal and about a quarter piece of toast. He liked the peanut butter this time."

"Oh, that's good."

That was that. By the time Sam got home, Kathleen would be standing at the door with her coat on and Jamie would be asleep.

"Okay then."

Sam took another bite of his sandwich and a slurp of his A&W. He pulled his laptop from his backpack. He deleted ten emails from fund raisers, five erectile dysfunction ads, seven graphs promising penis enlargement, four chairlift videos showing happy people who were relieved they could get to the bathroom in time, and another dozen random hustles. How had he gotten on these lists? He tried to unsubscribe but that only seemed to encourage them.

There was one personal message. It had been several months since he had joined a dating site. At first, he was suspicious about the offer — free for six months, plus $250 back if you weren't satisfied by your third date. He figured, what the hell? He filled in the profile and submitted all the data. Then the site went dark. He assumed it was a scam or it went bankrupt or whatever.

It wasn't like there weren't other options. Some dating sites even included pages for pharmacists. He looked at one post: "I hate my fucking job. Do you? If so, contact me after 10pm any night." Another one: "Do you ever wonder how you ended up a pharmacist? I flunked out of med school. Tried dental, but it sucked. So, pharmacy, what can I say? I never thought it would be so boring. Do you like to drink?" And: "Help! I'm dying inside." He decided not to fill out his profile.

Sam thought that if there was someone for him, they would find each other. It would be fated. There didn't need to be an online intermediary. And she didn't need to be a pharmacist. A woman who was kind, who was smart, who was funny, who was, well, interested in sex. Sometimes Sam was embarrassed to admit that this final thing—sex—was number one on his list. It had been for a long time.

He opened the message. "Humpr is back! And we want YOU!" The cover page was "Our Enduring Pledge to YOU!" The site was under "new ownership" and promised to be "an honest broker of your intimacy and happiness needs." Below the pledge was a sparkling red heart that said, "Click me, and I will beat again for you!!"

Sam took several Sun Chips from the bag. He wiped his hands on his white coat and then clicked on the heart.

CHAPTER 19

"At least you know what you're getting into. Thunderstone didn't tell me the truth. That's the crux of it for me. He lied and I was put in an untenable position. But at least this Ronnie guy was straight with you."

"Yeah, I guess."

"What?"

Sandy sat on the toilet while she ran her bath water.

"What woman in her right mind would do this?"

"Lilly seemed to be in her right mind."

"Kind of."

Sandy ran her finger tips through the steaming water. She turned off the faucet and slipped slowly in, the heat chasing her breath away. She curled her shoulders and then relaxed as her body simmered. Sandy lounged back, her cell phone almost slipping from her hand.

"Fuck."

"What?"

"Nothing, I'm taking a bath. So, you think it'd be okay to do this?"

"I mean, when you texted me, you sounded all kinds of into it. I'm trying to support you. I could just as easily argue for the opposite: Who wants grimy guys—"

"Excuse me: Rich executive grimy guys."

"Rich executive grimy guys glaring at you like you're a piece of candy or, worse, meat. I mean, it's not like you've had the best, like you've, I don't know."

"What, what are you trying to say?"

She could tell that Richie had shifted the phone to his other hand. Did that mean his right hand was perspiring? Was he twitching?

"Nothing, really."

"Come on, what is it?"

"I don't know, it just seems to me that from the beginning, guys weren't always that, you know, they did things…they weren't that good to you."

She sat up, water dripping from her elbows, goose flesh up her spine.

"Really. I know I haven't had the best luck, and I'm sure I exaggerated some of the stories a little so I wouldn't look like The Bitch. But—"

"I didn't mean anything. Really. Wrong words. I'm—"

"But did I ever imply someone had *done something*?"

"Done something? No, I'm just, I don't know, how would I know, like, anything? I was only assuming you must have, I mean, don't all girls, I mean women, don't they all have some awful story…"

He knew something.

"Yeah, well, we've all had our share of jerks. But I've learned how to handle the jerks. Anyway, I'm not going to *date* these guys. I just want to make some money. I'm still going to do my consulting thing, but I'm hanging by my nails right now."

She didn't want to know what he knew. Or thought he knew.

"Gentlemen's club" was a generous moniker for Venus's Flytrap. "Upscale" was also a stretch. At best it was "scale." There was a tool and dye shop on one side and an abandoned building on the other, smashed windows staring. It had a paved parking lot with actual dividing lines. All the Chicago towers—Willis, Trump, Vista—peered from a safe distance.

The building—red all-weather awnings, smoky block glass windows, and a gigantic nude in silhouette holding a martini glass (to hide a loading dock)—screamed beer distributorship. The lot was full.

Mostly pickups but a few beamers and Porsches, which made Sandy feel momentarily legit.

"Okay, I can do this."

She ran to the back entrance through light drizzle. When she opened the door, she walked into a dense fog of blue cigarette smoke mingled with weed. She gasped, then coughed, and held her breath. There was a dozen or more women in various stages of undress sitting in front of mirrors, Hollywood makeup lights glaring down at them. Ash trays, back packs, sequins, glitter, panties, spray tans, G-strings, hairless skin, stark ribs, long legs, short legs, veils, tassels, headdresses, spiked heels, butts of every shape and size, and breasts, more breasts than she had ever seen, including in her high school gym class. Suffocating music, screaming disco, pounded the walls.

Ronnie had told her to look for Bobby, the night manager.

"Hi, you must be Gemma." Bobby, maybe fifty, extended a fat little hand. He had short arms that stuck out when he let them rest. She was a full head and a half taller than Bobby, who wore his pants high on his belly; a worn leather belt, the top edge curled, gamely held Bobby's heft in place.

"It's Sandy, actually. You must be Bobby."

"Gemma when you're here, okay. Just better that way." He turned and headed to an office with a metal desk and two folding chairs.

"Have a seat."

Sandy smoothed her micro skirt and sat with her knees pressed together. Bobby laughed.

"When you're on the floor, you're gonna be bending, kneeling, crouching, squatting. Whatever. Your legs ain't gonna stay together. Don't bother trying."

He explained how to take orders, carry trays, bus tables. "And the table tips, they ain't all yours. Ten percent to the bartender. Something to the bouncer at the end of the night. You get the rest." News to Sandy…and Gemma.

Bobby put his clipboard and pencil on the desk and leaned forward, his elbows on the table.

"Any questions?"

"No, not really." Except: What am I doing here?

"Okay. Look, Gemma, here's the deal. You're gonna see floor to ceiling length red sheers located in four different places around the room. Behind them are the back rooms and lounges. These are where the executive sessions go on. The girls set their own rules back there. You know what I mean?"

"Uh…"

"No holds barred."

Sandy stared at Bobby, her mouth open slightly. Bobby frowned and shifted in his chair.

"Back there, guys and girls do whatever they wanna do for whatever price they agree on. Capisce? A cut to the house."

Sandy's eyebrows came together. "You mean, like…but…you know I'm just waitressing, right. I'm not—"

Bobby put one finger to his lips. "I'm just telling you what's what. Don't matter what kind of work a girl does out front. The back is always available…to any of you."

Sandy shook her head. "Look, I'm not—"

"Everyone who comes here to work gives me the 'Look, I'm not' talk. But it don't last." He coughed into his fist. "Anyway, here's the important thing. First, if we get busted, we don't know nothing about what's going on in the back. You're on your own. We deny everything. As far as we're concerned, everyone is obeying the rules posted on the walls—Guys can't touch girls; girls can't touch guys; curtains stay open; no fucking, no blow jobs, all that bullshit. Understood? Second, sometimes a guy can get, well, more insistent than he should; he may want to do something that the girl don't wanna do, you know what I mean? There's a white button in every lounge, every room. Push that button and if Razer isn't busy, he'll find you and get the guy outta there."

"Look, Bobby, I'm not going to—"

"Honey, trust me, I don't judge. I seen too many things to judge anyone, really. 'He who is without sin', so on and so forth. Whether you do anything more than serve drinks, that's your call. If you get hungry, if the landlord comes knocking, if that school loan comes due, if your kid needs vaccinated, whatever, it's there for you. Call it a benefit, like health insurance."

This was different than Sandy's first day at Facebook.

She walked down the hall to "The Room," music yowling. When she opened the door, it was like she'd been swallowed by a creature whose belly was lined with black velvet. She stood still, unable to see her own feet. She stuck one arm out, hoping to find a wall. "Jesus" came a man's voice as he pushed her arm out of the way. She closed and opened her eyes several times and shapes began to emerge. Silhouetted heads and shoulders and legs.

The runway jutted from the opposite wall. Piercing strobe lights assaulted the stage, like incoming fire from an attack helicopter. There was a round dancer with massive man-mades snaking her way back and forth between two poles. She sucked on one finger and pouted at the balding men who stared up at her, expressionless. A few tossed bills onto the floor. One man came forward as she lay on her back, legs akimbo, and gently placed money on her shaved altar.

There must have been forty tables, maybe more. Sandy was assigned twenty-six through thirty, wherever they were. There was a bar and buffet around the corner, two women pouring drink after drink, mostly draft beer. A brick wall of a man, arms folded, a permanent scowl on his face stood by the front entrance. Must be Razer, she thought.

She could see her feet now. She took a few steps forward, then stepped aside as a sweet-faced dancer holding the hand of a gray-haired business-type with loosened tie strode past her, disappearing behind the red curtains. Anywhere else, it could have been a grandfather and his granddaughter.

Sandy pressed her chest with the palm of her hand, trying to calm her breathing. She felt foolish, prudish. She took deep breath after deep breath, reining in her pounding heart. Stop it, she thought.

When she reached the bar, a stout woman wearing black nail polish, back eye shadow and a black unitard approached her.

"You new?"

"Yeah."

"Name?"

"S, uh, Gemma."

She pointed at a table where three guys in double-breasteds, wearing dress boots, and slouchy silk ties were sitting.

"Go ahead and try that table."

"What should I—"

"Just go, you'll be fine."

Sandy pasted a quivering smile on her face and crossed the room. The men looked more like boys the closer she got. When they saw her, foxlike smiles creased their faces; one poked another as the third stood. He held the back of his chair to steady himself. He bowed and swung his arm out, wrist dangling, as he tried to strike a dashing pose. They began to howl with laughter. Sandy wondered how many strip clubs they had already been to.

"Can I—"

She felt his eyes trying to devour her as he took her in his arms.

"Before we do anything, you have to dance with me."

"Fucking-A," said one of his friends.

He pulled her close and touched her nose with his. Sandy felt paralyzed.

"C'mon, loosen up, for chrissakes! I'm not gonna do anything to you." He glanced at the other two. "Unless you want me to." He swayed back and forth, pressing himself against her.

"Oh yeah."

Sandy looked at Razer, but he only watched. She tried to swallow.

"I'll be honest with you. I been looking for someone like you all night. Not like them"—he pointed at the stage—"with their fake tits and skanky asses. No, someone like you, the girl next door, you know what I mean? You must get that all the time. My God, look at you."

He reached into his breast pocket and pulled out a wad of money held tight by a rubber band. He removed a hundred-dollar bill.

"See that guy? That's Ben Franklin. History tells us a lot about Ben, but what it doesn't tell us is that he was a philandering old fuck who loved a good piece of ass." He leaned back and made eye contact. "He did. And he's an American hero." He glanced at his buddies, who were breathless. "I want to be an American hero like Benny here. It's *my* patriotic duty."

He grabbed her ass with one hand and clutched her left breast with his other. The lights were going out for Sandy. She couldn't feel anything.

"I've got ten of these Benjamin Franklins and I'll give them all to you for just one piece. Just one." He whispered in her ear. "Think of it as *your* patriotic duty."

Sandy pounded his chest and pushed him with both hands, but he held tight. She struggled as Razer watched from across the room. Gales of laughter rose from the table. She closed her eyes and leaned as far away as she could. She couldn't move. Time stood still.

Hands appeared, yanking the guy's shoulders. He let go of Sandy as she wobbled and began to slump. She watched as the slick linoleum floor rushed toward her face. She was in free fall.

She could see herself lying on a bed, the smell of someone's dirty socks filling the air. "No!" She cried out again, but his hand was over her mouth. She tried to bite him, but he shoved her face against the headboard.

"Help! Someone, please!"

"No one can hear you," the boy said.

"Please, don't."

"C'mon, you know you want this. Like, why else would you come up here?"

"It'll be fun," Roseanne had said when Sandy was reluctant about going to the party, especially when it was at some kid's house from another high school. Roseanne laughed and shook her head. "Lots of cute boys," she said, winking. In the end, it sounded too good to miss. But then it wasn't.

"Roseanne!" she cried, as perspiration puddled on the floor. "Roseanne!

Bobby told the pin-striped guy and his two friends to back off and give Gemma some space. He leaned in, trying to understand what Sandy was saying.

"Who? Rose-what? What are you talkin' about?" he said.

"Roseanne!"

But Roseanne didn't come. No one came. And she couldn't get away, and the boy, he wouldn't stop. She shut her eyes tight and held her breath. She felt the pain, like a knife, and gasped. His beer breath filled her lungs.

Afterwards, he put his pants on and didn't say a word. He left her there and went back to the party. She got up, her body numb; she went to the bathroom, washed her face, gathered herself together, and went back downstairs where she found Roseanne. Sandy told her that she had to leave. "My period."

Still sprawled on the Flytrap floor, Sandy opened her eyes and all she could see were shoes scurrying. The floor was damp and her face felt cool.

"Goddammit." Bobby's basketball-sized head leaned over her. "Just lay there, okay, until we know there's nothin' busted or nothin'."

"Let's get the fuck outta here." She watched as three pairs of scuffed boots disappeared into the dark, a toppled chair left behind.

"This ain't never happened before, I'm tellin' you." Bobby was on his knees now. "Your first fucking night. What're the chances, I mean, really, this *never* happens. Not to servers, it don't. I never seen those fuckers before in my life. Jesus." He leaned on his hands. "You're okay, right? I mean, nothin's hurt, right? You didn't give him some reason to do this, did you?"

"You're okay, c'mon. For real." The boy's voice echoed in her head.

CHAPTER 20

"So, where are you?"

Sandy lowered her window and stuck her head out. She looked in both directions. "Uhhh, just got off 90 at 490. The sign says I'm on 19 heading toward Leroy."

"Okay. You're sure it won't start."

Sandy tried to turn the engine over again. Her Honda Civic coughed like a sick cat working a fur ball.

"Nothing. It's done." She laid her head on the steering wheel. "Richie, I am so sorry about this."

"Why didn't you call me? We could have made better plans. Why didn't you fly?"

Sandy held the phone away from her face and scowled at it. "Because I don't have any fucking money." She sucked breath through her teeth. "It was...spur of the moment."

Long pause. "Sandy, what are you doing? I mean...well, what are you doing?"

After the disaster at Venus's Flytrap, Sandy had intended on going back to her apartment, showering, crawling into bed, pulling the covers over her head and never getting up again. But as she approached her apartment, she found that she couldn't stop. She kept driving. Soon she was on 80 going east, only partially aware of what she was doing. She was still wearing her Flytrap getup, though she had kicked off her spiked heels somewhere in Michigan. She stopped once for gas, a bagel and coffee. Truckers put down their burgers and watched. She looked like Alice Cooper, her blue/black mascara streaking her cheeks.

She drank her coffee and tossed half her bagel. She put her seat back flat and closed her eyes. She was awakened by the sound of seagulls scavenging the parking lot. In the west, the moon was full, while in the east the sky was faint orange. She went back into the rest stop, peed, bought a cherry pie and a bottle of water from a vending machine. Sandy hit the road again, now about two hundred miles from the western Ohio line.

As she crossed the wide-open farmland of Ohio, she began to cry. Where was she going? She felt like she was being chased and that no matter how fast she ran, no matter how far she drove, whatever was after her would stay tight on her heels, nipping, snapping, threatening. She felt lost. The directional arrows and mileage signs and numbered exits along the way were no help.

What *was* she doing? She hadn't been able to answer that question in years. In the beginning, her horizon line looked crisp, clear and inviting; eyes straight ahead, mind open, pace steady, if she headed toward that line, it would take her wherever she wanted to go. In those days, she thought of medicine or journalism or business. They were all within reach. Her options were as numerous as the leaves on the red maple in her family's front yard.

At some point, far too early in the journey, the horizon line faded in a fog so thick that at times it was invisible. Her eyes lost focus, her thinking became jumbled and she felt her life slowing to a crawl. No one else noticed as long as she smiled, danced fast and moved from one thing to another with such lightness of foot that she appeared to know exactly what she was doing. Actually, she was only running in place, the past so close behind that it could easily have been mistaken for the present.

Moving away and staying away, the geographical cure, hadn't worked. Her hometown, and all her accumulated baggage, was always with her.

"I don't know what I'm doing, Richie. I'm coming home."

"Do Mom and Dad know?"

"No. I didn't even know."

"You didn't even know?"

"No. Look, I know this is fucked up. It is. But I started driving and I couldn't think of anywhere else to go. You're home, aren't you?"

"Let's say home is nearby." Rich could hear air blasting through Sandy's flared nostrils. "Yes, I'm home," he admitted.

"So, could you just come get me? Please."

It was raining hard by the time Rich reached the Leroy exit and spied Sandy's Honda alongside the road. He could see a gray shadow behind the wheel. When he passed her, Sandy looked but didn't wave. He U-turned and settled in behind her. He pulled his jacket up over his head and sidestepped a swimming pool-sized pothole as he approached her car. Tapped on the window. He had never noticed how much his sister looked like their mother, especially the crinkles at the corners of her mouth and eyes. Worse, she looked the same age.

"Fancy meeting you here."

"What can I say, Richie. Thank you. And thank you."

"I was in the neighborhood anyway."

Sandy dashed to her brother's car as Rich got behind the wheel of hers. It took him three seconds to figure out the problem. No gas. He looked through the rearview mirror. She was huddled in the passenger side seat, her head against the window. 'Jesus, Sandy, what's going on?' he thought.

They drove into Bergen where a service station attendant let Rich borrow a can and buy some gas. He scurried back to her car. Once done, he hopped in behind the wheel. The rain was torrential by then, smacking the windows in stiff, pelting sheets.

"Better wait a little bit before…"

"I am so fucking sorry, Richie. I don't know. After a while, I was on the road so long, I don't know, I didn't pay attention to anything. Obviously. I just wanted to get away."

"Just wanted to get away?"

Sandy looked at her brother's quizzical face and began to sob. Rich leaned over and wrapped his arms around her.

"Jesus, what happened to you, Sandy?"

Sandy tried to speak but her breath came only in jerks and heaves and gasps. Her tear tracks swelled to overflowing. Her arms hung limp, boneless. Her hands were as puffy as her eyes, her cheeks. Rich held her tighter still. When had he ever seen her like this? When had she come so undone? He felt afraid for her, afraid that he couldn't help her.

In time, she grew quiet, still; her breathing changed, became thick, slow and rhythmic. "Sandy," he said. But she was asleep.

He shifted gently so that his arm could hold her more steadfastly. He kissed the top of her head. He looked down at her, at her skirt, her stockings, the back seams showing. An open-toed, clear-as-glass high heel remained on her left foot, its long spike digging into the floor mat. He leaned forward to see her face. Brilliant red lipstick, smeared onto her chin; and coal dark eye shadow, smudged across her cheeks. She seemed shrunken, a mini-version of herself, as she pressed awkwardly against him. He squeezed her and rested his head on hers. He looked at the rain coursing down the windshield as tears reached his chin.

Here they were, he thought, going nowhere. He had tried to reframe his move back as positive regrouping, rather than retreat. He had contacted some old friends, reached out to some tech and healthcare startups. He sold himself as experienced in healthcare, preventive healthcare or health maintenance, which ever seemed to work best. He picked up a few gigs sorting data for researchers, nothing big, but enough to live on. He had furnished his townhouse from Salvo and Helping Hand. He had a bedroom, bath, kitchenette and a tiny living room, featuring a sagging couch facing a twenty-inch TV. He could see a Tops grocery store from his front window. There was a used bookstore for times of desperation. And a pet store that featured a single cockatoo. These were his stops when he walked through the village.

He spoke to his parents daily and visited them a couple times a week. When he'd asked how things were going, they'd sidestep his inquiries. They acted like everything was normal, even though it was obvious to Rich that it wasn't. His dad had a patchy, grizzled beard and seemed to be wearing the same Bills sweatshirt every time he stopped by the house. His mother was — he hesitated to think it — odd. Unusual was a generous word to describe how she dressed.

"Mom?" he had said when she came into the kitchen wearing a snakeskin turban. His father didn't bat an eye.

"How do you like it?" she said, her arms outstretched.

Before he could answer, his father shot him a warning glance.

"Love it, Mom."

And that's the way it went. At least until recently. Last Saturday, he stopped by with takeout from Grandpa Sam's. They were both eerily quiet. His father was clean shaven again. He was wearing an actual shirt with a collar and everything. His mother didn't have a shocking wig on her head; her hair was almost two inches long and regaining some luster. She wore jeans and a pale-yellow crew necked sweater. He almost cried — "Jesus Christ, what happened?" — but thought better of it when his parents seemed unaware of how different they looked.

"The gnocchi looks delicious, honey," his mother said. Once so tentative about putting anything in her mouth, she dove in, throwing caution to the wind.

"Wine?" his father said, holding a bottle of chianti in his hand.

"A little," said his mother, her mouth full.

She was either cured or dying.

Growing restless beside Rich, Sandy groaned, her face contorted. She jabbed an elbow into his ribs; her head tossed back and forth.

"Sandy. Sandy, are you okay?"

She mumbled and heaved and pushed away from him. She sat up, gasping for air.

"Sandy?"

She tried to catch her breath as she turned to look at him. How had she gotten from the floor at Venus's to Richie's car? She rubbed her eyes and licked her lips.

"Here." Rich opened a bottle of water and handed it to her. He laid his hand lightly on her shoulder. She gulped the water and coughed. Then she remembered. She lay back in the seat again and closed her eyes. She took another drink and then another. Rich watched, not knowing whether to speak.

"My first day at work didn't go so well."

"Oh," said Rich.

She remembered Bobby's sour breath, as he sat beside her on the floor. He asked her if she wanted to go to the hospital, but then suggested it probably wasn't such a good idea, like it might make things worse. She remembered that he said something about the newspapers and her reputation, and how he was only thinking of her, how it's hard to make these things go away, if you know what I mean, what with the internet and all.

Sandy got on her hands and knees, then sat in a heap on one of the chairs at the now empty table. The music wailed, a dancer was shaking her boobs at two men, and servers tiptoed around her, not wanting their customers to go dry. Stout-woman-from-the-bar approached, a scowl on her face.

"What did I tell you, asshole?" At first Sandy thought Stout Woman was talking to her, until she saw the finger flipped at Bobby.

"What?"

"Don't 'what' me, you fat fuck. I told you she wasn't ready! Did you even ask her if she was ready to go solo? I mean, look at her eyes. Fucking Bambi had more balls. You should be fucking ashamed."

At first Sandy thought Stout Woman was being supportive, but then not so much.

"Could I have a glass of water?" No one noticed.

"If I was her, I'd sue your ass." Stout Woman was pointing with her fist now.

"Look, Candy" —Stout Woman seemed like a more apt moniker— "shut the fuck up or you can take a hike, okay?" Bobby glared, his eyes reminding her who was in charge.

Stout Woman demurred, stepping back while giving Bobby one final finger. Again, this wasn't Facebook.

Sandy was on her feet by now. How she got there was anyone's guess. Bobby stood beside her, Sandy's heels dangling from his fingertips.

"Don't listen to her, I'm tellin' you. She's got issues, you know what I'm talkin' about?"

Sandy straightened her back and held onto a chair. She looked around the room, fearful that everyone was staring at her. Not to worry, their numbed faces and vacant eyes were focused on the strobe lit stage.

"You'll be okay," called Bobby as she staggered away. "Can I do something for you?" Sandy kept walking. "Maybe you oughta just go home, you know, rest up. I'll put you on the schedule for tomorrow night, okay? Don't want you to be penalized for this...Hey!"

Sandy turned. "Here you go." Bobby tossed the shoes to her. They fell at her feet. "You're gonna need 'em."

Rich said, "You're fucking kidding me" at least five times while she recounted the events of the last twenty-four hours. The story came out in staccato shards, jagged phrases, barbed words and sentences. In the retelling, though, the fever broke. Rich hugged her again; this time, though, her jaw was set, the tears were gone.

She followed Rich back to his apartment. On the way, they stopped at McDonald's, Sandy's hunger finally catching up to her. Once at the apartment, she collapsed on Rich's bed. Rich stood over her. He removed her shoes and tossed them in the wastebasket. He covered her with a comforter, pulled the blinds and closed the door. He took a Corona from the fridge and downed it in three gulps.

CHAPTER 21

He had suggested that they go out to a movie at the Little and then dinner at Gray's. Sounded like a perfect evening to Sam. Very public. No pressure. Not suggestive of anything.

Rhonda was his first date on Humpr. He'd connected with several other women but they'd been far too aggressive. Things had changed since he first dated Gayley and then Marianne. He should have known that was the case from watching TV, movies and scanning the internet. But when faced with it, he was shocked. He felt unprepared for the twenty-first century hook-up culture. On Humpr, it seemed like everything ran in reverse. Instead of dating someone to see if you'd eventually want to become intimate, now you immediately had sex with someone to see if you wanted to date them. Everyone was in a hurry to do what once took weeks or even months to accomplish. At first this had discouraged him. He wasn't that kind of man.

Sitting at home night after night eating Lean Cuisine in front of the TV with Jamie. Then going to bed alone, trying to visualize that actress from *Modern Family*, the one with the accent, so he could at least achieve some release, if not satisfaction. Watching, with lascivious intent, as some of his female customers walked away from his counter. Googling porn sites that he was too embarrassed to enter. Was this what he wanted in life?

After Marianne died, he didn't have a sexual impulse for at least two years. He was numb, inside and out. He focused on Jamie and finding the right care for him. He went through a handful of home health nurses before he found Kathleen. Kathleen—he shook his head to think how foolish he'd been, how off the mark, how pathetic.

It was the Kathleen Fiasco that made him think about branching out, exploring the field, so to speak. If he could find someone else, it would reduce his preoccupation with her. It would make it easier to accept that she was beyond his reach. Enter Humpr. Once the site reopened, he read online that the previous owner was being sued by former employees claiming he'd created a "hostile work environment" and had "systematically forced" them into "unwanted sexual behavior." Who knew? The new ownership was on the up-and-up, as far as Sam could tell.

There were still some questionable listings, men and women who were offering more than dating and companionship. Rhonda didn't fall into that category, even though a red flag went up when she suggested he come to her house for their first date. This was too forward for his taste. She seemed excited with the alternative he had suggested, though. Her profile indicated she had two grown sons; that she had been married twice and twice divorced ('Why did she include that?' he wondered); that she was an "office manager"; that she was "late-forties-ish", which probably mean early fifties. She had a broad, crooked smile on her profile, one eye nearly closed, like whoever took the picture snapped it a second too soon. Rhonda wanted to "have fun," "not take life too seriously," and find a man "who knew how to make a woman feel good." This last item kept him awake at night.

Sam tried to spruce up the bouquet of mixed flowers he'd bought from the grocery store; then he knocked on Rhonda's door. He could hear her running about inside. She called, "I'll be there in a minute!"

He shuffled. Her door began to open. His heart sputtered and hopped like a rabid bunny.

Rhonda looked like, well, a real person. She had shoulder length brown hair, parted in the middle. Blue-gray eyes—both open an equal amount. She had some wrinkles, but her face had perfect symmetry. She smiled easily, her imperfect teeth, oddly attractive. She wore a blue sweater and a paisley scarf, of some sort, and tightish gray slacks, perhaps a size too small. Some kind of shoes. While he didn't want to appear obvious, he snuck looks at the rest of her and liked what he saw. She wasn't a stick, by any means. He liked her fullness, her curves, very proportional. He smiled.

He was surprised to notice her scanning him in return. He knew that her view was not as appealing as his, so, hoping to compensate, he smiled even more broadly.

"Well..."

"Well, indeed," replied Rhonda, sounding breathless.

"You are Rhonda." He stuck out his hand. She ignored it and stepped closer to give him a hug. If it had lasted another second it would have been too forward, but it felt good. He forced a friendly laugh.

"So nice finally to meet you, Sam," she said. "You go by Sam, right? Not Samuel."

"Either is fine. Most people call me Sam. And you? Rhonda?"

"Actually it's Mary Alice." Sam's forehead furrowed. She reached out and patted his chest. "No, it's Rhonda. Just being silly. You never know on that site, though. Most people aren't who they say they are. It's like they're lying, you know? I don't like that. I'm always honest. Or try to be." That explains why she had listed the divorces, thought Sam.

"Yes. Yes, I agree. Entirely." Why did he sound dishonest?

The movie was a subtitled, dark, Swedish fantasy, when what Sam had hoped for was something light, something they could laugh about over dinner. Instead, he felt like he needed a nap as soon as the credits started to roll. But Rhonda seemed unaffected by the gloom. She took his arm as they walked around the corner to the restaurant.

"The Swedes are so deep, aren't they?"

"Yes, I suppose so."

They were seated by a glass wall, Sam in a chair and Rhonda on the long, burgundy, leather cushioned seat that spanned the length of the restaurant like a church pew. Everything was sleek and silver and wrought iron. When a brigade of waitstaff approached the table, Sam thought he should have Googled the prices in advance. She ordered some kind of steak with some kind of fancy sauce. He ordered broiled lobster. Also, with some kind of fancy sauce. Rhonda liked Malbec so they ordered a bottle, Argentinian, he thought. He wished he had worn a tie.

Rhonda's face glowed as she surveyed the room. Meticulously quaffed and manicured men and women tipped their glasses to one another. They talked in low tones, probably about the stock market, Sam assumed; when they laughed, it was as if a bomb had detonated in the middle of their tables; they leaned back, heads tossed upward, as if to avoid the shrapnel of cleverness as it burst forth.

Rhonda's eyes were wide. She twisted her head slightly to one side. "Fancy-shmancy!"

Sam lifted his glass. "Nothing but the best. Here's to both fancy and shmancy."

Salads finally arrived. And soon thereafter, entrees.

"So, you're a pharmacist?"

"Guilty as charged," said Sam. He swallowed, then wiped his mouth with the linen napkin. Without being asked, he dove into pharmacy life, where he'd gone to school, how long he'd been at Walgreen's, what his average day was like, how many people worked there. At one point, he stopped, trying to identify an annoying droning sound, only to realize it was him.

"Interesting," she said.

And so it went.

Rhonda grew up in southern Ohio, near the Kentucky border. She married young and moved to the Rochester area when her husband got a job at Kodak. "Bang, I got pregnant." She went to night school to get a teaching degree, but then—"Bang again"—she got pregnant. Two boys. "They were my life." She raised them, they both went into the service, one in South Korea and the other in Germany. "Never call."

"You know, it was about then that I took a good look at Ralph, my husband, and thought, 'What in the world am I doing with this guy'? You know what I mean?"

"Well…"

"So, I says to him, I says, 'Ralph, I don't want to be married to you'. I moved out. Got a job in a dentist's office. Went to community college for office management and started my life over again."

"Wow." Sam seemed always to be mid-chew when a response was required. He gulped. "That's quite a story. How long have you been on your own?"

"Married again about six years ago."

"Oh." He put his knife and fork down, since there was more to come. "What was your second husband's name."

"Christine."

Sam's face froze, not sure what expression was fitting. "Okay."

"Never knew I could swing that way until I tried. And swing, I did. Got drunk at a friend's party and Christine kind of swept me off my feet."

"Uh huh. Well, that's good, right?" 'Why are we out on a date together?' Sam wondered. He finished his glass of wine in a gulp and didn't wait for the waitstaff to pour more. He tipped the bottle toward Rhonda, as if to say, 'Fill 'er up?', but she was mid-story, so he poured himself another. The glass was so full that he bent over to sip it, like a kid slurping at a drinking fountain. No spills. Success. Then he drew the glass to his mouth and guzzled some more.

Rhonda told a minutely detailed and disturbingly explicit tale about her "killer" sexual relationship with Christine; she also enumerated the ways in which her orgasms differed depending on whether she was with Ralph or Christine, "though never at the same time." Sam poured himself more wine.

"Once the state okayed same sex marriage, we tied the knot. It felt good for a while. But marriage wasn't really my thing." Another divorce decree on the wall. "Don't get me wrong, we still see each other. Like I said, some things were very good. But..." She shrugged.

They ordered a sweet potato souffle with a lava center and vanilla bean ice cream for dessert.

Sam's three glasses of wine had made Rhonda adorable and her stories delightful. "You sure have had yourself a life! Maybe a life and a half!" Several tables turned to glare at Sam who was finetuning his outside voice. "I just love it!"

Sam had difficulty spooning his dessert, keeping the sweet potato, the lava and the quickly melting ice cream in place. "Fucker," he whispered.

Rhonda, catching up to his wine consumption, guffawed and snorted. "Look at you. You are the funniest man I've ever met! And I've met my share!" She winked, the side of her mouth opening wide.

"What about you, Samuel Cunningham? You haven't told me anything about your life. Married? Children?"

"Yes, I was married to a wonnerful woman and we had ourselves a wonnerful son." He grinned. She nodded, encouraging him to gone on. "We were married...a great many years. Our son's almose thirty."

"Okay."

He grinned again, raised his eyebrows and licked his lips. He picked up his spoon and went at the souffle again.

"There's got to be more, Sam. I mean, right? What's her name?"

"Marianne."

"Where's this wonderful woman at?"

"She's gone away."

"Left you, did she?"

Sam laid his spoon on the table and raised his napkin to his lips. He balled the napkin and tossed it onto his dessert.

"Yes, I guess she did."

"Another man?"

"Nope."

"Don't tell me it was a woman."

"Nope."

"So?"

"She found herself a big old oak tree out on Town Line Rd. and she ran her car into it."

Rhonda put her spoon on the table and dropped her napkin onto the floor. "Oh, my God, Sam, I'm so sorry. Why would she do something like that? That's awful." She reached across the table and placed her hand on his. Sam looked at it. Her skin was soft and warm, her fingers wide. Sam was confused by how the words had come out of his mouth, matter-of-fact, chill, indifferent.

"I mean, she died...terribly." He reached for his glass again. Rhonda withdrew her hand, her face sagging from the weight of his words.

"Sam, I'm..."

Sam gulped the last of their second bottle and looked around for waitstaff. He smiled.

"Everyone thought it was Jamie, because of Jamie."

"Jamie?"

"Our son. Hurt playing football. Never the same again. Thirty but like two, really, maybe three, four...who's to say. Broke her heart, it did. But it didn't kill her. No...it didn't kill her." He leaned on the table with both elbows, his head drooped.

"Sam, really, you don't—"

"Bet you didn't expect this much fun, did you?" Sam tried to sit up; he waved one arm, hitting someone at the next table. "Sorry," he said.

"Maybe we should go." Rhonda reached for her bag.

"It was me..."

"I don't think—"

"It was, you know...it was me..."

Sam fell asleep in the car. When he woke up, he was in Rhonda's driveway lying in the back seat. His breath smelled like the inside of a trash barrel; his tongue was swollen, his head throbbed. 'How long have I been here?' he wondered. 'Where was she?' As he sat up, a wave of nausea overtook him. He opened the car door and vomited on the driveway. Rhonda was standing at the front door.

"I've brewed coffee," she called.

CHAPTER 22

It was 2:00am by the time Sam pulled into his own driveway. The light was on in the living room. He had put Jamie to bed before he had gone out. Gretchen had probably finished her homework long ago. Sam had told her it would be fine to have her boyfriend come over while she babysat Jamie. Not wanting to walk in on anything, Sam shook the door when he opened it, stomped his feet and announced, "I'm home." His warning signals weren't necessary. He found Gretchen curled up on the couch, fast asleep. He clicked off the TV.

Sam reached for Gretchen but then pulled his hand away. He called to her softly. At first, she didn't move. He tried again. She startled and sat up, rubbing her eyes.

"Hi Gretchen, it's just me."

She stared at him but didn't speak. She yawned and wiped the drool from her cheeks.

"Okay." Her eyes were still struggling with the light as she headed for the front door, slipping her shoes on as she went.

"Did everything go okay?" But she was already out the door.

Sam picked up a bowl with Dorito crumbs in it. Several empty beer cans were on the floor near the TV. The boyfriend must have made an appearance. He shook his head. He would never have thought of leaving cans behind when he was dating Gayley. Nowadays, kids aren't afraid of being caught.

He dumped it all in the wastebasket under the sink and then went back into the living room, the reading light on by his easy chair. His head was thumping yet he didn't have the energy to go up the steps. He tumbled into his chair, the crinkled leather engulfing him. The lamp felt like a spot light burning a hole in the back of his head. He turned it off and settled into darkness. A street light shown through lace curtains. He closed his eyes and leaned his head back, sighing at the relief he felt. He grimaced at what he could remember of the evening.

He learned one thing about Rhonda. She was kind. Two things, actually. She was tolerant. For a long time, he sat at her kitchen table, head on the Formica, a cup of coffee simmering at the end of his nose. His eyes dribbled tears. Rhonda drank her coffee slowly. One cup, then two. Biscotti with the second. She didn't ask him anything. She didn't suggest he go. She waited, seemingly unconcerned about whether he would ever raise his head again. Would she eventually have to explain to some future realtor that, yes, he comes with the house?

He couldn't remember what he'd told her. He knew Marianne's death had come up. That she had hit a tree. On purpose. He hadn't gone on, had he? He hadn't mentioned Gayley, had he? He remembered that she had been studying her biscotti as she chewed. If he had told her the whole story, surely she wouldn't have been so focused on her cookie.

His mouth still feeling mossy, Sam got up from his easy chair and went to the kitchen for a glass of water. He took one sip, then another. It tasted so good that he drank the rest in a single gulp. But then his stomach revolted. He started coughing, then gagging and finally he vomited into the kitchen sink.

He'd been at the same spot the night that Marianne died. The police had finally left. Waves of guilty nausea enveloped him; he leaned over and out it all came into the same sink and down the same drain. The contents of his stomach along with his life.

He breathed slowly and looked over the sink and out the window at his neighbor's back door, their porch light still on. "Shit," he said

better make lunches. Nellie would be late for her shift in the morning. He had to be there early to cover the front end before the pharmacy opened at 9:00am.

But first, there was the problem of trying to get out of his chair. He closed his eyes.

CHAPTER 23

Eddy had longed for the Treatment Talk. He had dreamed about it for months, fantasized about it, had numerous imaginary conversations with Gayle about it. He had kept his secret hopes on life support. Perhaps she would finally come around; she would finally return from her self-imposed exile, from her abandonment of the only thing that might save her.

In recent weeks he had felt hopeful. Gayle was her old self. No flamboyant wigs. No ostentatious Hawaiian ponchos. No garish lipstick. He didn't say a thing to her about it, but he crossed everything he could cross, hoping that whatever had whisked her away had lost its grip.

Gayle entered the kitchen quietly and watched Eddy bent over the stove, scrambling, brewing, frying, and toasting. Good as he was, he couldn't possibly understand what her life had come to. Not that he hadn't tried. His face, his eyes, there was empathy in the way he sighed, the way he fell quiet. But he never came close to seeing, hearing, feeling what it was like to lose your life right in the middle of living it. How could he?

It wasn't only Eddy who was at a loss; it was the doctors, as well; doctors who had seen this disease thousands of times but hadn't lived it. Even the commiseration of other patients—"I know what you're talking about; I know this thing and what it does"—even these patients, who faced the exact same diagnosis and treatment, only touched her aloneness fleetingly. Every person's suffering is singular, no matter how much we want to believe otherwise.

Eddy caught her eye and she returned his smile. She loosened her clenched jaw and took a deep breath. There was comfort in knowing that she would rather be with him during her aloneness than anyone else.

Eddy filled plates with waffles and bacon and toast from real bakery bread. His freshly ground coffee was brewed to perfection. He set the table with their good china, and even made mimosas served in champagne flutes. She could have told him he didn't need to stack the deck, but she appreciated his effort.

"So," began Eddy, linen napkin spread on his lap, syrup cruet in his hand. "You wanted to talk about treatment."

Gayle almost laughed at Eddy's practiced nonchalance. She imagined him standing in front of a mirror rehearsing the proper intonation, the noncommittal yet earnest facial expression, closeting every personal desire to influence or coerce. She knew that it was all he could do not to have the car running in the driveway so they could dash off to the cancer center at the slightest encouragement.

Eddy studied his wife's face with a jeweler's precision, loupe to his eye, looking for sparkle, looking for light.

His goal this morning was *not* to do anything that Gayle might need to resist or oppose. Not to suggest a course of action, not to lean in one direction or the other. He would be Switzerland, presenting neutrality over a delicious breakfast. Appearing to be neutral and curious was the best way to influence her, to persuade without persuasion.

"Yes, I did. I wanted to talk about what to do next."

Eddy took a deep breath, held it and then let it out slowly through wheezing nostrils. 'What to do next' did not include the all-important word — treatment. Where was she heading with this? What should he say?

"Okay." He reached for the coffee pot, resting on a warmer. "More?"

"No thanks, honey."

He topped off his cup to near overflowing.

"That's the question, isn't it?" Okay, that's good, he thought.

Gayle sipped her coffee as she chewed a piece of bacon. "This is delicious."

"Thanks." Eddy moved his waffle around on the plate.

"I've been doing some research on immunotherapy." It was still rather experimental with ovarian cancer, she said, although it has showed great promise with other cancers. Eddy hoped she didn't see his jowls sag. Was she preparing an evidence-based explanation for doing nothing?

She reached across the table and patted Eddy's limp hand. "I know this has been hard on you—"

"No, no, really."

"Yes, it has. And I appreciate how patient you've been." She pressed her napkin to her lips. "I left treatment because I wanted the freedom to live in the moment as much as possible; do things I wouldn't normally do. The time seemed short and I didn't want to miss out, all that sort of thing. But I found that I missed *this* life. I missed you, I missed the kids, I missed my office, I missed standing on the front porch and watching the traffic in the morning, cup of coffee in my hand. I guess, for a while, I ran away from all that, because it was so hard to think of having it, you know, taken away. I don't know if that makes any sense, but..."

"I think I understand." He didn't, but he assumed the longer he listened, there was a chance that he would.

"The thought of having things taken away, the things I love...my life...it was too much to bear. It was great fun to run for a while, but running, trying to be someone else, wasn't the answer, no matter how much I wanted it to be. So, I've decided to come back to my life."

Eddy was still in a fog. "That's good, that's good that you've decided to come back. I couldn't be any happier." He forced a grin. He reached for the syrup cruet and handed it to Gayle. She took it and put it beside her plate. "Thanks," she said. Eddy added a pat of butter to his half-eaten waffle, but it didn't melt. He laid his fork down.

"Eddy, what's the matter?"

"Nothing, everything's fine."

"I've known you too long to believe a single word you're saying. What is it?"

Eddy wiped his mouth with his napkin. He cleared his throat and placed both hands on the table.

"Well, I don't know exactly. I mean, I was worried that you had gone away and that I'd lost you forever, so I'm happy you're 'coming back'." He said this with air quotes, something Gayle hated. She held her breath. And her tongue. "But, it's like, are you back because you're resigned to, I don't know…"

"Dying?"

"I guess. Are you settling in for the final stretch of the road, so to speak, or are you hoping to pave more road, make it longer…I'm sorry, this metaphor doesn't—"

"Look, Eddy, I am resigned to dying. I have to be."

"Okay." Eddy felt his stomach roll over.

"You can be both, you know. I could die. I know that. It's what usually happens with this, this thing. But at the same time, I'm ready to move forward, keep going, or, what did you say?"

"Make the road a little longer…"

"Yeah, maybe we can do that…"

Eddy was standing at her side now. Gayle stood and he kissed her forehead and took her in his arms. He wasn't resigned to anything, but he knew better than to argue the point.

Gayle could feel her husband's heart beating against her chest.

"So?"

"So, I'll call the center tomorrow, see when I can get in to talk about where to next."

"Okay. Okay then. Let's do that, I mean if that's what you want to do…then that's what we'll do…maybe we could call today." Gayle squeezed him around the waist so hard that he held his breath. "Or we could call tomorrow."

CHAPTER 24

There was a bounce in Eddy's step as he hotfooted it to the pharmacy the next morning. It didn't matter that a spring snow, icy and piercing, pelted him as he went. The air was delicious, he thought, gulps of it fueling his buoyant stride. He found himself whistling. When was the last time he had whistled? Who knew he could whistle so loudly? He waved at a passing garbage truck and then a FedEx truck and a UPS truck close on its tail. He laughed for no reason other than he could.

It was Sam who had insisted that Eddy push Gayle to change her mind, to get back into the game, which is the most that anyone can do when fighting cancer. Push on! Pushing, all by itself, may be enough to win the day. You can't deny someone their life when they take each and every breath with unwavering tenacity. Can you?

Their conversation had ended exactly as he had hoped. Life was good again. What were the chances? He felt electrically charged from head to toe. They made love twice that night. It had been a decade, maybe two, since he could have made that claim. 'Made love' was a genteel way of putting it. A younger Eddy might have said they 'effed each other brains out', and that would still have been an inadequate representation. They were animals! He was on top, she was on top, they were sideways, backwards; there were penetrations, explorations, every nook and cranny, tongues and teeth and fingers and, my God, toes. Groaning, moaning, whimpering, howling, grunting, wailing. It was a raucous, cacophonous event horizon from which Eddy thought they might never return. And that was before they even made it up the stairs to the bedroom. There were orgasms on top of orgasms; orgasms so strong that Eddy thought someone was banging the side of the house with a wrecking ball.

When they finished, Gayle rolled over, smiled and then began to laugh so hard her whole body shook. Eddy couldn't move. He couldn't feel anything between his legs. His privates in full hysterical paralysis. What did it matter? If he died right now, it would have been worth it. He rolled onto his side and laid his hand on Gayle's stomach. She looked at him. Her face was the face of that girl he first fell in love with, innocent, unfettered.

"What?" she said.

"You are beautiful."

She turned on her side and kissed him, wet and slow and deep.

This time they didn't eff each other's brains out, they made love.

•   •   •

When Eddy headed out for his morning walk, Gayle retreated to her office. She locked the door. She hunched over her computer, and started reviewing her spread sheets, examining her clients' tax accounts, the refunds, the fees. She opened the folder labeled "Other" and scanned their own accounts and holdings, estimating as best she could how much money they had. Only she could discern the broader picture within these details, the ocean beneath these waves. Eddy knew nothing about any of it. It was best that way. The whole thing would scare him to death. She knew she'd have to open the book and tell him the story at some point, but the thought of it made her shutter.

She became short of breath as she perused the numbers and tried to make sense of all she had done. She closed the computer with a thud. 'Too much', she thought. Too much to deal with when a new treatment was hanging over her head.

•   •   •

Sam watched as Eddy walked back down the aisle to the exit, his step steady and determined. Sam hadn't seen 'the old Eddy' in months, not since the world had caved in, not since their surreal powwow together at the foot of Jesus. Sam was glad that his pep talk had played a part in getting Eddy to urge Gayle back into treatment.

"I'm here to tell you you're a good friend, the best," said Eddy, his eyes glistening.

"Well…wonderful…"

"She's going back into treatment."

Sam grinned. "That is the best news ever."

Sam's heart skipped. He pressed his palms onto the counter top to steady himself. 'Gayley', he said in whisper to himself as his friend disappeared through the exit.

Eddy and Sam had never talked meaningfully about the past; how Sam had left for college and had asked his best friend to "watch over" (his exact words) his girlfriend. It was clear to both of them that the goal of this assignment was for Sam to maintain his relationship with Gayle, a relationship that he assumed would lead to marriage, children and a life of happiness. There was no better person to ask than Eddy, honest, respectful, a friend whom he trusted implicitly.

He was so stunned by what happened during his first semester at college, a mere three-and-one-half months, that he froze when confronted with the new reality — Eddy in, Sam out. His stoic demeanor was misunderstood as magnanimity. He was generous by nature, but not so generous that he would give his love and his future away, not even to his best friend. The illusion of hunky-dory-ness surrounding this changing of the guard forced a bereft Sam into hiding during his semester break. Christmas morning found him curled up under his covers unwilling to come down for breakfast, despite the urging of his grandmother. 'Fuck you, Grandma', he had thought.

His father tried to come to the rescue, reminding young Sam that there were "plenty of other fish in the sea." Sam stared at his father for a long time, waiting for him to laugh at his own words, but instead, his father gave him one confident slap on the back and returned to the kitchen for his mom's Christmas coffee cake.

Sam returned to campus a week early so he "could get a leg up on the new semester." Instead, he discovered a dozen bars and liquor stores within a half-mile radius of his dorm. He procured a passable ID and with nothing better to do, sampled the offerings of each establishment, drinking so much and so often that some bartenders refused service as soon as he entered their bar. "Nope, go back to your dorm and think about what you're doin'. This ain't healthy." 'Fuck you, grandma', he thought.

Sam didn't go to classes for the first three weeks of the semester; he seldom made it to the cafeteria. Or the shower.

Half-way through the semester he met a girl. She was a junior, actually three years older than Sam, which is to say, a real woman; from New York City, no less. They were in a speech class together. She told him how much she enjoyed his assigned talk about oral hygiene. "The mouth is such a fascinating place." She smiled and cocked her head. "Would you like to get together...we could explore this topic further?" meaning, 'Would you like to see my dorm room?' meaning, 'Would you like to get a little busy with me?'. He said "Sure," thinking he'd better practice his kissing. He rushed back to his dorm and accosted the pillow on his bed.

He met her that night in front of the library. They walked in silence to her dorm. How well he kissed mattered not. Almost immediately he was touching her above her clothes, then below her clothes, and then without any clothes. Later he felt embarrassed that he'd asked, "What's that?" when she got the condom wrapper out. She was an experienced teacher and he left her room well-schooled and grateful.

When he called her for another date, her roommate said she had only been "trying to make her boyfriend jealous" and that they had gotten back together again. So, b-bye. As cliché as it sounds, something about the whole experience made him grow up on the spot. Being caught in romantic intrigue, behaving illicitly had shaken something loose inside. It cleared his mind and steadied his gaze about life. He felt like an adult, which is to say he felt like he'd been sucker punched by life, the wind knocked completely out of him. But he'd be okay.

Once he caught his breath, there was no more playing. He stopped drinking, hit the books and ignored girls altogether. For six whole weeks. Just before spring break he started dating. What was her name? He proudly announced the news to Eddy and Gayle when he came home. The best 'fuck you, grandma' he could muster.

It wasn't until pharmacy school that he met Marianne. She felt like a haven, a safe place where he could learn how to love. Eddy and Gayle, Sam and Marianne. Friends, raising kids together, making their way in life. Past be damned.

For years he observed Gayley from afar, hoping this self-appointed role as watchman on her tower contributed in some way to her well-being. When he got news about her cancer, he was unsure whether to contact her directly, but in the end he did. He never told Eddy. Gayle must not have told him either, since Eddy never mentioned it, an odd reversal of the long-ago secrecy. She was formal about her illness and appreciative of his calls, little more.

When Eddy told him she had stopped treatment, he couldn't bear the thought of losing another woman he loved.

"But Gayle...I can't let you—"

"*You* can't let me! Don't be ridiculous. I know what I'm doing. I don't want the treatment to destroy me, and that's how it feels. Like I'm killing myself...so that I won't die."

"But...you can't give up—"

"I'm not giving up! Where did you get the idea I was giving up?"

And so it went. How could it have been otherwise? He felt foolish. He bent over the pill tray. Five, ten, fifteen, twenty...

"Excuse me, excuse me. I don't mean to interrupt, but I need service. Immediately, please?"

Sam dropped his spatula and huffed. He took another deep breath and gathered himself before heading to the counter.

"Rhonda," he said in a breathy rasp. He could feel his face turning toasty. "I didn't expect...I mean, well, I'm surprised to see you."

"I'm just as surprised as you are."

•　•　•

Eddy was a little more flatfooted as he approached the Presbyterian Church. Sam's words echoed in his mind: "That's great news, Eddy. Let's hope she hasn't waited too long." Eddy had felt so ecstatic over Gayle's change of mind that he had overlooked the most obvious dilemma facing them: Time had passed. Could they catch up?

Eddy entered through the side door and walked up the stairs to the second floor. At the end of the hall was Rev. Goff's office. He knocked on the door and waited. He had never gone inside before; had never sought Peter out because he always showed up, like a prowling apparition. Today was different. He wanted company when he stood before the Consoler. With Rev. Goff beside him, he would have more gravitas, more street cred, or was it pew cred? Whatever it was, he needed it, because he was going to pray again, this time for all the marbles.

"That is the best news!" Peter invited Eddy in.

Eddy was impressed by the floor-to-ceiling mahogany bookshelves that surrounded the room, a veritable canyon of knowledge. He mistakenly assumed that Peter relied exclusively on the Bible for his wisdom. Peter smiled: "Wisdom comes from everywhere, if you look. The Bible has two testaments." He stretched both arms out. "This is what might be thought of as the third testament." He chuckled. "The trick is assimilating it all and using it to guide how you live, neither of which have I mastered."

"Neat."

Down the back stairs and out another exit they went. The holly around the Consoler was in need of trimming; leggy branches jutted everywhere. The grass beneath the bushes was high, the weeds even higher.

"Tell me, tell me again this good news you've brought today." Peter leaned forward on the stone bench, his hands gripping the edge of the seat.

"Well, it's like I said, Gayle's decided to go back into treatment. She's ready to continue the fight."

"This is a blessing, that's for sure."

"Yes, that's how I feel," said Eddy, although 'blessing' was not a word he would have chosen. 'Terrific', 'fantastic', 'unbelievable'. 'Unbelievable' was probably the most apt, because Gayle wasn't one to change her mind once she made a decision. Whether it was a movie to watch on TV or who she was voting for ("Not that orange one.") or where to shop for a good cut of meat, it didn't matter how large or small the decision, once made, it was made and unmaking it was near impossible. He was happy to think that maybe, just maybe, he had some influence on Gayle unmaking her treatment decision. Maybe not his words, but his, well, how to put it? His water dripping on her stone.

"We haven't met with the treatment team yet and she'll have to have some tests and stuff, but we're getting started again."

Peter shook his head and patted Eddy on the back. "As the saying goes, the Lord moves in mysterious ways."

"We'll have to see if that's true." This time Eddy patted the good reverend's back.

"What do you mean?"

"For a long time, you've been urging, actually pushing me to believe in God, to pray, to come on board, so to speak. And I have been hesitant—"

"Hesitant hardly captures it!" Peter said with a gentle scoff.

"Hesitant, reluctant, skeptical, whatever. Things change."

"That's good."

Eddy wasn't listening. "Something bad comes along. Worse than bad, really; and you try to steady yourself; and you think, 'Okay, I just have to hang in there and this will go away at some point. I can do that'. And usually that's the way it goes. Bad things pass. Good things, too, I know, but mainly bad things pass. In life you have to grit your teeth and go forward. Most of the time, that's enough."

"Well—"

"But sometimes, it's more complicated than that. You have one bad thing going on—your wife has cancer. Then another bad thing comes along—you lose your job. Not only did you lose your job, but you can't find another job for love or money. You're, all of a sudden, too old. It's like one day you're a crew foreman, a boss, and the next day you can't do anything. Worse, you're too proud to take a shit job at McDonald's, you know what I'm saying? Along the way, health insurance evaporates. So, you keep thinking, you think—'Just take it one day at a time, things will work out'. Then out of the blue your wife decides she doesn't want to do treatment anymore. And you have no idea why. You ask and you listen and you still don't understand what you're hearing. But you know one thing—if she's not getting treatment, she's going to die, simple as that."

Eddy paused, fire burning his throat. His chest heaved and he licked his lips before speaking again. Peter didn't appear to be breathing.

"And so, it's like—fuck. What do you do? Well, you follow the rules—you put that one foot in front of the other, because that's always worked, and you keep your head up looking for some kind of break to come along. But one foot in front of the other is too slow. Time isn't on your side. The clock is ticking, the sand is passing through the damn hour glass. And you realize the whole one-day-at-a-time thing isn't going to cut it."

Eddy turned to Peter, his face moist, his eyes piercing. He pointed at him.

"And that's when it happens. All that patience and hopefulness and grim determination melts and all you have left is bottom-of-the-well desperation. It's quiet down there, I'm telling you. There's no one to turn to. You're looking up from the bottom, you know what I mean, and you can't see a goddam thing, just blackness. You're about to give up. Game over. But then you see something. At first you think it's just a figment of your imagination. But you keep looking. Sure enough, there it is, just a pin prick in the velvet, the slightest hint of light squeezing through that tiny opening. And you think, 'Okay, that'll have to do'."

Eddy stopped. Peter opened his mouth and then closed it again.

"You might say it's like a burst of noonday sun slicing through the cloud cover. But, not really. We've lost so much time because of Gayle's...because she stopped. We don't have any idea what's going on with the cancer. None whatsoever." Eddy clenched his fists. "For a while, I thought she looked better; maybe stopping treatment had been a good idea. But lately, I don't know. I can't put my finger on it, but something's going on. She doesn't complain at all. But she doesn't look at me when I ask how she's feeling." Eddy stood and took a step toward the statue. He looked up. "So, we've got a pin prick, that's all; just a little bit of light." He looked over his shoulder at Peter, then turned. "Don't get me wrong. Any light is good light. I just wish there was more."

"Yes, of course, anyone would want more."

Eddy turned back to Jesus. "That's why I'm here. I want more light."

"Okay...What—"

"You told me I should pray; that praying would help, if only to relieve the burden a little, right?"

"Well, yes, I—"

"I thought about this a lot. I even did a little research. I Googled 'Jesus and miracles' and I was pretty amazed. Healing the blind and raising the dead. Impressive stuff. And I thought, 'Why not Gayle?', you know what I mean? Why not Gayle and me? Why shouldn't we expect a miracle, huh?" He turned again, a grim smile, eyebrows raised, a question on his face.

Peter looked down, then rubbed his face and huffed. "Well, Eddy, I don't know if it works exactly like that. The Bible reports these miracles, but they were like gifts."

"What's that mean?"

"It's hard to explain. The miracles demonstrated God's grace. They were a foreshadowing."

"Foreshadowing of what?"

"Well, many believe they were a foreshadowing of what would happen when Jesus came back, you know, the end of world."

"That's perfect, because that's what we're dealing with here, the end of the world."

Peter's face looked hollow, empty. "But..."

"But what?"

"But, well, I don't want you to put all your hopes in this...I don't want you to be disappointed...or hurt."

"Look, I'm about to lose everything in my life, so I've got nothing to lose."

Peter rose and stood beside Eddy, both men looking up at the impervious face of Jesus, his not-really-a-smile gazing down on them. Eddy collapsed to his knees in the dirt. Peter carefully kneeled beside him. Eddy clasped his shaking hands together and held them up to Jesus.

"Look, Jesus…or God?" He checked with Peter.

"Either will do."

"The end of the world has come. The clock is winding down on Gayle. Here's what I want: Heal my wife. Please. Do you hear me? Heal my wife." There was a long silence. A crow cawed in the distance. Both men held their breath for fear of being clobbered by a willful and jealous God. "Okay, so that's it. Up to you now. Amen."

CHAPTER 25

"What's that?" Sandy was lounging on the foldout couch in pink sweats and a black hoody. Her hair was pulled up into a loose ponytail. Her knees tucked into her chest as she carefully painted her toes blood red. "Looks very official. What is it?"

Rich's face tightened. Sandy was like a child who needed to know everything about every move you made, no matter how insignificant. He loved his sister, but, my God, things had gotten claustrophobic in the last several weeks. Rich's apartment was supposed to be a launch pad. Sandy would quickly find work and then just as quickly move to her own digs. But every time she was ready for launch, the weather changed, postponing indefinitely her departure to parts as yet unknown.

Not that she hadn't looked, she had. Not that she hadn't had some luck, she had. She was working as a contractor for two marketing firms in Rochester, mostly with car dealerships and restaurants. For what seemed like pennies. She hovered over the launch pad but didn't take off, at least not as Rich had hoped. Some days she worked hard. Other days she slept, not checking her messages, Instagram, anything. She seemed to disappear. She had nightmares. He could hear her struggling, crying. When he'd check on her, she'd act like nothing had happened. In the morning all would be forgotten.

There was so much about her that he loved. She ate with her mouth open. She loved old movies, like *Casablanca* and *Citizen Kane*, though she talked through them, often mimicking the dialogue. She ate cinnamon toast every morning for breakfast, along with a cup of tea. She was a bath person. She made detailed exercise plans but never followed through on them. She read fiction voraciously, mostly fantasy. She was sharp-tongued and fleet of mind. She talked with the speed of a magpie, but then would fall silent for hours. She had a wonderful laugh, high and uncontrolled. She could cook. She smiled every time he looked at her. She made him feel both cuddled and smothered.

Some things about her had changed, though, since high school. Not the normal changes that occur after you go to college and enter the world. These were more fundamental, like she had a crack in her foundation and the floors were slanting this way and that, so much so that when she walked, she wobbled and couldn't keep her balance. Growing up, nothing could topple her, nothing stood in her way, but now it seemed she was lost and wandering, not knowing where to go or how.

He frowned at himself when he thought about Sandy this way. He felt like he was criticizing her. Who was he, with his chronic twitch, his questionable professional choices, his failed relationship, to comment on anyone, let alone his sister? His launch plans weren't any more successful than hers. He had small contracts with a law firm, a pharmaceutical company and two local breweries. Mostly research or platform development. When he told new acquaintances about his work, they were impressed. He never mentioned that he could barely pay his bills. Together, he and Sandy brought in as much as a newlywed couple scratching out their first year together.

He opened the envelope; it's return address was a law firm in Washington, D.C. He unfolded the crisp letter.

"So?" Sandy, toe spacers in place, waddled on her heals to the kitchenette where Rich sat at the breakfast bar.

"Nothing."

"I'm telling you, it'll be years before you see any money. You know, they're back up and running again?" Sandy pulled a piece of bread from the bag and dropped it into the toaster. She took butter from the fridge, sugar and cinnamon from the pantry.

"So I heard."

Sandy tried to read her brother, who, when he was deep in thought, didn't make eye contact. He was more private than she remembered. They used to hide out in his bedroom and talk for hours not so many years ago. He'd always been the kind of big brother a girl would want. Thoughtful, encouraging, patient. She looked up to him, never wanting to disappoint him, something that would have come as a surprise to Rich.

Rich re-read the letter. "The lawyers are going to make a mint off this. I won't see anything, maybe a few hundred dollars."

"You did the right thing."

"I suppose." Rich didn't feel better for having done 'the right thing'. Left the job, had to move back home, was living in a generic small town outside a second-tier city.

"No, really. You did. It's just that sometimes doing the right thing doesn't get you much."

She'd said little to Rich about what had happened in Chicago. She felt too conflicted, embarrassed. She hadn't told him about the panic attack, about collapsing on the floor in a sweat. He'd have been surprised that it was still happening. She was sixteen when he'd found her on the bathroom floor, perspiration dripping from her sheet white face. "I just need to lie here," she had said, passing it off as hunger. He sat on the floor holding her hand. But they never talked about it.

Even before the bathroom incident, Rich had noticed other changes. She startled for no obvious reason; she stayed in her room a lot; she hesitated to go out with friends.

He'd drop by her room to check in:

"I'm allowed to be quiet, Richie."

"I know. It's just…"

"It's just what?"

"Has there been any trouble or anything lately?"

"No! What's up with you?"

"Did everything go okay the other night?"

"What?"

"Did you see Jamie?"

"Jamie?" she said, shaking her head quizzically. She got out of bed and rushed the door.

"Jesus Christ, back the fuck off." Then slammed it.

Sandy cut her cinnamon toast into quarters and poured herself a cup of tea. She sat across from Rich. She took a bite and closed her eyes. "The best."

"I can't believe you're still eating that."

"Some things don't need to change. Some things are perfect just the way they are."

Rich poured himself another cup of coffee. By then, Sandy was already putting her third slice of bread in the toaster.

"How are you doing?" There was that old question again. He'd been waiting for weeks to ask it.

Sandy stared at the toaster. "What do you mean?"

"Well, when you called me from the road, things were, like, pretty bad. Everything's been a blur since then. And I realized I never asked how you were doing post-Chicago."

"I'm okay." Sandy stuck a knife into the toaster to fish out her toast.

Rich was going to let it pass, but couldn't. "Sandy, you told me a little about what happened at that place—"

"Venus's Flytrap."

"But not much."

"I wasn't stripping, Richie."

"I know that. That's not what I'm asking. I'm asking about you, Sandy, you're my sister, for chrissakes and something bad happened to you."

"Like I told you, this guy got aggressive and then my boss got up in his face and I had to leave." The toast came out in pieces. She tossed them into the sink and turned on the disposal. "What can I say; I got very upset, I had to get out of there. That's about it." She tried to be nonchalant, but her hands were trembling now.

"I'm sorry."

"Not your fault."

"You know what I mean."

"It's over." She filled her mug with more water, tossed a teabag in and put it in the microwave. She stared at the mug, then closed her eyes. When it dinged, another round began with Rich.

"Look, Sandy. These things are never just over. They loiter in your life. They're always hanging around. They come back and go away and come back again."

Her back to Rich, Sandy added a teaspoon of sugar and some half-and-half to her tea, then stirred it. She held her breath.

Rich cleared his throat and shifted in his seat, his chair squeaking. Sandy turned to face him, her eyes half-mast.

"I didn't know you were an expert on sexual harassment."

Rich met her eye-to-eye. He was tired of pretending. He tried to control his every facial muscle. "I'm not. But I am an expert on sisters who have been sexually harassed...or more." His words came in a whisper. "I know what happened."

"What do you mean, you 'know what happened'?"

"I know what happened to you."

Sandy pressed her palms together.

"Richie—"

"Back then, I mean. Back in high school." He hoped for some recognition in his sister's eyes, some permission to go on.

"I don't know what—"

Rich reached across the table top and took her hand in his. "Look, I know."

Sandy pulled her hand away. "What do you know?"

"I'm sorry, Sandy, but I heard you. It was that night, that Friday night after you came home from that party you went to with, what was her name, I don't know."

"Roseanne."

"Yes, Roseanne. I was in the hall. I was in the hall and I heard your voice. At first, I thought you were just talking on the phone but you didn't sound right. I came to your door and I listened. You were crying to someone. You were crying and telling them what had happened at some party. I wanted to go back to my room, but I couldn't. I wanted to open the door but I didn't. I didn't know what to do, but I kept listening, I had to."

Sandy froze. Did she want to go back there? Did she want to go back to her bedroom again?

"I'm sorry, Sandy. I heard it all. I heard you say you couldn't get away, that the door was locked and you couldn't get away. And he did things to you...he did things...things you didn't want to do. I felt sick, Sandy, I felt so sick, I didn't know what to do."

Sandy could feel her insides being pried open again; she remembered that her bedspread smelled like Downey softener that night; and that her nails were a mess because she could never wait long enough for the polish to dry; she remembered that her jeans were torn and her underwear was gone and she didn't know how she would explain it to her mother. She couldn't remember anything that she told her friend, Roseanne, but she remembered that Roseanne screamed so loud that Sandy had to hang up because it was too upsetting. She remembered her mother calling to her the next morning, 'Hey sleepy head, time to get up', like she always did and how she wanted the day to be like every other day, but it wasn't and never would be again.

Sandy wrapped her arms around her stomach. She wanted to smile at her brother. She couldn't. She didn't ask for this. What to do? Running away had been her best option in the past. She felt too tired for that. She opened her mouth and started to talk, to tell her story as best she could.

"I had never been to a house party, you know? I mean, I was only a sophomore, I didn't know anything. But Roseanne, she was going to this party and she invited me to go and I said 'Sure', what did I know. She said it'd be fun."

"You don't have to—"

"And it was. I had a beer, and started to loosen up, so I had another. It was great, it was. We danced and laughed. Sometime in the evening I was upstairs, I don't remember how I got there, but I was upstairs and he kept telling me how much he liked me. He was so nice. But then he wasn't. I mean, he locked the door and then he was on me, I don't know how else to say it, he was on me and I couldn't move and he was pulling at my clothes, and I was screaming, but no one came. And then he did things—"

"Sandy, you don't have to tell me this, you don't. I just wanted you to know I knew —"

"He did everything. He laughed at me. I asked him to stop and he laughed at me."

"Jesus, Sandy, I wish I —"

Sandy's body knotted, her fists clenched, her jaws locked.

"And then it was over. And I was sitting there by myself, trying to find my clothes, trying to get dressed. I didn't feel a thing. And then I started to cry and I couldn't stop. I got home somehow. Later I called Roseanne, you're right, that's who I called." Sandy's hands were folded in her lap. She spoke quietly, distinctly. "I've been angry and afraid for a long time, Richie. You know, the one thing I'm most angry about is that I never got the chance to confront him about what he did to me."

Rich gulped air. "Wait a minute. What...what did you say?"

"I never got a chance to tell him what I thought of him, what a piece of shit he was."

"You mean because of his injury."

"What injury?"

"You know, the football injury."

"He didn't play football. He enlisted right after high school and got killed in Afghanistan. There was a big memorial service at the Gates High School gym. Flags at half-mast. Must have been thousands of people. Speeches, local politicians, everything. I didn't go. Mom and Dad didn't understand why, since they thought he was a friend. I got drunk instead. As drunk as I could get. Not to drown my sorrow, but to drown my relief, my happiness."

Rich's mouth hung open.

"When I went to that party, I was just a girl, a kid, really. I didn't know anything about anything. I was just living my life, you know? And then this boy took me upstairs and it didn't matter what I said or how much I begged. He just did what he wanted. I was nothing to him. I was zero. He killed my insides. I've been piecing myself back together ever since."

"You mean, Jamie, right? Tell me you mean Jamie Cunningham."

"What are you talking about? Jamie? Are you kidding? It was JB Hannaford, some senior asshole at Gates."

"It wasn't Jamie Cunningham?"

Sandy's face tweaked. "Jamie Cunningham? Absolutely not. What would make you think that? Jamie Cunningham, he'd never hurt a fly."

Rich's head hung. He kept swallowing but there wasn't any saliva. He lifted his gaze and tried to smile. "No, he wouldn't. You're right. He was too good, he was."

"Richie. Richie, what's wrong?"

CHAPTER 26

"So, here's the deal, Sam." It seemed to Sam that Rhonda framed all human interactions as business transactions. A matter of reasoned give and take, mostly devoid of emotional considerations, at least superficially so. If this, then that. In this case, the 'if-this-then-that' was out of the ordinary. "If you're horny and I'm horny, then we could probably get together to alleviate each other's…problem."

Since what's-her-name in college, he had never met a woman who was so direct. He looked around the pharmacy, hoping no one was listening. Mrs. Eady approached the counter. Rhonda was about to continue her rationale until Sam's wide eyes suggested she wait.

"How are you today, Mrs. Eady?"

Mrs. Eady thumped her purse on the counter and tried to collect herself. "Do I need to answer that question?" She cackled and winked. "Mister is sick again, I'm telling you. The man is always down with something. The rheumatism or the arthritis or the bursitis, anything with an 'ism' or an 'itis'. This time he's got the pneumonia, just to change things up."

Sam wondered if Mr. and Mrs. Eady had ever had a conversation like the one he was having with Rhonda. He looked at Rhonda, who also winked, though her wink seemed to carry a different message than Mrs. Eady's.

Sam reached for the bin behind him. "I'm very sorry that he's sick again, Mrs. Eady. That's just as hard on you as it is on him. He's lucky he's got you."

She leaned forward and, in a stage whisper, said, "Why don't you stop by sometime and tell that old man." They both laughed and Mrs. Eady ambled back down the aisle to the exit.

"Wow. You're good. I mean, you actually care about these people."

"Well, I do; I want to be sure that they —"

"It's making me wet."

Who says that? thought Sam. He was still thinking about it when he got home after work. And later, when he was getting Jamie ready for bed.

"Here you go." He pulled Jamie's pajama tops over his head. He helped him to the bathroom and then sat him on the toilet.

Jamie smiled, "Oooooooohhh."

He'd moved his bowels, a relief to both of them. Sam cleaned his son and pulled his pajama bottoms over his feet before helping Jamie off the toilet. Once on his feet, Sam held him with one hand and pulled his bottoms up with the other. Jamie grabbed his father and held him tight. "Pa."

"Yes, it's me, son." Sam wrapped an arm around Jamie and gently hoisted him to his feet. Jamie laughed —"Uh oh" — like this was a game. "That's my boy." Sam huffed as he half carried his son to his bedroom. They fell together onto the mattress. "And there you have it, right?"

Jamie's mouth opened wide, his yellowing teeth bared. "Yaaaaay, Pa."

Thoughts of Rhonda disappeared. He looked into Jamie's deep brown eyes and wondered what was going on behind them. Did he know that Sam was his father? Did he wonder where his mother was? Did he understand how he got here, how he got into this predicament? Was he suffering?

"What should I read tonight?"

"Moooooo."

"Okay, Mooo, it is." He took the book from the shelf and began to read. "In the great green room…" It was Marianne who read Jamie bedtime stories when he was small. Sam's work schedule usually meant he got home long after Jamie was asleep. Sam always went into his room, re-tucked him in, and gave him a kiss on the head. It was so routine that, as Sam remembered it now, he often didn't even look at his son. He was tired and hungry from his long day. Satisfied that he had at least made the effort, he'd return to the kitchen where Marianne would be making him a grilled cheese sandwich or something else simple.

"...Goodnight moon..."

Sam had started reading it again to Jamie a year or so after the injury. He'd heard that reacquainting someone with familiar objects and stories might awaken parts of the brain that seemed dormant. He'd asked Marianne what she thought of the idea and she'd said, "Sure," impassively. He'd been reading it to is son for twelve years. Not every night, but almost.

Mouth wide open, one arm sticking out over the side of his bed, Jamie was asleep before Sam reached the end. He closed the book and placed it on the shelf. He took Jamie's arm and laid it across his chest. Then he pulled up his covers and kissed his head.

He glanced at the clock on the wall. It was almost nine. He sat for a moment longer, listening to his son breathe. He got up, flicked off the light and closed the door.

In the kitchen, Sam rummaged through a bottom shelf, eventually locating two dusty bottles, one gin and one vodka. He had bought a lemon and a lime, which he cut into wedges and put in small separate dishes. He opened the refrigerator to check for tonic.

Sam went around the corner to the small pantry between the kitchen and the dining room. There he found a bag of Fritos and a two small bags of Lay's. He opened them and dumped the contents into two larger than necessary bowls. He got the cutting board from beside the oven and put it on the counter near the sink. He opened the fridge again and took cheese from the bottom shelf. He sniffed it twice, then stared at it and sniffed a third time. His eyes watered. He dumped the cheese into the disposal and returned the cutting board to its place beside the stove.

He cracked open several ice trays and put the cubes in an ice bucket he'd found on a shelf in the basement. He discovered tongs in the bottom drawer behind an array of spatulas.

Sam arranged everything on the glass coffee table in the front room. He fanned the napkins, laying them beside a small stack of paper plates. He decided the bowls were too large and replaced them with smaller wicker baskets he found in the spare bedroom closet. He lined them with napkins and poured the chips into each.

Shoot, he thought. Drink glasses. Did he have anything suitable? In the dining room hutch he found a set of four leaded glasses, short, wide and heavy. Perfect.

He thought again about what Rhonda had said at the pharmacy. He felt his ears getting hot. He sat on the couch and watched the clock. At 9:00pm he got up, pulled the curtain back and looked out the window. He sat down again and at 9:15 headlights shown through the lace curtains.

When a few minutes passed and no one knocked, he headed to the front door, only to find Rich Kimes standing there, looking lost. He stared at him, confused, like he had stepped through a time warp. Then he blinked several times and smiled. Sam opened the door and leaned out. Richie, shuffling back and forth awkwardly, wanted to talk.

"Well, I'm just about to—"

"How's Jamie doing?"

"Good, good, you know, as well as can be expected..." Sam felt embarrassed by his own lack of hospitality. After the accident, he hadn't seen much of Richie. Eddy had said it was too hard for him. Sam tried to accept this explanation.

Another car pulled into the driveway. Rhonda bounced out and strode up the sidewalk, nearly turning an ankle in her heels. She looked Rich up and down.

"Well, what is this? Have you invited a friend?" she said with a gravelly laugh.

Sam seemed only able to inhale.

"I'm very sorry; this is a bad time; I..." Rich looked at Sam, his eyes beckoning.

"Rhonda, this is Richie; Richie, Rhonda…a new friend…Uh, Richie was Jamie's best friend back in high school. Before everything. It's been so long…"

"Look, Mr. Cunningham, I should have called. I'm sorry." Rich smiled at Rhonda and turned to leave.

"Look, Rich, I'd love to catch up. And Jamie, I'm sure he'd like to see you. Why don't you try again?"

"Sure." Rich waved back at Sam as he headed to his car. Once behind the wheel, he looked again at the front door, now closed. He could see the silhouettes of Mr. Cunningham and his 'new friend' gesturing and then sitting.

"Fuck," breathed Rich. He'd come on an impulse, his conversation with Sandy fresh in his mind:

"What's wrong?" she'd said.

'What's wrong?' he'd thought. Everything. "I could have sworn you said, Jamie. 'Jamie— something something—did it to me'. And you were nearly hysterical. And I heard 'made me', like, 'made me' do it. I know I did. And you said 'Jamie'. Didn't you? I know that's what you said."

Rich ran his fingers back through his hair and bent over, holding his head. He paced back and forth.

"Richie, are you okay?" Sandy got up from her seat and placed her hands on his back. "Come on, sit down." She guided him to the fold-out, but he wouldn't sit.

"Sandy, there has to be some kind of mistake. Jamie's the one. I heard you say his name, I know I did."

Sandy stepped back, afraid, her hands clasped in front of her. "Sit down, Richie, please."

"You don't understand—"

"You're scaring me, Richie."

Rich grabbed her by the shoulders, his face contorted. "Look, Sandy, really, it's, it's…I figured I knew enough, you know…I heard you on the phone…I heard you say his name—Jamie…so, I had to do something; you were my sister, for chrissake…somebody had hurt you…Jamie, I thought it was Jamie…so I had to, I had to…someone had to pay…"

Sandy tried to speak calmly, slowly. "Rich, listen to me. I don't understand. What are you trying to tell me?"

"I'm the reason Jamie's...I'm the reason Jamie's the way he is. I did it."

"What are you talking about?"

"I didn't want to. But I couldn't stand the thought of what he did to you. I couldn't let this happen to you without...I had to do something. So, when he came through the line, I hit him...I hit him with everything I had...I kneed him in the side of his head as hard as I possibly could...and I heard him groan. And I thought, 'Good'. I got him. But then..."

The corners of Rich's mouth fell. Sandy put her arms around him, trying to hide the fear in her eyes.

"No, no, no, Richie, it's okay; you're okay. I'm sure..."

Rich laid his head on her shoulder.

Returning from Sam's, Rich could see Sandy standing at the window of their apartment as he pulled in the lot, his mind still racing. By the time he backed into his spot, she was at the front door. She had told him not to go, that too much time had passed, that this would only upset things in ways that no longer mattered. But he had insisted.

Sandy was at the car door now. Rich sat still, clutching the steering wheel. She tapped on the window. He got out of the car and leaned back on the hood.

"So?" Sandy's arms were wrapped around her shoulders, chill wind blowing her hair. "How'd it go?"

"It didn't."

"What do you mean, it didn't."

"I have to go back. There was someone else there."

"Shit."

•　　•　　•

Sam poured vodka into a glass, then reached for the tonic.

"Half and half, please," said Rhonda.

Sam added more vodka and dropped several cubes into the glass and handed it to her.

"Thanks," she said, stirring her drink with the tip of her finger. She took a sip. "Perfect."

She kicked off her shoes and curled her legs under herself. "So, that was quite a handsome young man."

Sam poured tonic water into a glass and added a splash of gin. He put the drink on the table. "Yeah, my best friends' son." He crossed his legs. Rhonda moved closer. "Haven't seen him in years." Sam stared absently at his glass. His body felt slack.

He'd missed seeing Richie. He'd been a fixture in their house. Sam could almost hear their voices, Jamie and Richie, as they roughhoused on the wrestling mats in the basement.

He never came to the hospital, though.

Rhonda put her hand on Sam's thigh. He looked at her, then smiled.

"You went away for a moment."

"I'm sorry."

Rhonda kissed him softly on the cheek and then on the lips.

"Are you back now?"

Sam took her into his arms. "Yes, I'm back now." And kissed her long.

CHAPTER 27

"When do you think you'll try again?"

"I don't know?"

Rich and Sandy clicked their seat belts and Rich pulled out of the parking lot.

"Maybe you don't need to go back."

"I have to."

"But it's making you crazy. I can tell. You're fidgeting all the time; you can't sit still. And…"

"And what?"

"Nothing."

"Go ahead, say it."

"Okay. You can barely keep your eye open because of…"

"Because of what?"

"Never mind."

Sandy turned on the radio. Then turned it off again. She put the window down several inches despite the cold. Rich's eyes were glued to the road.

"Maybe slow down a little, okay."

"Do you want to drive?"

"No, I just don't want to die before we get there."

· · ·

Eddy put a filter into the coffee maker. He added coffee and water and pushed the button. Gayle was bent over the oven as the timer went off.

She opened the door and closed her eyes as the heat hit her face. She put on an oven mitt and removed the tray of chocolate chip cookies, placing it on top of the stove.

They caught each other's eye and smiled tentatively.

"Well?"

"Well what?"

"Are you ready for this?" Eddy's voice sounded more like, 'I'm not ready for this'.

"Please don't say anything...crazy."

"I won't. I promise."

"When they left the last time, they thought the next get-together would be around my coffin."

Eddy winced. He took several mugs from the shelf and arranged them beside the coffee maker. He filled a small bowl with packs of Splenda and added the sugar bowl. He took a carton of half-and-half from the refrigerator, but decided that a small milk pitcher would be a nice touch. He found one in the pantry, wiped it out with a napkin and filled it.

They had decided that Gayle would do the talking this time. She would tell them what had changed and what was coming. He was glad to be relieved of any communication duties, especially since he was feeling less optimistic today than when Gayle had told him she was going to re-enter treatment.

Eddy had no illusions that the cancer had taken a break. He was sure it had continued its relentless march. Recently she looked gaunter; she seemed less stable on her feet; she spent more time in the bathroom. When she stopped giving him straight answers about how she was feeling, he stopped asking.

Rich and Sandy needed to know what was going on, but Eddy worried that their hopes might be raised and then dashed quickly. The test results should come back in another two to three days.

"This is terrific news." the oncologist had said. "I mean, fantastic."

Her enthusiasm was infectious. Eddy sat up straighter and leaned forward. It was as if she was saying, 'Great, let's hook you up and finally get rid of this thing!' Simple as that.

"We'll need to do a few more tests. As you may recall, your CA-125 levels were in the 75-80 range when we first started treatment. Normal range is under 35. We want to see where you're at now, so we know how to proceed. You'll need a pelvic, of course, and I'll be referring you to Dr. Washington, who's our lead oncologist in immunotherapy. She will design the treatment, depending on the outcome of your tests."

Eddy and Gayle looked at each other.

"We want to get started as soon as possible," said Eddy.

"Of course," said Dr. Chen. "We do, as well. But there are a few steps first. It shouldn't take long. We'll draw your blood today. I'll have our secretary set up an appointment with Dr. Washington before you leave."

"How long will the wait be?" Gayle's left leg was wrapped around her right.

"Typically, we can get our patients in within two weeks."

Gayle felt like a plug had been pulled inside her and everything had emptied out. Her face turned pale.

Dr. Chen reached for her, placing a hand on her knee. "I know you're in a hurry. I'm sorry this takes a little more time than you thought."

Eddy took Gayle's hand, entwining his fingers with hers. "Time just seems short."

Gayle and Eddy had had a plan in mind, an expectation. Make the appointment with Chen; meet with the kids to give them the news; start the treatment. They thought it would take a few days, little more. Now they would be meeting with Sandy and Rich with almost nothing to tell them.

"Let's tell them not to come," Eddy had said.

"That'll just make them worry more. They have to know we're meeting about the cancer. They have to. If we call and say, 'Hey, no need to come', it'll just make it worse."

Gayle slid her spatula under each cookie and arranged them in circles on a China platter that had belonged to her mother. For a brief moment, she wished her mother was there. She wished she didn't have to be an adult, a mother with children of her own, a wife. She wished someone else could take over, could quiet her, could tell her everything would be okay in a way that she could believe.

•   •   •

Once the greetings and initial small talk subsided and everyone poured their coffee or tea and balanced their cookies on their knees, Eddy sat forward on his easy chair, about to speak, already overstepping his bounds.

"Your mom and I can't tell you how much it has meant having you so close by again. I know it's been a sacrifice for both of you to come home..."

Sandy glanced at Rich, who widened his eyes slightly. Do they dare say they had no other choice? That Sandy had been assaulted in a strip club? That Rich had been working for an escort service that was being sued? Should they tell their parents that they had needed to retreat from their lives?

Sandy watched her mother, who looked small, like a girl in a woman's body, her hands almost translucent. Sandy hadn't noticed how deep set her mother's eyes were, how hidden from the light, how dark. She felt a pang, a longing for her mother to be the mother she remembered, the one who threw her head back and laughed, who smiled softly, who listened. Where had she gone?

She wanted to say, 'Mom, I was hurt; that's why I've stayed away; I was hurt and had to run; had to get away'.

"...and this thing, this journey has reached another fork in the road. Another decision point..."

Rich watched his father's fumbling hands, his forced smile. 'Just say it,' he thought. He knew what was coming. He could tell by how his mother looked, how his father's brow moistened as he talked. Just say what we know you are going to say! He felt his knees lock, his lower back stiffen, his shoulders clench, as if the sky were about to fall on him, crushing him. Brace yourself, he thought. The last meeting had been an unmitigated disaster. 'Your mother's dying; don't be a stranger' was how he remembered his father's words, his attempt at guilting them into coming home more often, calling more often, being there while everything unraveled.

Gayle nudged her husband with her knee. He stopped talking. She looked at her son and daughter in turn. There was still a little boy and a little girl in their uncertain eyes. Could they ever have been babies in her arms? What had they looked like on the very first day of their lives? There were so many days she couldn't remember. She felt the sharp blade of fear cut through her. If she died, they would disappear. She would never see them again. She would never see anything again. How could she have ever walked away from treatment?

Gayle slid forward on the edge of her seat.

"Mom, what is it? You can tell us," said Rich.

Eddy put his arm around Gayle.

"Well." She swallowed twice, trying to get control of her voice. "Sorry to be so dramatic. It's just…it's so good to see you here. I mean, so good to *really* look at you…It's hard to explain." She bowed her head.

The air in the room seemed to vibrate. Mail fell through the slot on the front door and slid across the entryway.

"I stopped treatment because I thought it was the best thing. I thought it would give me the best chance of living normally for a while. I thought it would be less difficult than continuing the misery of treatment, especially since it wasn't working. I wanted to let things happen as they were meant to happen; and try to live a little bit while I had the chance. I wish I could say I was thinking of you. But it was for me. Of course, it would have been easier in the long run for you, as well. At least that's what I thought." She turned to Eddy. "My mouth is dry, honey. Can you get me a glass of water?" Eddy patted her back and got up.

"But things changed. I didn't think it mattered how long I lived. I mean, I always wanted a long life, but to live it in constant suffering, I didn't want that. And that's what I imagined it would be."

By then, Eddy had returned. She'd asked for a glass of water and Eddy, being Eddy, brought her a tall glass of iced water with two wedges of lemon, one in the glass, the other on the rim.

"Thank you," she said, kissing her finger tips and touching them to his cheek. She took a sip. "I found, though, that the thought of not being here, not being in the world with you, not sitting on the porch with your father watching birds at the feeder, not standing in the middle of the street to catch a glimpse of a full moon, not sitting like this, just visiting; even not being bent over tax forms and talking idly to my clients, well, it seemed completely impossible to give it all up." She pursed her lips, the pretense of a smile. "I'm not foolhardy; I know it will happen someday. But to give it up, to give up all the bits and pieces of life, all the moments, all the love, even all the struggles and goddam torment, wasn't right, at least not in my mind."

Tears filled Eddy's eyes.

"What are you saying, Mom?" said Rich.

"Your father and I met with Dr. Chen. I told her I wanted to get back into treatment. I wanted to try this immunotherapy."

"Fantastic!" said Rich. "I mean, this is…this is terrific, right? How soon will you get started?"

"Well…" Eddy fidgeted, wanting to jump in.

"We thought it would be immediately." Gayle explained the steps she would need to take and the amount of time that may pass before treatment began. While she didn't say it directly, it was clear that what remained to be seen was whether additional treatment would be warranted.

"Are you saying that this could turn into a big nothing?"

"Sandy!" Rich glared at his sister.

"No, I didn't mean…I mean, is there a chance that even though you're ready to go, it may be too…?"

"Too late." Gayle leaned back in her chair, needing more support.

"I mean, I'm sure it's never too late, right, but…"

Gayle's voice was firm, steady, like she might be explaining changes in the tax code to a client. "Could it be too late? Yes, it could. I may have waited too long. A mistake I would have to live with. But we can't be sure, can we? In the end, we don't know. We have to decide and go forward even though there's no way of knowing what will come of it. It's the way it is, Sandy."

"I think this is great news." Rich rubbed his hands together as if he were about to eat a gourmet meal. "I mean, they're experts in this, right, they know what they're doing and you're still, well, strong enough to take this on. And with all of us…" He looked around the room and recognized how far apart they had been for so long, how distant they were even as they sat together in the same room. "We can see this through," he said, a little too confidently.

Sandy sat with her hand over her mouth. "Mom, I didn't mean anything."

"I know," said Gayle.

Ready to burst, Eddy finally spoke. "I totally agree with you, Richie. This is great news and your mother can do this. The doctors are great. We've been told the immunotherapy doctor is like the best in the country." He looked directly at Sandy. "But I understand that we need to be cautious; we need to be circumspect, but hopeful."

"Yes, hopeful's the right word." Sandy watched her mother, how still she sat, unmoved. "I, for one, am hopeful," she said.

"I'm trying to be neither hopeful nor despairing at this point. I'm trying to take one step, then another, that's all. That's what I'm doing. Later, I'll decide whether I'm hopeful or not."

"We're all with you, Mom," said Rich.

"Absolutely," said Sandy.

Sandy's and Gayle's eyes met. Sandy widened hers, hoping her mother could see her support.

•　　•　　•

When Sandy and Rich got in the car, it was quiet for ten seconds.

"What the fuck was that all about? 'A big nothing'? Jesus, Sandy, what were you thinking?"

"I didn't mean anything. You know that. I just…"

"You just what?"

"I don't know. It's like there's a wall between us. I don't know how to talk to her. When I try, well, you see what happens."

"Whatever it is, work on it. Mom needs all the support we can give her."

Rich breezed through an intersection on yellow, a car blaring its horn at him.

Sandy looked out the passenger window. She closed her eyes. She could see herself standing at her mother's office door. So long ago. She was still in tears that following morning. She felt afraid, confused. She knocked.

"Mom?"

"What is it, honey?"

"Can I talk to you?"

"Not right now, honey, I'm busy. A little later, okay?"

Sandy stood at the door for a minute longer, then walked away.

•   •   •

Eddy looked at the sky. Neither moon nor stars. He could barely see. He entered the garden. The ground was so damp that he slipped and fell at the foot of the statue. "Shit," he said as he got up, fingering a hole in his jeans.

He was breathing hard as he looked up at the face of Jesus. He didn't know whether Jesus was smiling, frowning or indifferent. Who knew? Who cared?

"Look, I'm telling you." He took a deep breath. "Look, it's this way." His hands quivered. He tried to speak, but couldn't. He began to weep. He opened his mouth to scream but nothing came out.

•   •   •

After Eddy left for his walk, Gayle retreated to her office, her refuge. She sat at her desk for a long moment, then turned on her computer. She stared at the screen saver, a random photo of a beach in South Africa. She closed her eyes briefly, then opened the "Other" folder as she had done hundreds of times before. She scrolled slowly through file after file, page after page, over twenty-five years of data, information organized in ways that only she could understand. Bottom line after bottom line. She hoped it would be enough. No matter what happened next, she hoped it would make a difference.

CHAPTER 28

Sam couldn't remember sex ever being quite like it was with Rhonda. Marianne had been modest. They were comfortable together, but they seldom diverted from the usual sequence of things. There was always some foreplay, although he never knew if she enjoyed it or not. He hoped she did. He was always on top and she lay below him, half-smiling, eyes closed. And that was that.

Rhonda's body was like a national park. There were so many ways in, so many vistas, so many awe-inspiring places to stop, to linger. She was eager for him to explore every single one. She guided him to the best spots. She encouraged him to go where he wouldn't have thought he was allowed. He could pitch his tent wherever he wanted. He felt like an explorer discovering a whole new world.

When she came, she growled like a wrestler body slamming someone to the floor. He heaved and heaved and then collapsed on top of her. She laughed and slapped his back, as if they had just finished an Iron Man triathlon. He looked around for oxygen.

"My God, Mr. Pharmacist!" She kissed him hard and slapped his back again. He grinned and started to roll over. "No, no, stay put. I want to feel you inside me a little longer." 'What in the world?' thought Sam.

She came to his house almost every night once Jamie was asleep. He stood at the window, peeking out from behind the curtains, trying to be discrete, but feeling like the family dog waiting for someone to come home with his bag of treats. This went on for several weeks.

He was in an extraordinarily different sort of routine, one that included whipped cream and feathers. But a routine nonetheless. It wasn't that he was getting bored. He never told her not to come. But there were nights when he would rather have sat and talked or watched a movie together. Clothed. And with some popcorn.

He wondered if there was something wrong with him. If he told Eddy what was going on, would Eddy have said, 'I can see how that would get pretty old'? Absolutely not. He'd have said, 'Merry effing Christmas!'.

Marianne was smart, she had ideas about things, politics, religion; she could talk and was funny. They could spend an evening doing nothing, and he would feel great by the time his head hit the pillow. It wasn't that Sam wanted Rhonda to be Marianne, not exactly, but he wanted something more than sex, which surprised him. He had felt like a dead battery for so long that he thought all he needed was a jump start. At first, he was right. He felt great, lighter, less morose. But after a while he could feel his battery dying again.

He watched from the front window and when she didn't come, he called her. No answer. This seemed odd, but not alarming. She had her own life and didn't need to check in with him when her plans changed. But when a few days passed without a word, Sam called her again. No answer again. A couple of days later he drove past her apartment. Her car was gone. He called again and then again, but after a few weeks, he stopped calling. He stopped watching from his window. He settled back into his evening routine, prepping Jamie for bed, reading him a story, sitting beside him until he was snoring, watching some TV, then going to his room to read himself to sleep.

One night when a car pulled into his driveway unannounced, he felt his heart skip. He watched for the door to open, but when he saw that it was Rich again, he stepped back, not wanting to be seen. When the doorbell rang, he grimaced, waited, but then went to the door.

"I should have called ahead," said Rich.

Sam waved his comment away. "No, really, come on in." He'd found his customer service smile. "Go on in the living room there. Can I get you something to drink?"

He returned with two glasses of ice water. They then struggled through some idle chatter about how long it had been, what Rich had been up to, how pleased his parents must be that he's back in the area, Sandy, too, isn't that great. They both ran out of patter at the same time.

Rich took a long drink. He was surprised how much older Sam looked than his own father. His sagging lids and bushy eyebrows, his yellowed nails in much need of care.

"Can I get you some more?" said Sam. He felt his chest swell. This is what Jamie would have been like as a young man. Bright eyed, clean-cut, fresh-faced. He watched Rich's every move, how easily he took the glass in his hand, switched it to his other hand, drank it effortlessly, placed it back on the table without a spill. He didn't need any help, any encouragement.

"No thanks, Mr. Cunningham, I'm fine."

Not knowing what else to say, Sam excused himself to fill his already full glass.

"Is Jamie here?" called Rich.

"Yes, yes, he's in bed, but he may not be asleep yet. Usually he's gone in a minute, but sometimes..." Sometimes he doesn't sleep at all. Sometimes he grinds his teeth and cries without ceasing. Sometimes Sam holds him in his arms and talks to him, even though he never answers.

Rich was relieved. He didn't know what it would be like to see Jamie after all these years.

"He may be awake. We could check."

"No, no, that's okay —"

"No, really, it's fine. I know it's been a long time since you've seen him." Sam found himself reaching back for that faint hope that something might shock Jamie into being the Jamie of old.

Mr. Cunningham stood.

"Okay, well...if you don't think it will bother him, I could..."

He followed Mr. Cunningham up the same stairs that Rich and Jamie had climbed together so many times before. Studying together, watching porn, sneaking beers, smoking weed out the window. This time, though, Rich felt like he was trespassing.

Mr. Cunningham opened the door slowly. "Jamie? You awake? Someone's here to see you." But Jamie was asleep.

Sam motioned Rich into the room. Rich stood at the door. A beam of light from the hall framed Jamie's face. His mouth was open, his eyelids fluttering; his hair was disheveled and looked dirty. He could barely recognize his old friend. His face was pocked and pasty. His fingers were balled around his thumbs; his wrists were curled. With each breath came a deep grating snore. It sounded like residue from the groan he'd heaved on the day he first collapsed. It sounded like the summing up of all the ensuing years.

A sad smile crossed Sam's face as he gently pulled Jamie's cover up to his chin.

"Well...I'm sorry he's not awake. I think he would have liked seeing you."

Rich's gaze passed from Mr. Cunningham to Jamie once more. There was no way Jamie would have known that he was Rich; there was no way he would have known that Rich was anyone or anything, for that matter.

"Yeah, I'm sure."

"Maybe another time."

"Yeah, another time."

Sam closed the door slowly. He put his hand on Rich's back, ushering him toward the stairs.

Maybe this was enough, thought Rich. Maybe coming to see Jamie and his dad was all he needed to do. It was clear that Mr. Cunningham had everything under control, that life had gone on somehow, that Jamie was loved and cared for. What good would it do to rummage around in the past? Would it make life any better for Jamie, for Mr. Cunningham? No, it would not. His being there after all these years was enough.

When they got to the bottom of the staircase, Sam put his arms around Rich. Rich didn't move. He didn't return the hug. He froze. Sam stepped back.

"I'm sorry. It's just so good to see you; so good to know that after all these years, you remembered; you came. I just wish that Jamie could have…"

Rich could feel a knot in his stomach. His face glistened with sweat. He tried to lick his lips but his tongue felt too thick and arid.

"Well…" Sam touched his temple with the palm of his left hand.

Rich looked at the front door. "Look, Mr. Cunningham—"

"Really, Rich, you're too old to be calling me Mr. Cunningham. It's Sam."

"Okay. Sam."

"That's better."

"It's this way. I'm sorry I haven't come to see Jamie in such a long time. It's just—"

"No need to apologize, Rich. I know how it is. Life starts happening and you just have to go with it."

"Yeah, I guess that's true. But, still, I feel bad. I mean, Jamie and me, we were best friends."

"Yes, you were."

"And what happened to him, it's, I don't know, it's like he died but he didn't, you know what I mean? The Jamie I knew, we all knew, was so alive and now, it's just hard to look at him and remember who he was."

Sam's smile faded, his real-life face emerging behind it, darkly resolved.

"I like to think that Jamie's still in there, that everything he used to be is still in there, just asleep or something."

"Yes, yes, no, I didn't mean—"

Sam's eyes were puffy, not from crying, but from the exhaustion of things that never changed.

Rich sat down on a bench near the door. He leaned forward, his face in his hands, his elbows on his knees.

Sam reached for him, but then pulled his hand away. "Are you—"

"Mr. Cunningham, I have to tell you something. It's about that day."

Sam slipped his hands into his pockets.

"It was just a hard practice, you know, but nothing out of the ordinary. We had a game the next day, so we were extra pumped and ready to hit each other, you know what I mean. Jamie was really feeling it. We were running our goal line offense and defense. Jamie ran several plays off tackle and then Coach called for a dive play. Fourth and goal on the one kind of thing..." Rich tried to read Mr. Cunningham, but he wasn't sending signals. He could have been standing in line at the DMV waiting to be called. He's heard all of this before, thought Jamie, but he couldn't stop. "I wish I could say that I talked with Jamie at practice, but I didn't. I mean, I saw him every day. But somehow...I don't know...we didn't cross paths that day." Rich stretched his fingers and then let them rest on his knees. He was lying now. He'd avoided Jamie all day, even when Jamie tried to get his attention at practice.

"Anyway, Jamie hit the hole head down, driving hard, just like he always did. I was at linebacker, on the outside. All of us collapsed to the middle and he barely made it to the line. I mean, he got hit, hit hard by I don't know how many guys." Without thinking, Rich raised his hand. "I was one of them. I think you knew that I was in the pileup." Mr. Cunningham tipped his head forward slightly, his expression somber.

"Mr. Cunningham, when I came down on Jamie, it was with my knee: I hit the side of his head with my knee. I mean, I hit Jamie with everything I had, like I was trying to hurt somebody." Rich was surprised to hear his voice crack. He put his hand over his mouth. "I don't know how to say this, but I'm the one, Mr. Cunningham. I'm the reason Jamie is the way he is today." His head fell into his hands.

Rich heard Mr. Cunningham's deep sigh and the creek of the floor as he shifted his weight back and forth. When Rich looked up, Mr. Cunningham's eyes were full of tears, his mouth turned down at the corners. He didn't say anything. Instead, he took Rich by the arms and helped him up. Then he put his arms around him again and held tight, his body shaking. 'Will he crush me?' thought Rich.

Sam let go, stepped back and tried to gather himself. He coughed, wiped his eyes and forced a grin. "Sit," he said. Without looking, Rich sat, Mr. Cunningham standing over him.

"I'm sorry, Mr. Cunningham. If I could go back—"

Mr. Cunningham waved him off.

"You're the sixth one."

"Sixth what?"

"All you boys, you cared so much..."

"I don't understand. Sixth what?"

"You are the sixth one to take the blame for what happened. Six of you have come forward over the years, each with his own story about how he'd hit Jamie so hard that it...broke his brain, that's how Elijah Jackson put it. He was the first one."

Rich stood again and shook his head.

"Remember Johnson, what was his name? He said he was the first to hit Jamie. He said he hit him helmet to helmet. And Dave Jameson, he was playing safety or something, I can't remember now, but he said he speared Jamie and heard him groan. Just a year ago, Billy somebody, back from the service, stood at the front door telling me he was the one."

"But Mr. Cunningham, this is different—"

"And now you." Sam's eyes glistened. "To think that after all these years..."

"But I think I *was* the one." Rich let his chest settle, his stomach sag. "I wasn't being completely honest with you. I didn't talk with Jamie that day because I was, I was angry at him...you know, it happens...and when I hit him, I really tried to mess him up, I did."

Sam sat down beside Jamie. Jamie didn't look at him, but he could hear him breathing shallow.

"Look, Rich...when the MRI came back, they said, well, let's just say it wasn't a single blow that did the damage."

"But—"

"Look son. I still have part of Jamie with me. He smiles. He's not in pain. When he seems sad or afraid, I can hold him. He doesn't remember. He's not really suffering. I don't want anyone else to suffer either."

•　　•　　•

Rich sat in his car, the twitch below his eye running its course. He felt relieved. He had told Mr. Cunningham what he'd done. He had made his confession. And Mr. Cunningham hadn't blamed Rich at all. In fact, he absolved him of any responsibility. It was an accident, a terrible accident that happened and, no matter how awful people felt, no one was responsible. 'This kind of thing happens all the time', thought Rich. People want to believe that everything is ruled by cause and effect, that someone is always to blame. But that's just in our heads. It's not real.

He looked at the front window of the Cunningham house just as the curtain fell back into place and the lights went off. Rich started down the street and then pulled over to the curb. He turned off the motor. He leaned back against the head rest, his feeling of relief fading.

He closed his eyes. Maybe it hadn't been him. Maybe it was just a thing that happened, just a bunch of boys playing hard without any concern about the consequences. He kept thinking about the absolution Mr. Cunningham had given him. It was like a gift from God, or something. Why then did Rich's head ache? Why did his insides feel straightjacketed? Why did he want to hide, to wipe himself away?

Rich looked into the rearview mirror at his bloodless face. 'Evil intent', he thought. 'You went after your best friend with evil intent'. The rest—the exonerating MRI, the blind kindness of Mr. Cunningham, the detergent effect of time—didn't matter at all.

CHAPTER 29

Eddy and Gayle stepped onto the parking garage ramp as the sixth-floor elevator door closed behind them. For a moment they didn't know which direction to go. Eddy put one hand on Gayle's back and pointed. "I think we're that way," he said. They pulled the collars up on their spring jackets as the wintery wind sliced through them.

They walked up the ramp beyond the protection of the parking garage roof and onto the nearly empty lot, a slate sky above them. Seagulls fluttered and perched on an overflowing trash receptacle. The wind blew Gayle's hair back and pinched her face. Eddy put his arm around her as they scurried to their car.

Earlier they had been late for the appointment with Dr. Washington. They had left in time but an accident on 490 waylaid them. Eddy had worried that this was an omen, that somehow the accident was a sign of bad things to come.

Gayle stared at the line of cars, heads and arms sticking out here and there in protest. She could feel her body react, her muscles tightening, her teeth grinding, her lips pursed, her breathing faint. She shook her head. "Are you okay?" said Eddy.

"Yes," she said without looking at him. She tried not to think, not to predict what might be said about the results of her tests. She looked at her hands, her cracked nails; her sneakers, the rubber curled in places; her old lady slacks, why had she worn them? Their car began to move. She felt lighter for no reason.

They were ten minutes late to Dr. Washington's office. "We could have gotten here faster if we'd have walked," said Eddy. Out of breath, Gayle checked in and then they waited twenty more minutes to be seen.

The visit lasted little more than fifteen.

Back on the sixth floor of the parking garage, they sat in silence as the wind shuddered the car. Gayle called Rich who put the phone on speaker so Sandy could listen. There were questions for about ten minutes, then some awkward laughter to close.

• • •

Sandy and Rich, sitting together on the roll-out couch, looked at each other and then looked away. They looked at each other again, as if now they were ready to speak, but then said nothing.

"Tea?" said Rich.

"Yeah."

Coffee mug and tea cup warming their hands, they returned to the roll-out, assumed their positions and watched the steam rise.

"So," said Sandy.

"Yeah."

"I don't know what to make of this."

"Mom sounded…"

"Flat."

"Yeah, flat, like she was reading a script…poorly."

"Considering the news, you'd think she'd have…"

"Shown a little more emotion."

"Or any emotion."

"Makes me wonder."

"Yeah, me, too."

• • •

Dr. Washington had greeted Gayle and Eddy with a firm handshake and a broad smile. She motioned them to the plush chairs opposite her desk while she searched her computer for Gayle's record. She wore a crisp white coat, her name embroidered on the pocket. A stethoscope was coiled around her neck. She took off her horn-rimmed glasses, placing them in her lap.

Gayle and Eddy, balanced on the edge of their seats listened for the news. Dr. Washington began with a question. "I'm sure you've thought a lot about this visit and these tests. What are you expecting from the results?"

'Cut the crap', thought Eddy. He looked at Gayle to answer first.

"Well, I guess I thought it would be one of two things. Either the cancer could still be treated; or we were too late."

Gayle watched Dr. Washington's face for a clue, but saw nothing.

"And you, Mr. Kimes, what were you expecting?"

'Jesus', thought Eddy. 'What kind of bullshit game is this?' "I don't know."

"You must have come with some expectation." She raised her eyebrows as if to say, 'Come on'.

"Okay. I'll tell you what I'm hoping for. I'm hoping the cancer is gone. I'm hoping that's what you are going to tell us. I'm hoping we don't have to come back here ever again. I'm hoping we can return to our lives and do what we want, because this whole thing is over. It may sound foolish or stupid, but that's what I want. That's what everyone wants." He turned to Gayle whose lips bore a faint smile.

Gayle looked at Eddy as if she were seeing him for the first time. His face was taut with determination, even anger. His words came from his heart and he didn't care at all whether they were what the doctor was looking for. His love was like a fist swinging at the sky, trying to punch a hole through the clouds to make room for some sunlight.

Dr. Washington shifted in her seat, looked at the computer screen and then back at Gayle and Eddy. "Well, you have given me three answers. I can tell you that one of them is correct."

Eddy, no longer listening to what Dr. Washington was saying, watched his wife. He studied the line of her jaw, her head tilted up slightly, the surest sign that she was listening intently; he watched her soft brown unblinking eyes, how they never moved, never shied away once they found you, captured you; a look that had unsettled him in the beginning. It was so plain, so honest, so beautiful. He noticed a pinkish cast to her cheeks which quickly turned rose. She blinked and her eyes became moist. She touched her face, as if to cool it. She looked down and then up again. She tried to smile as she turned to Eddy.

"What?" said Eddy, looking first at Gayle and then at Dr. Washington. "What's wrong?"

"You weren't listening?" said Gayle.

"Of course, I was…what did I miss? What happened?"

Dr. Washington leaned forward, her arms braced on her knees. "Mr. Kimes, your answer was the right one."

•   •   •

Eddy clutched the steering wheel. Gayle sat with her hands in her lap. The Rochester skyline peeked at them. In the distance, dark clouds were racing from the west.

"It's going to rain," said Eddy.

"Uh huh."

A van pulled in beside them. A mother, father and three young children tumbled out, the kids racing toward the elevator. It started sprinkling.

"Gayle, honey, did she say…?"

"Yes."

They both shook their heads, took deep breaths and exhaled laughter. Then tears. Followed by more laughter.

Dr. Washington had told them that Gayle's CA 125 level had "fallen through the floor." It had gone from "nearly 80" to "15, which is totally unheard of." She said "the scans showed nothing, I mean nothing." She presented "the case" to her colleagues, "who just shook their heads. They've never seen anything like it." They redid everything and got the same results.

"How is this possible?" said Gayle.

"Your guess is as good as mine. Sometimes there's a lag between treatment and outcome, but not this long. We're trying to figure it out, find a medical explanation. I've sent these results to colleagues across the country. I hope that's okay. Maybe we'll find out. But for now, we don't know why this happened."

"I guess it's a miracle," said Eddy.

"That's as good an explanation as any."

She went on to say that this may not be predictive of the future; there is always the chance of a recurrence, so she would schedule Gayle every six months for a complete assessment. Gayle and Eddy shook their heads, still trying to digest the news. Eddy realized that, despite what he had told the doctor, he never expected the cancer to go away. In fact, considering how Gayle had looked recently, he thought they wouldn't be able to do any further treatment. He assumed the next step would be planning how best to use whatever time Gayle had left. What did they want to do that they hadn't done before? Was there a trip they wanted to take? All the things people do to cram as much life as possible into a thimble full of time.

"Why does she look like she's still...not well?" Eddy glanced at Gayle to see if he had crossed a line. Dr. Washington turned to her patient.

"Have you been eating, Gayle?"

"Not so much."

"Sleeping?"

"No."

"There you go."

Eddy had figured that Gayle wasn't sleeping or eating because she was dying. When cancer ravages your body, you don't eat; you don't sleep; you don't do much of anything; you don't even dare hope; you wait. Turns out she was afraid; she was anxious and afraid and, as he looked at her tinker toy frame, probably depressed. He looked at his own belly, bulging over his belt, his tucked shirt trying to hold everything in.

•   •   •

Eddy started the car and put it in reverse. Then back in park.

"What?" said Gayle.

"I don't know. Seems like we should do something. Something to celebrate."

"What do you want to do?"

"I don't know. What do you want to do?"

Eddy placed the palm of his hand on his jaw as he gave her question some thought.

"You want to go out for breakfast."

"Okay."

"Great."

"We should stop at the store, too. Need bread, milk, a few things. Shouldn't take long."

"Okay."

Eddy put the car in reverse. He started whistling as he headed down the first ramp and around the first turn.

"I'm going for broke this morning. The platter—omelet, hash browns, pancakes, juice and coffee."

Gayle placed her hand on Eddy's arms. "Yeah, pancakes sound good."

CHAPTER 30

Gayle poured tea for both of them. She had made coffee cake, which she'd sliced and covered with Saran Wrap. She undid the saran and put the cake on the kitchen table, along with two dessert plates and two forks. She put the napkin holder on the table, as well.

"My God, Mom, did you and Dad jump out of your skin? I mean, it's like you got a 'get out of jail free' forever card. I'm so happy for you."

"Well…we went out for breakfast. And then to the store."

"Oh my God, you are two crazy people! Breakfast and Wegman's. In the same day, no less. I hope you were able to handle the excitement."

Gayle chuckled. "Yeah, complete madness."

"I'm sorry if Richie and I sounded, I don't know…"

"That's okay…"

"We were shocked. I mean, we hung up and looked at each other, not knowing if we'd heard the same thing, you know what I mean. It was just so unexpected, and I couldn't tell for sure from your voice; well, anyway, it's the best news ever, I mean ever. I couldn't be happier!"

Gayle hadn't heard this much enthusiasm in Sandy's voice since she was a teenager. Sparkling, melodic, delighted.

"And you made cinnamon fluff."

It was a family recipe, something Gayle only made on special occasions. Sandy always had it for birthday breakfast, even on school days.

"Well, like you said, I've gone crazy."

"I bet you never thought you'd be making cinnamon fluff because of something like this." The words sounded wrong as soon as they came out of Sandy's mouth. "I mean…"

"I know what you mean. You're right. I would never have thought I'd get cancer. And I never thought this would be the outcome."

"You didn't?" Sandy put down her fork. "Why's that?"

"There are 'not so bad' cancers, 'bad' cancers and 'awful' cancers. Mine fell into the last category. I think that's one of the reasons chemo seemed foolish after a while. But the more I thought about it, about dying, I wanted to try, you know, try to make time stretch as far as I could."

In the silence that followed, they both took bites of coffee cake.

"My God, Mom, this is delicious."

"More tea?"

"Sure. So, what do you make of the news? I mean, this doesn't just happen, does it?"

"Your dad is convinced it's some kind of miracle." She wiggled her hands in front of her face when she said this.

"Well, Mom, isn't it?"

"I don't believe in miracles. Just because you can't explain something doesn't make it a miracle."

Sandy cocked her head to one side, as if confounded by her mother.

"Don't get me wrong, honey, it feels miraculous. I don't think I've ever felt this relieved. Not since I found out I was pregnant with you and your brother, have I ever felt such gratitude. And it's fine with me if your dad wants to believe it's a miracle. It makes him happy. That's good. He's had a pretty awful year, too."

Sandy was embarrassed because of how little concern she had showed for her parents' travails. Somehow, she hadn't believed it was real.

"I hope you can be happy, too, Mom."

There was such tenderness in Sandy's voice that for a moment Gayle could barely catch her breath.

"So, well, how are you? I've been so caught up in everything that I don't know what…"

"I'm fine, Mom." Sandy sat up straight. "Actually, things are going very well for me. I got a job. Like a real forty hour a week job with benefits and everything."

"You did, that's wonderful."

"Yeah, you'll never guess."

"So, where?"

"The medical center. In human relations, if you can imagine. I'll be developing some software for them and maybe doing some marketing stuff."

"Oh my, Sandy, I'm so happy for you."

Gayle stood up and took Sandy in her arms. She held her tight; she could feel her warm, grown-up self, so vibrant it brought tears to her eyes.

"Are you okay, Mom?" Sandy leaned back, but her mother pulled her closer.

"This is just…good…holding you…"

"Mom?"

"I've missed you, Sandy. We used to be so close, remember? We were like buddies when you were just a girl." Sandy lay her head on her mother's shoulder. "And then it changed. I knew that when you and Richie got older, things would be different, that you'd both pull away, find yourselves, and then we'd all come together again, you know what I mean…but…it seemed we, you and I, never did. And I always worried that we wouldn't, that we wouldn't find each other again."

'She doesn't know a thing,' thought Sandy. 'She has no idea what happened'. Sandy couldn't speak, her throat choked by so many lost years. How could she have thought that her mother knew and didn't care? It had been ten years and Sandy was still standing at her mother's office door, wanting to tell her everything, wondering why her mother couldn't talk.

"I'm sure it's just me being sentimental. It's just me, but I always worried, you know; it happens sometimes in people's lives, it's like there's a tear between them and it never gets mended." She let go of Sandy, feeling self-conscious. "I'm sorry, honey, I guess I'm a little…"

Sandy saw pain etched in her mother's creased forehead.

"It's the news, I'm sure of it. It's made me a little…careless with my feelings."

"No, Mom, it's, well, it's real, you know, and I love it."

"I love you." Gayle caressed Sandy's cheek.

Sandy opened her mouth. She wanted to say 'I love you' but there was something in the way. She sat down. She took several breaths, hoping to clear her voice. But the words wouldn't come. She could feel her insides twisting, slowly contorting. She remembered how she had laid awake that night, wrestling with herself. What to do? She hadn't planned on talking to her mother, but when she got up that morning, she drifted down the stairs to her mother's office, her hand gently knocking, unsure of what she would say if her mother opened the door.

When her mother called to her, when she told her she couldn't talk, Sandy had felt sad, but also relieved. It was as if she had opened Pandora's box a crack, but just as quickly, the lid had been closed before anything frightening came out. Only later, when she had no one to run to, did she feel hurt, angry. 'If only', she thought. But it was too hard to go back. Too easy to go forward. At least for a while.

"Mom, sit down, please."

"What is it, honey?" Gayle's legs bent slowly, she sat cautiously, the tone in Sandy's voice so foreign.

"Mom, something happened a long time ago…something awful."

Gayle's face went ashen. She slid her hand across the table, reaching for her daughter's fingertips. Sandy felt the nausea she often felt as a kid when the family would gorge themselves on pizza; she'd go to bed and her stomach would knot and then aching waves of belly pain would follow. She'd become afraid; afraid that she wouldn't reach the bathroom in time; afraid that everything would come out uncontrollably, and there she'd be sitting in her own mess. Her words came slowly, almost incomprehensibly at first.

Sandy described that night, how she'd gone with her friend to a party. She stopped to see if her mother remembered but there wasn't any sign of recognition. How could such a night not be remembered? She reminded her mother about JB, the boy who was killed in Afghanistan. She told her mother she had had a couple of beers. She felt a child's guilt when entering a confessional.

She looked down at the table as the details poured out. She was reporting now, objective, unfeeling. It was the only way. She hated each word. But she let them out, the nausea slowly abating. And then there weren't any more words.

There wasn't a sound in the room. Not the floor that usually creaked, not the hum of the refrigerator when it turns on, not a car passing, nothing. She wanted to look at her mother, but she didn't dare. Then her mother stood and pulled her chair to Sandy's side and sat down. She rubbed Sandy's back and then she took her in her arms and kissed her head and cheeks. She rocked slowly back and forth and she whispered—"It will be okay now"—and Sandy began to weep, first tears of fire, then solace, then cleansing. "I'm so sorry I didn't open that door, my sweet girl. What he did to you..." Her voice cracked. "What he did to you was a vicious hateful thing, a crime. Goddammit." Her breathing was thick with anger, rage. "Come here." She pulled Sandy closer. "I hate that you've had to carry this, this burden so long. I will carry it with you now."

Sandy shuddered, bending over and laying her head in her mother's lap. Gayle continued to rock her slowly. She ran her fingers through her daughter's hair.

Gayle remembered. She had been a young girl once, too. Young, happy, carefree, in love. She, too, had come home once after a date wanting to talk to someone. But not daring to. Her mother told her every time she left the house with him—"You be careful, I'm telling you"—her voice sharp and cutting. Gayle passed it off as being old fashioned. Anyway, Gayle knew how far was too far. But this night was different. He was more...excitable. He kept telling her what his friends were doing with their girlfriends.

They were in the backseat of his car. He kept saying "I love you, I love you, what's wrong? Don't you love me? I mean, I'm leaving for college. We won't see each other for, like months…" She didn't know what to do. But when he started to penetrate her, she knew she didn't want to do this; she knew it was too far. "No," she had said. "Please, Sam, no." But it was too late. The whole thing was over in seconds. He told her how wonderful she was and how much he appreciated her doing this for him. All she said was, "Please take me home."

"Come on, Gayley."

"No, really, I need to go home. It's getting late…" She looked out the window and didn't speak again.

At first, she was angry at herself for being so cold to him, for making him beg. He told her how much he loved her, how this would seal their love, especially since they wouldn't see each other for so long. She knew other girls did it all the time. She almost called him to say she was sorry. But she felt too sad to talk with anyone. She went to sleep instead. And that was that.

As it turned out, Sam came home the first weekend after leaving for school. He wanted to do it again. Though it wasn't true, she told him she was having her period. The following week, Eddy stopped by for the first time.

It was ten more years before she understood that she had been raped. She had made it clear to Sam that she didn't want to do it. She had said "No," and it hadn't mattered. She felt dirty for the longest time, and hated Sam for longer than that, but in the end, made peace with things, as best she could, and kept a wary friendship with her old boyfriend and his wife.

She looked down at her daughter, peaceful now as Gayle continued to caress her hair. How good this would have felt, she thought. She lay her head on Sandy's and closed her eyes.

CHAPTER 31

"Of course, it's a miracle. What else could it be?"

Sam sat with Eddy in the 'breakroom'. He felt perplexed by Eddy's story. What had really happened at the doctor's visit? The facts were blurry, but the message was clear: Gayle was healed.

Perhaps it was his friend's religious zeal that made Sam unsure of the story's veracity. He had too many filled prescriptions languishing in their bins waiting for customers who never claimed them; customers who insisted that they were depending on a Higher Power to pull them through. Later when he'd find their obituaries in the paper, he'd shake his head and dispose of their medications. He hoped this wasn't another version of the same thing. He'd never known his friend to be religious, but in the last year or so there was an emergent spiritual something about Eddy.

"What exactly did the oncologist say? Did she talk about test results?"

Eddy explained the test results. "And she said this type of thing can happen, like it's kind of possible, but very rare."

"Did she say it was a miracle?"

"She said that was as good a word as any."

Eddy was puzzled by his friend's skepticism. The proof was there — no sign of cancer for no apparent reason. If that's not a miracle, what is? In years past, Eddy would have been as doubtful as Sam. He was never much for faith healing, televangelism, laying-on-of-hands (through the TV screen), all those fraudulent attempts at capitalizing on the suffering of people. He rejected all of it out of hand.

But this was different. This wasn't a carnival side show. This was the product of sincere prayer and (mostly) abiding hope. He asked and it was given. What were the chances?

It's not like Eddy was a devout anything. He was afraid and lost and desperate when he kneeled in front of that statue, in front of Jesus the Consoler, and made his appeal. Afterwards he worried he'd been too pushy, too demanding, but then he figured how else could he get the attention he needed. There must be a lot of prayers flying around up there. He wondered if there were prayer controllers, like air traffic controllers. There had to be some mechanism.

"Well, I'm so happy for you, Eddy; you and Gayle. It must feel like you got a reprieve, like you got a new lease on life."

"Does for sure."

"Who would have thought, you know? It's wonderful."

Eddy's smile could not have been bigger. The bell at the counter rang once, then twice.

"Well, old friend, duty calls. My best to Gayle."

He embraced Eddy who floated out of the store. Sam washed his hands before heading out front again.

He looked up as he approached the counter and stopped dead in his tracks.

"Hi, Sam." Rhonda's smile was thin. Gone was the ruby red lipstick, the cloudy mascara, the low neckline. She wore a new pair of glasses with dark purple frames; a pearl blouse, hair pulled back in a pony tail, tied with a purple ribbon. Her hands were clasped at her waist.

Sam closed the pharmacy for an hour. "I'll be back," was all he said to Nellie. He and Rhonda settled into a corner booth at the Union Street Coffee Shop, mugs in front of them. Neither spoke at first.

Sam broke the silence. "Where have you been?" His tone was sterner than he intended.

"Long story."

He never expected to see her again. She'd always seemed like a mosquito, flitting and fleeting, lighting and leaving, biting when you least expected it. When they first met, he'd wanted to swat her away, but he was also drawn to her. She was so uninhibited, so playful, so unabashedly carnal.

He came to accept her eccentricities, her hyper-reactivity to almost everything, like the time she exploded into tears when he'd killed a squirrel with the car. 'You bastard!' she'd said. But within five minutes, she was laughing and pawing at him as he struggled to keep the car on the road. What did *he* know? He hadn't been with a woman in decades. Maybe this wasn't out of the ordinary.

"I've got the time."

Rhonda tried to read the look in Sam's eyes. Did she want to do this? Did she want to open herself up to a man she barely knew. What would he think or say? And did it matter? She'd been here before. Hot and heavy and then disappearing until she could cool off and come back to earth. Was this any different? Was it ever a good idea to tell a guy what was going on?

"I've been away."

"Vacation?"

"Not exactly." Rhonda leaned back and looked at the couple in an adjoining booth, how they ignored each other. "I've been sick."

A worrying frown crossed Sam's face.

"What's wrong, Rhonda?" said Sam, thinking of Gayle.

"It's something I've had for a long time. Usually, I have it under control. Sometimes, though, I don't. I didn't when we first met. I hadn't had things under control for months. I lost a job, found a job, lost one, found one. Same with men."

Sam felt the color retreat from his face. He clutched his knees.

"I've had this since I was a teenager. The cost of having it has been steep."

"What are you talking about exactly, Rhonda?" Again, not how he wanted it to come out.

"I'm bipolar, Sam. It's a mental illness thing—"

"I know what bipolar disorder is, Rhonda. I fill prescriptions for it every day." He felt his chest heave. How had he not recognized this? "I'm sorry."

"When I'm manic, it's like I'm riding a comet. I'm soaring, I'm alive, I'm imaginative, I'm sensual, sexual. I'm everything I'm not when I'm at my baseline. It feels so good. For a while. I get to be someone other than myself. But the comet doesn't last. It burns out or it crashes or however you want to put it, it disappears and I'm left in midair with nothing below me. I fall for a long time."

"You don't have to tell me—"

"I met a lot of men on that site, what was it, Humpr? You were one of them. All of you were kind of blurry. When I found myself alone in a motel, not having any idea what I was doing there, I knew that the bottom was coming fast. My psychiatrist admitted me to a hospital in Buffalo. That's where I've been."

She wasn't looking at him any longer. He couldn't see her eyes. She closed them when she talked. "It took a while for the meds to kick in. For me to feel normal again. Or as normal as I get." She looked up and smiled, her face tired.

"I'm so sorry. I wish I'd known."

"Nothing you could have done." She shrugged. "You know, when the fog began to lift and I started thinking about what I had done, who I had been with, you were the only one I could see clearly, the only one who had left a mark, if that makes sense."

Sam raised his eyebrows and held his breath.

"Remember that night, the night I came to your house and this young man, I don't remember his name, he came to the door wanting to talk to you?"

"Yes, it was—"

"While you talked to him, I was watching you. And you seemed so regular, so average, so just-a-person, that I felt, I don't know, safe. I didn't always feel that way when I met guys. But I felt it with you. I thought, 'He won't hurt me'. Of course, I didn't know, but it's what I felt. And it's what I remembered when I was in the hospital."

Rhonda's arms lay on the table top, her hands knotted together. She opened them and splayed her fingers, then tucked her hands in her lap. Her face seemed grayer, older than he remembered. She looked like all the customers that came to his counter for their prescriptions. Plainly dressed. No bells. No whistles.

"Are you hungry? I don't have to go back right away. We could have something to eat? How would that be?"

Rhonda's shoulders squared and she released a breath she didn't know she was holding.

"Yes, that would be nice."

"Good. That's good."

CHAPTER 32

Eddy found Peter in the church sacristy, a dusty smelling room full of benches and chairs stacked with Bibles and hymnbooks, white choir robes and red stoles hanging on wire hangers against the walls. Peter stood over a table. He held a cloth in one hand and with the other, he picked up shot glasses to be dried and polished. He studied each one before placing them gently in their appointed holes on a golden tray.

"Good morning," said Eddy.

Peter startled, dropping a glass to the floor where it shattered into innumerable pieces. Peter turned. His glare softened when he saw Eddy.

"I'm so sorry," said Eddy.

"Not a problem, really." Peter kneeled and swept the pieces together with his bare hands. "We have others."

"Looks like a drinking party."

"It is in a way. I'm preparing for communion this week. Each one of these glasses will be filled with wine, nonalcoholic, of course. The wine represents the saving Blood of Christ. I will bake a loaf of hearty bread, multigrain, and it will be broken into pieces and placed on several platters and then passed among the people. The bread is the Body of Christ. They will pray, then eat the bread and drink the wine. It's a reminder that God is with us, that God is inside us, that even these tiny pieces of bread and little glasses of wine, all of it, like all of us, is sacred."

"I guess it's a little more than a 'drinking party'." Eddy was embarrassed and tried to smile but his face couldn't quite do it.

"Maybe the 'party' part is right. It *is* a celebration." Peter smiled and cleaned another glass. He put it on the platter. He waited for Eddy to speak but when he didn't: "So, how's it going?"

This time Eddy's smile was involuntary. It closed his eyes and lifted his ears. "We got great news the other day."

"Really."

"Gayle is cancer free. I mean, it's gone."

"My God!"

"Exactly my thought, too. It's a miracle."

"And the doctors, what are they saying?"

Eddy shrugged and tilted his head to one side. "The tests, the tests didn't find a thing. Nothing. They've sent the results out to some other doctors around the country, or something, because it's so unusual."

Peter was ashamed that he was skeptical. Throughout the years, dozens of parishioners had claimed miracles. A cousin who coughed up a tumor; a great-aunt who regained her sight; a man who'd stopped breathing for an hour, then woke up. These were among the believable ones. Most were laughable, but it was impolitic for a pastor, a believer in the Word of God, to suggest that these tales were rubbish, not to be believed.

In recent years, his skepticism had turned to cynicism. He saw in such miracles a sad attempt to gain attention otherwise denied. But he kept his mouth shut, applauded the reports of parishioners who stood during announcements to share their good news, even when he knew they hadn't been ill a day in their lives.

And, yes, ashamed was the right word. How could a man of God have so little faith? He *wanted* to believe. But that was the closest he could get.

"They said — 'No evidence of cancer' — you're sure?"

Eddy didn't seem to hear him.

"We've got a fresh start on our lives. And I have you to thank."

"Me?"

"Yes, you. You're the one who told me to pray, to turn to God. And that's what I did. I asked God to heal Gayle and, as far as I'm concerned, he did." He shrugged as if to say, case closed.

"And that's...well—"

"I was desperate, I'm telling you. When I walked away, it wasn't like I felt —'I don't have to worry anymore'—but at least I felt that I had said my piece, you know, like Job, remember?"

Peter listened closely but said nothing.

"I think he was smiling, though."

"What?"

"You know, the researchers and Mona Lisa's smile. Was it a frown or a genuine smile? You wondered the same thing about the statue. Well, I'm telling you, it was a smile that day, I know it was."

"Eddy, I'm so very happy for you. I can see why it feels like a miracle. This, indeed, is good news." If you couldn't hear the reverend's voice and could only see his face, you'd think someone had just told him there'd been an automobile accident. His mind had already fast-forwarded, perhaps five months, perhaps five years, to the day when the doctors would tell them the cancer had reappeared. He closed his eyes to scold himself and to erase the thought. As he re-opened them, his smile rose with his lids.

"So, I, well, I want to do something."

"What do you mean, Eddy?"

"My good fortune, I want to show my gratitude somehow."

"You mean pay it forward?"

"This is what I was thinking. You know how awful the statue looks. It hasn't been cleaned in decades. It's filthy, really, covered in dirt and bird crap and who knows what else. Hasn't been white since I don't know when. It should look better, you know what I mean?"

"I guess—"

"Maybe if it was shinier, more people would pay attention." Eyes wide, Eddy waited for the reverend to respond. "That would be a good thing, wouldn't it? I mean, people would come and pray or sit and think, whatever they needed. Who knows, maybe there would be more miracles."

"I don't know if we can count on that, Eddy, but…cleaning it is an idea worth thinking about."

Eddy could feel the whole thing slipping away, like Peter didn't get it for some reason.

"Look, I'm serious. I was this close to losing everything. I didn't have a job. My wife was dying. I was up to my eyeballs in debt." He swallowed hard. "And I came here with nothing to hope for; I mean nothing. And then this happens. I don't deserve it. I know that for sure. But it happened anyway." Eddy's eyes were narrow and fierce now. "I want to do this one thing."

Peter could see in Eddy's eyes how an unwarranted gift could leave a person unsure of what to do, yet believing that there was some way, no matter how small, no matter how incidental, to say thank you.

"Look, Eddy, here's what I'll do; I'll take it to our Ruling Elders. They have to approve this sort of thing. They don't meet again, though, for a few weeks."

Eddy beamed. He put his hands on Peter's shoulders and shook him gently.

"Now, I can't promise you—"

"I'm sure you can make this happen. I know it."

CHAPTER 33

"So, it's true." Rich scanned his mother top to bottom. She looked different, like a weight was no longer crushing her. Her face gleamed; the lines in her forehead were not nearly as deep. When she hugged him, he could feel her strength.

"As true as can be." Gayle was pleased that Rich's face was calm. He looked unruffled, relaxed, almost happy.

"Did they say anything about the future?"

"Like whether I'm going to get it again?"

Rich's lower back tightened at the thought. "Well—"

"Look, it's gone. They can't find it. Whether it's hiding in me somewhere, playing Where's Waldo, who knows. The only thing that matters is that right now I don't have cancer. The future is anyone's guess." The only thing Gayle was sure of was her last comment—The future is anyone's guess. She was struggling to believe everything else. She had been sick for so long, she had been in this awful wrestling match for so long, that it was hard to believe the cancer had slipped away without a trace. It was hard to free fall into life as if she could trust it again. There was no doubt she wanted to. And while she didn't embrace Eddy's staggering confidence, his reckless happiness, she did find him inspiring in his way. It helped to live with someone who was listening to the same song but hearing such different music.

"Well, I couldn't be happier. In fact, I can't remember *ever* being happier than when I heard the news."

"Thank you, sweetheart."

There was a pause where their eyes didn't meet.

"And, so, how are you?"

"Well, I've got good news. Not as good as yours, but good. Looks like Sandy has scored me a job at the medical center."

"Wonderful."

"Yeah. I'll be working kind of in her area. Doing a bunch of different things. Helping produce the medical center's newsletter, fielding media requests for interviews with hot shots, helping departments with web design. Kind of a jack-of-all-trades gig."

Gayle didn't say a word. Instead, she took him in her arms again and squeezed. She felt both happy and relieved. Finally, he was doing something that she could understand, a job that she could explain to her friends.

"Wonderful. What about your other jobs, your contract things?"

There were no other jobs, no 'contract things'. Everything had dried up three months ago. He would have been knocking on his parents' door two months ago if the Humpr settlement hadn't come through. Fifty-five hundred and change. Not a lot, but enough to pay rent, fill the tank, buy some groceries and go out every once in a while. Mostly with his sister.

Turned out Felix Thunderstone was really Harold Banky from Jersey City. A high school dropout with a talent for money-making schemes that skated on the other side of the law. Married twice, skipped out on child support both times, moved often, changed his name even more often, but had the charisma to seduce people into following him. Humpr was not an illegal venture, but his abuse of employees violated their civil rights. Not good. Five years jail time and a five hundred thousand dollars in fines. Then, in all likelihood, back into the game.

"I've told them about the change. I'll work with them on my off time until they can find someone else."

"Can you stay for dinner? Your dad will be home in a while. I can make homemade mac and cheese."

"I'd love to, Mom, but I got to get going. Stuff, you know."

"There's always stuff, isn't there."

Rich kissed his mother's forehead and turned for the door. Then:

"Hey, before I go. Do you know about this thing Dad wants to do?"

"With the statue, you mean?"

"Yeah."

Eddy told Gayle about it a week earlier:

"What do you want to do?"

"I met with the reverend, you know, Peter, and I told him, I said I wanted to do something, a kind of thank you for everything." Each word made Eddy feel foolish. He raked his lip with his teeth and then winched his mouth to one side. He knew that Gayle wasn't keen on miracle talk. He took a breath. "You know, because...because you all of a sudden don't have cancer."

"Okay..."

"And I think the, uh, I think that praying to the statue, maybe that's what did it, I don't know."

"No one knows."

Despite Gayle's doubts, she loved her husband's willingness to believe. There was always an 'It'll-Work-Out' sign pinned to Eddy's heart. Every time he was laid off, he said it. Every time he got a new job, he said it again. Never mind the months of cutting coupons, paying some bills and ignoring others, the months of hunching over her books fretting about their finances, working as many angles as possible, and massaging the accounts. He always shone a brighter light on things. She always found a reason to carry an umbrella on a sunny day.

How could she not support him, after all he had done during the illness? "I think it's a wonderful idea." She hadn't heard much about it after that.

Rich took a breath. "Well, he's asked me to help him."

"Help him, how?"

"I'm not sure. He said something about cleaning it, or something. I didn't understand."

Gayle told Rich what his father believed about the cancer. Rich tried to control the corners of his mouth, hoping to get a sign from his mother that it was okay to laugh. When she didn't give one, he reined it back in.

"Is he serious?"

"Dead serious."

Rich's brow furrowed. "Is that what you believe, Mom?"

"I don't know why the cancer went into remission...or went away, I guess."

"Hm. I never thought of Dad as, like, religious."

"It's not like he's joined a cult, Richie. It's been a long, hard haul. For both of us." He is still so young, she thought. He doesn't understand that when there's nothing left to hold onto, you grasp. You reach out as far as you can until you find something, anything. It doesn't matter what other people think if it makes sense to you, if it helps you get up and go forward. "I admire your dad."

"But he wasn't the one with the cancer."

"Yes, he was." She looked at Rich, her eyes unblinking. "If your dad asked you to help, help him, okay?"

"I told him yes. I just didn't—"

"Good."

·   ·   ·

Eddy opened the van and studied the contents. There was a ladder, chamois cloths, sponges, water buckets, marble cleaner, ammonia, and marble polish. He sat on the bumper and read the directions he'd Googled. He folded the paper and tucked it into his jeans pocket. He looked up when he heard a horn blow. Eddy waved. Rich nodded as he pulled his car into the nearest spot.

Rich got out of the car and stared at the steeple.

"You know, I've driven past this hundreds of times but never looked at it." He tilted his head back further. "Something, isn't it?"

They shook hands and Rich joined his father on the bumper.

"So, what are we up to?"

Before Eddy could answer, Peter came around the corner.

"Gentlemen," he said.

Eddy stood and took Peter's hand. They shook vigorously and patted each other's shoulder. Rich sat, his hands in his lap, a sheepish look on his face. Eddy introduced Peter. Rich stood quickly at attention. He bowed slightly, as if he were meeting the pope. He put his hand to his chest and shuffled it around, approximating the sign of the cross.

"Oh," said Peter. "No need for that."

They all coughed up a laugh.

"I wanted to stop by to reconfirm that the Ruling Elders have given their enthusiastic approval to your plan, Eddy. They couldn't be happier. They send their blessing."

After a minute or two of weather talk, Peter retreated to the church, saying he'd peek in on them from time to time. Before he left, he thanked Rich for helping his dad and, in turn, providing a much-needed service to the church.

"Blessings on *you*, as well."

"I am very much glad...that this could...that I...that I do this," said Rich.

Eddy patted his son's back. "Maybe we should have paid for another month of speech therapy when we had the chance."

Eddy hoisted the ladder onto his shoulder and grabbed the bucket. He pointed to the other items and Rich took them in his arms awkwardly. Eddy walked ahead of Rich. They went down the sidewalk and around the corner to the back of the church. Rich could see Jesus's head above the newly trimmed bushes. When he stepped inside the garden, he was taken aback by the size of the statue.

"I had no idea."

They dropped everything on the ground.

"Yeah, really." Needing no prompting, Eddy told his son the statue's history. What a big deal it was in the 1950s; its controversial 'look'; and the notch near the shoulder blade.

"Yeah, it was the size of a man's thumb." He looked up at the statue. "Gotten bigger since then."

"Too bad it wasn't perfect." Rich was looking at Jesus's face, the eyebrows shading its eyes.

"Everything's imperfect."

"I guess."

Then he told Rich about the Mona Lisa and the smile.

"What do you think? Happy or sad?"

Rich wanted to say something, anything. What was the right answer? Happy Jesus? Sad Jesus? His dad's face was alight with pride. He realized his father was introducing him to his new best buddy. Rich studied the face. There wasn't the kind of crinkle in Jesus's eyes that would suggest a smile. His mouth was impassive, almost indifferent, like someone waiting in a check-out line at the grocery store.

"Happy," said Rich.

His dad nodded with satisfaction. "Yeah, he's smiling today." Eddy was pleased that his son could see it too. It was so subtle that it could easily be missed unless you gave it time, let it awaken slowly before your eyes.

Rich sat on the bench. "Dad, I'm still trying to understand—"

"I know. I don't think your mother gets it completely either. It's hard to explain. I been coming here for over a year. You knew that?"

"Mom told me."

Eddy told Rich that, in the beginning, he would come there for a breather when he felt like everything was closing in. Sometimes he needed to get away, simple as that. But after a while, he visited whether he needed a breather or not. He couldn't say why. All he knew was that he felt different after each visit. Replenished. Hopeful. The statue became a lifeline. He talked about his conversations with Peter and how he had encouraged Eddy to pray, no matter how pointless it seemed.

"So, I came here, I came here one night and I said, 'Do it, heal her.'" He turned to his son and shrugged.

"Really? That's what you said."

"Basically."

"What did you think would happen?"

"I didn't know."

"Huh."

"You know, Rich, sometimes things that never made sense before start to make sense. Call it the ultimate hail Mary pass, whatever, but it worked. Your mom is all better. And it's time for me to say 'thank you', you know what I mean?"

Rich didn't know what his father meant. Not once during the travails of the previous year had Rich thought, 'I'll ask God to get me out of this mess'. Not once.

"Yeah, I know what you mean."

Eddy reached for his son and squeezed his arm. He could tell by the blank look on his face that he didn't get it at all, but Eddy appreciated his thoughtful lie. "I'll be right back." He went to the spigot near the garden and filled the bucket. When he came back, Rich had already put up the ladder.

"So, what's the deal? How do you do this?"

"A bunch of steps. First thing is you wipe it down with that marble cleaner there." He pointed and Rich retrieved the plastic bottle. Eddy squeezed it onto a sponge and climbed the step ladder while Rich steadied it.

Eddy was startled by the massiveness of Jesus's head and had to grab hold of the ladder as it shook back and forth.

"You okay, Dad?"

"Yeah."

The closer he got the more magnificent Jesus appeared. His face exuded compassion, his eyebrows nearly blanketing his downcast eyes. His hair, like bands of ribbon, were tipped in curlicues that draped his bare chest. He leaned back slightly to get a better look at Jesus's mouth, the grimy lips partially open, chisel marks left in the corners, his cheeks pocked from years of snow and rain and beating sun. His eyes, half open, seemed sad, yet peaceful. From below the folds of his robe, Jesus's arms emerged. Sinewy muscles defined his forearms and the hollow of his wrists. His hands were thick, with long slightly curled fingers, each joint delicately lined, details that only the sculptor would see. How much he must have loved this mass of marble.

Eddy placed his hand on Jesus's cheek, then caressed his hair. He ran a finger across his lips, those mysterious curls of marble that he and Peter had often speculated about. He put one finger in the notch, that long-ago imperfection that helped define the statue for all time. He smiled as warmth seemed to encircle him. He dabbed his eyes with the back of his hand. "Hi," he said in a whisper.

"If you're okay, I'll start on the bottom," called Rich. He put his hands on his hips and studied the task at hand. "Jesus." He grabbed a sponge from the bucket, doused it with cleanser and started on the base, then the feet. Dirt came off grudgingly. Rich rubbed harder. The texture of the stone was uniform, except for subtle differences in color. He bent over to examine a small section of cleansed marble, finding whites and creams and blacks and charcoals; greens and reds and rose, almost every color he could imagine. When he stepped back, it was as if they disappeared. So many beautiful impurities.

Despite the cool temperature, both men were perspiring when they took a break to refill their buckets. New sponges in hand, both men returned to their places and wiped the statue clean of soap residue. When they were done, they looked at each other and laughed, pleased with their progress, impressed by the nearly resurrected Jesus.

They wiped the statue dry with chamois cloths and then rinsed it again. More chamois cloths. Both men were breathing hard now. They worked in unison, father-son, the statue seeming to enhance their harmony.

They sat on the bench enjoying the lunch Gayle had packed for them.

"I thought you were crazy, Dad, but wow." Rich gestured with his sandwich. "I don't know, but it sure is something, isn't it?"

"It's like I'm seeing it again for the first time." He looked at his son. "Having you here makes it even better, you know."

Eddy opened a jug of pure ammonia. They both winced and stepped back as the smell snatched their breath away.

"You're kidding."

"Put these on," said Eddy as he handed Rich a pair of rubber gloves. "And this." He gave him a surgical mask.

"You're not kidding."

They made sure the statue was dry and then like detectives probing for evidence, they cleaned the statue again, this time lingering over every crack and crevice. When they were done, they rinsed and dried once more.

The morning had come and gone. The afternoon was slipping away when they came to the final step in the process.

"The guy at the gravestone place said this stuff should make it pop," said Eddy as he opened a bottle of stone polish. "Let me give it a try first."

Rich held the ladder again as his father climbed with one hand while holding the sponge and polish in the other. He applied the solution to Jesus's face as if her were baptizing a baby. After a few minutes, he stopped, looked at Rich and both men shook their heads in satisfaction.

"I'm telling you, Dad, it's gorgeous, really."

Jesus's face gleamed in the late afternoon sun. "It's like the 1950s all over again, and this guy's being installed for the first time." Eddy had never felt the kind of pride he felt on that ladder. He'd been a pretty fair husband and the best dad he could be; he'd been a damn good cableman and a dependable friend. But this was different. He felt like he was reaching beyond himself in a way he never had before.

"Okay, I'll start down here."

"Don't miss any crevices."

"I won't."

Rich drenched the sponge with polish and started on the base and feet again. It was quiet in the garden, just the sound of sponges on stone, until Rich was startled by a sharp crack, crisp as a gunshot. Then another and another. He heard his father gasping. Rich watched from the corner of his eye as his father's ladder tumbled to the ground. His father clutched Jesus's arm and shoulder when another snap as loud as a thunderclap filled the air.

"Dad!" Rich jumped to his feet, but he was too late. There was panic in his father's eyes as the right side of Jesus's torso, including his arm, gave way at the notch, and crumbled to the ground, like the collapse of an ancient tree.

Eddy lay in the dirt, several hundred pounds of Jesus crushing his legs. He'd lost his wind in the fall and his eyes bulged with fear. Something pressed hard against his cheek. He reached for it and felt the palm of Jesus's hand bearing down on his face.

Peter burst into the garden. "Oh my God, no."

CHAPTER 34

Gayle guided the wheelchair carefully over the step and onto their screened-in back porch. "I can do it," said Eddy. The sun sat on the neighboring rooftops, its light casting lengthy shadows across the back lawn. A nuthatch and a cardinal pecked at the feeder that hung by an aging maple. Rich and Sandy sat quietly as their father shuffled toward the table, grabbing the leg and pulling himself the final few inches. "There." He was breathing hard. "Good."

Gayle's face was fuller than Sandy had seen in two years. She'd gained weight and was going to an exercise class at the Y. Her cheeks were pink. "Need to keep my strength up," she'd said, a reference to the unanticipated requirements of her husband's plight. Sandy looked for sadness or exhaustion in her mother's eyes, but could only find resolve.

•   •   •

It had been almost four months since the headlines hit the papers: "Jesus Crushes Faithful Servant"; "Man Loses Wrestling Match with 'Heaven-weight' Champion." Four months since Eddy found himself numbed with shock as he lay beneath a gargantuan chunk of Jesus the Consoler. Four months since the surgeon had explained that of the twenty-six bones in Eddy's right foot, every single one had been broken, many pulverized; not to mention his femur, tibia, fibula and patella. "The whole shootin' match," was his final diagnosis.

A half dozen surgeries followed in rapid succession. His leg was now held together by pins, screws and plates. The specialist tried "as best I could, considering the damage" to set, piece together, jerry-rig, do whatever he could to bring Eddy's foot back. His toe to hip cast had been removed a week earlier. "This should help with the pain," said the surgeon as he handed Eddy a prescription for oxycodone that remained in Eddy's wallet. He settled for handfuls of ibuprofens instead, which only scratched the surface of his pain.

Eddy had memory glimpses of the accident. He had lost his balance. The ladder wobbled and then tipped over. He grabbed for Jesus, but fell, as if in slow motion, the Consoler close behind. He couldn't breathe. His heart seemed to stop beating. There was vice-like pressure, but no pain. He could see his son's feet. Then a voice; was it Peter? Flashing lights, siren sounds, firefighters' helmets. The grinding torque of the crane. Then, the pain. Then the blinding pain and the darkness behind his eyelids.

•   •   •

When they rolled him to the front of the hospital at discharge, Gayle met him in a shiny new jet-black wheelchair van, tricked out with plush red leather interior, TV, surround sound stereo, moon roof, tinted windows, the whole deal. Once he was locked and loaded into the van, they headed home. "My God, Gayle, we can't afford this." Gayle looked at him through the rearview mirror and then back at the road. "Not your worry."

'She's made of steel', he thought, tempered steel, hardened by life's extremes of heat and cold. She never frowned, but it was a month, maybe more, before she smiled. Her mind had been humming, planning, concocting, scheming, figuring. Something in her clicked, because when he woke up one morning, she was standing over him, a grin on her face.

•   •   •

On the way home from the hospital, Eddy asked if Gayle would drive past the church. At first, she pretended not to hear him. He asked again. The corners of her mouth tightened. "Is that necessary?"

"No, it's not necessary, but I'd like to go by anyway."

226

She headed into town. When she stopped at the light across from the church, she saw Sam staring out the pharmacy window. "Hey, look." Gayle leaned on the horn several times until Sam looked up, confused. Then he started waving his arms back and forth over his head, as if a war had just been won. Eddy lifted himself to get a glimpse of his old friend. Gayle pulled around the corner as Sam strode across the street to meet them.

Gayle pushed a button and the door beside Eddy eased open and the ramp slid out like a tongue.

"Very impressive," said Sam. "Welcome to the club." His eyes and Eddy's locked briefly. When Sam and Marianne had grudgingly conceded that Jamie's progress had plateaued far sooner than they'd hoped, Eddy had gone with Sam to buy their first wheelchair van. It was too much for Marianne who had gone to bed for nearly a week. "They sure have come a long way…Permission to come aboard, sir."

"Permission granted."

There was an air of celebration among the three of them that lasted for a few minutes. Smiles became difficult to sustain. "Better get back," said Sam.

•   •   •

Gayle cruised slowly down the street as Eddy craned his neck. The right side of Jesus the Consoler's body was decimated at the collarbone, a jagged crater left behind. Workers had long since piled the rubble in a corner of the church lot. With a law suit under consideration, nothing had been done to repair the statue. In ways that Eddy couldn't explain, he grieved the damage done to the Consoler more than he grieved his own. Neither would ever be the same again. "Can you park the van?" he said.

•   •   •

Peter had visited Eddy every day while he was in the hospital. He prayed over him. He sat silently in the corner while Eddy slept. He tried to comfort Gayle but she was immune to his efforts. Peter wanted to explain how dismayed the church was, but Eddy was in too much pain to hear anything he had to say and Gayle was too angry.

When he wasn't at the hospital, Peter often sat in the church sanctuary alone, praying, thinking. What did it mean? Why had it happened? Was it simply the result of a flaw in the marble that had worsened over the years? Or did it indicate something more? He had encouraged Eddy to pray. Prayer would give him strength, endurance, hope. He had not anticipated that Eddy would transform the delicate flower of prayer into a cudgel, a club to beat God into submission, to wrest from the Almighty a personal reward.

He never believed that Gayle had been saved by Eddy's prayers to Jesus the Consoler. But he never challenged Eddy's belief. He'd learned that it was unwise to question true believers, those special few whose wholehearted devotion, delicate as a glass menagerie, could be reduced to shards by a someone with challenging doubts, someone such as him.

And yet, it was true. Gayle had, by all accounts, been healed. He'd seen her himself. There wasn't even a remnant of disease. She looked vibrant, stalwart, younger even. It had happened, just as Eddy had prayed.

And the cost? The price for challenging God, for forcing God's hand? Eddy would never walk again. Eddy would never be free of pain again. Peter didn't dare believe in such a God. The statue's collapse had to be the fault of the sculptor. It had to be the fault of the minister who refused to send it back decades ago, to replace it with something perfect, something unblemished, unmarred, unbroken. Eddy's fall was not the act of an arrogant God. It was bad luck. It had to be.

Peter had led a church campaign to raise money to help Eddy and Gayle. Several of the Trustees had enthusiastically supported this effort. One, speaking candidly, said, "Perhaps he will, well, perhaps Mr. Kimes will not feel litigious when he sees how much the congregation cares." Peter went to the hospital and presented them a check for seven thousand, six hundred and twenty-four dollars.

"We don't want your money, Peter." Eddy's face seemed full of grace. Or was it exhaustion, bewilderment?

Gayle reached for the envelope in Peter's hand. "Thank you, reverend."

Eddy opened the van door so he could listen to the birds nesting in the holly. Gayle leaned on the arm rest and didn't speak. He closed his eyes, remembering. He could still see Rich's face as they sat on the bench talking. It felt good to be doing a project together, father and son. He knew Rich was skeptical about the statue and the miracle. But Eddy appreciated his willingness to stand by his father, to pitch in, to help him give something back in response to how much he had received.

The work was tedious. Their arms and shoulders knotted and ached as they reached the final stages. But the results gave them energy. The statue's brilliance was breathtaking. The reward made everything they'd done seem effortless, in retrospect, the soreness they felt seem soothing, gentle.

Eddy could see it in Rich's face. His eyes bright with innocent expectation. Something he hadn't seen since he was a boy and Eddy was a new father.

Eddy opened his eyes and looked at Jesus's face again. There was no smile to debate about any longer. There was only an empty stare. He shook his head. When he was lying on the ground, he saw pieces of the statue scattered all around him. Then, with Jesus's cold hand on his face, he knew. He had destroyed it. He was the one.

"Ready to go, honey?" said Gayle, trying not to sound impatient. Eddy's eyes were on the statue, or what he could see of it. He wanted to go into the garden. But she refused, saying it would be too difficult to navigate. Although his dejection was obvious, he felt too weak to argue with her.

If she had gone into the garden with Eddy, she might have smashed what remained of Jesus the Consoler. When she had reached the hospital, Eddy was already in surgery. She found Rich in the family waiting area, hunched in a chair. "What happened?" she said.

"I don't know." Rich had lifted his hands and let them drop. "We were almost done." He opened his mouth and closed it again. "I mean, I was standing on the ground and Dad was polishing Jesus's head. He was so proud of how it looked. I was, like, let's just keep going; it'd been a long day. He told me to go ahead with the bottom part, so I did. Next thing, I hear, like, these sharp blasts, like lightning hitting a tree or something, and I look up and there he is falling like a rock. His face looked confused. And then the goddam statue, it just crumbled into a million pieces. All of it on Dad. I couldn't get to him in time." His voice cracked and he covered his eyes.

"It wasn't your fault, Rich. You know that. The statue was defective from the beginning."

"I know."

But was it his fault? Should Rich have been the one lying under the rubble of Jesus? He was the one with the dark secret. He was the one with a stain, not his father. He thought of Jamie. Why hadn't he told Sam that there was nothing but malice in what he'd done? Sam had forgiven him. Rich stayed silent and walked away. And now this.

When he talked to Sandy about it, she'd taken his side. "Don't be ridiculous, Richie. You went to Sam's house. You told him you were the one that caused Jamie's brain damage, for chrissakes. You took responsibility. You didn't even have to. And you know what? Who's to say it was you? You heard what he said—everyone hit him; everyone thought they did it. No one knows, Richie. That's the truth— No one knows."

Rich was unconvinced.

· · ·

Gayle placed cups, cream, sugar and a carafe of coffee on the porch table. She poured a cup for Eddy. Sandy and Rich followed. Eddy commented on the yard, how much work there was to do and who he would get to do it. Rich offered. "Yard work? You?" said Sandy. Everyone laughed. "I'll take you up on that," said Eddy. "You're on," said Rich.

It was quiet for a moment. Eddy nodded at Sandy and Rich: "Well, you two called this summit. What's up?"

Rich and Sandy looked at each other. Rich said, "I guess we're curious, you know, about how things are going, that sort of thing; what your plans are about the accident; whether you've given it any thought.

"It was a terrible thing, what happened, Dad, and I know a lot of people who've said you deserve something for it, for your suffering. We thought maybe it had been long enough that you and Mom may have…"

Eddy had taken his last sip of coffee. "Can I have another, honey?" Gayle poured another cup and topped off her own.

"Anyone want more? I can make some?"

"No, that's okay," said Sandy. "I'm fine." She looked at Rich. "We're both fine." She wanted to say more but didn't.

Eddy stirred his coffee but didn't take a sip. "What you're asking is, are we going to sue?"

CHAPTER 35

"Eddy, I want to talk to you about something." Gayle was putting the dinner dishes into the washer.

"What's that?" He didn't want to know.

"Our finances." She hit the start button.

"Not now, okay?"

This had been weeks ago.

"We've got to talk about this, Eddy. We can't ignore it." But ignore it, he did.

His hopes had been high after Gayle got her news. The future, closed tight for so long, was reopening. A miracle had given them their lives back. The road ahead was full of promise.

Then the catastrophe. Could it have happened at a worse time? More medical bills. More debt. The pile was so high they needed Sherpas to reach the top.

At one point, Rich had said, "I'm sorry to ask, Dad, but what are you and Mom living on?" Good question. "I mean, Mom has her business, but that's what, three, four months out of the year, right?"

Eddy stared at his son.

"I know, it's probably none of my business…"

When Eddy hadn't disagreed, Rich backed off. What Rich hadn't known was that his father's silence was a show of ignorance, not offence.

He had never been the money person in the family. Gayle started paying their bills the first month after they married. It worked. Things moved along. They bought a house. Had children. Vacations. Never missed a mortgage payment. She started doing taxes, which added moneys to the coffer. How much, he didn't know. He didn't need to know, so long as things went well. He seldom asked about money matters, because when he did, his eyes glazed over ten minutes into Gayle's explanation. She was better at it, plain and simple.

All the more reason to be suspicious when she brought up the tender topic of their financial standing. There could only be one reason for this: We are going down the tubes at lightning speed. Did he need to know this right now? Would it matter that much if they waited just a few weeks (maybe months) longer; time enough to get his head together, to figure out what normal might look like in the middle of so much abnormality?

There was only one plausible source of money. "Payday Ahead for Injured Man?" one headline blared. They had received plenty of calls from personal injury lawyers, including some TV favorites: "You waiting for the other side to do the right thing? (a choir in ruby red robes begins to laugh in harmony); Don't hold your breath! WE'LL FORCE THOSE (Bleep) TO DO THE RIGHT THING...OR ELSE!" He knew Gayle was fuming over what had happened. She blamed the church, but she never brought up suing. She didn't urge him to do anything, one way or the other.

He appreciated her giving him room to think. It made sense to sue. Even Peter privately told him that he had grounds. A thorough examination of the statue found that the notch was much more than a minor imperfection. "Yeah, it looked like a long narrow snake hole that stretched from Jesus's shoulder blade, through his chest, to what looked like a pool of water in his lower left abdomen. Water works slowly, but it always wins." Peter had wiped his face with a handkerchief. "The statue should never have been placed."

"You should definitely sue their asses off," said Sam over a Heineken on his back patio. Jamie sat nearby, watching the neighbor's corgis. "What's Gayle think?"

"I haven't asked and she hasn't said. She wants to talk about our finances, though." Eddy sighed and stared at his beer.

"Sounds like she wants a decision about a lawsuit. How else can you survive this thing? Who knows, if you get one of those mean-assed TV shysters, you might be able to get enough to pay off all your medical debts." Eddy took a sip of beer and put the glass down. "What's the matter? This isn't rocket science, Eddy. It's pretty simple. Sue for negligence. Listen to your minister. Eye for an eye."

Sam pulled his Bills ballcap down to shade his eyes. He glanced at Jamie. "Look, Eddy, do you think Marianne and I could have made it without some help? Our lawyer raised questions about practice safety, sufficiency of protective gear, a bunch of things. We settled very quietly with the school district. Didn't make us rich; didn't bring our Jamie back; didn't stop Marianne...But I'm still using interest off a trust fund to help take care of him. Let's face it, your 'accident' was even more blatant. It should never have happened, period."

"I know. I know."

"So?"

"I don't know."

What was he supposed to say? If it hadn't been for the statue, Gayle would probably be dead by now. He'd be alone. His life would be all but over. Instead, Gayle was back to a hundred percent. He couldn't remember her looking so good. There's no denying that he's a mess and will be a mess for the rest of his life. But he's alive, right? That statue could have fallen six inches one way or the other and he might be dead. But it didn't; and he's not.

He'd called one of those TV lawyers, the ones with the phone numbers that are all the same digit. Eddy didn't even have to meet the representative face-to-face. He described what happened and before he could finish his story, the guy said, "Geez, I've heard this a million times. Churches trying to avoid responsibility for anything that happens on their property. They always claim it was an 'act of God'." He scoffed at this. "Come on! That doesn't fly in the real world. Look, I'm telling you, if you sue them, their insurance company will settle in a hurry, and not only will your hospital bills disappear, you'll be living on easy street, if you get my meaning."

Eddy got his meaning, but he wasn't sure he liked it. Was gutting the church the right thing to do? It wasn't like they put up the statue knowing it was going to collapse someday. They acted in good faith. But good faith doesn't prevent disasters. Sometimes they happen no matter what your intentions are.

"What kind of crazy are you?" Sam didn't understand Eddy's reasoning. "They should have paid attention to that thing. They should have known it was faulty. But the Ruling whatever-they-call-themselves gave you the all clear, without ever checking. That is total negligence on their part. If we hadn't sued, Jamie would be in some state-run shithole right now. You've got to protect yourself. No one else will, Eddy. No one else can possibly care about you and much as you do."

"You're right, you're right," said Eddy. He understood Sam's fury. His son's life had been taken away, and Sam had been left to witness it every day of his life. He would have felt the same if something had happened to Rich or Sandy, but it hadn't. It had happened to him. That made it different. He had gone to the church to clean the statue as a way of saying thank you. The statue cracked and fell on him. Who could have predicted that? It just happened. Terrible outcome, for sure; but anyone's fault, not so sure.

Money remained an Empire State Building sized problem. If she argued for suing the church, he didn't know how he could resist her reasoning. She understood their plight better than him. He girded his loins and sat down with Gayle in her office. It smelled of cardboard boxes and stale air, of metal cabinets and ink cartridges. She sat at her desk with a pile of manila folders in front of her and a spreadsheet opened on the computer screen. 'Not the spreadsheet', he thought. Eddy sat to the side, like an elementary student about to be tutored by his teacher.

She took a breath and was about to speak.

Eddy jumped in. "Look, honey, I don't have any folders, nothing, I don't have a good argument for not suing the church. The whole thing happened on their property. Jesus the Consoler turned out to be defective. We desperately need the money. It all lines up. It all makes sense."

He stopped. Gayle wasn't looking at him. She wasn't listening. Instead, she was organizing sheet after sheet of bank statements while scrolling through the data on her screen. She cleared her throat.

"I'm sorry, Eddy, what were you saying."

"I know you think we should sue. It makes the most sense—"

"You don't want to sue. I get it. I'm not sure I completely understand it, but I get it. So, we won't." She soft shrugged.

"What?"

"Look at this."

Gayle began explaining all the papers and numbers. She did it in a whispery voice as if she were afraid someone might be listening. At first, he wasn't paying attention because he was digesting what she'd just said.

"Eddy, are you listening to me?"

"Yes."

She started again to explain how they could make it through all their financial problems; how, in fact, they didn't have any financial problems, if they were careful, that is.

"What are you talking about?"

She slowed down, enunciating every word clearly, stopping at the end of each sentence, leaning back in her chair silently as she punctuated each paragraph, letting Eddy catch up to what she had been doing and how long she'd been doing it.

"Are you saying what I think you're saying?"

She looked at him without a blink. "Yes."

"But isn't that—"

"Shh, just listen."

CHAPTER 36

"Well, suing looks like the only option," said Sandy, echoing Rich. "I mean, it makes total sense. They should have to pay. And you guys, I'm assuming you need the money, right?

Rich and I could help out some, but not as much as we'd like to. We think a suit would be wise. It's not selfish. It would be, well…just, fair." She looked at Rich.

"Yeah, you deserve a little justice for what you've been through. I mean, Dad, look at you. Don't take it wrong, but, you know, you're not the same anymore. You've got this constant pain and it's hard to get around and you can't do the things you like, you know, working in the garden, that sort of thing, and we think that someone should be held to account for this." He looked at his mother. "Mom?"

Gayle looked at Eddy and then back at Rich. She exhaled heavily through her nose. "I agree that what happened to your father is awful." She cleared her throat. "I mean, I hate to see your dad in this, this situation, this condition, it isn't right. It isn't fair. It's…" Gayle gazed across the backyard at her neighbor's above ground swimming pool, still covered.

"It's what, Mom?" said Sandy.

"I don't know." Gayle reached for Eddy's hand. Eddy squeezed hard. They looked at each other, unsure of what else to say. "I don't think your dad is inclined to sue anyone."

Rich shook his head. Why was Dad so passive? So...weak? He wanted to say something, but he knew that if he opened his mouth, a torrent of incoherent ranting would flood out. He bit the inside of his cheeks, trying to control a twitch that was shifting into overdrive.

He looked at Sandy, whose mouth hung slightly open.

"Dad, for real? You've got to be kidding." Her arms stiffened.

Eddy glanced at Gayle who nodded imperceptibly, as if to say, 'Go ahead'.

"A law suit is off the table. We're not going to do that."

"But why?" said Sandy.

"I know this isn't the majority opinion in the family, but if it wasn't for that statue, or God, or whatever, your mother wouldn't be sitting here today."

"Jesus, Dad—" said Rich.

"Anyway, it's not necessary. Your mother and I aren't on the brink of financial collapse."

"But—"

"Your father and I have gone over everything, all our finances. We'll be fine."

"How's that possible? You have tens of thousands in medical bills alone. Dad's got no job and won't be able to work again. No offense, Dad. And Mom, doing taxes, that's not going to be enough." Sandy's lower back ached. "Really."

Eddy and Gayle's eyes locked. What was Eddy to say? 'Not to worry; we've got plenty of money; your mom's been stealing from her clients for years. Everything will be fine.'

"I'm not stealing from my clients. Don't be ridiculous." Gayle had been offended when he first said this. Her devotion to her clients would never allow her to do something so heinous as to cheat them. She always played it safe and sound. She knew the laws inside and out. And all the quirks that arose with changes each year. She got them every penny they deserved and never cut any corners. As she had explained to Eddy, she'd been audited five times without any problem whatsoever. "The auditors know me. They trust me."

Eddy couldn't speak. 'Who was this woman?' he thought. What had she been doing tucked away in her office all these years?

"So, who are you stealing from?"

"The government."

"Jesus Christ, you can't be serious."

"They'll never miss it. It's like a grain of sand on the beach; a tiny ripple on the ocean; a few pennies hidden under trillions upon trillions of dollars; it's like—"

"Enough, enough." Eddy wheeled back and forth in her tiny office, his hands tearing at the wheel rims, his head down.

"Just a few hundred dollars here; a few hundred dollars there."

Eddy stopped. "Okay, okay, that's not so bad. You're right, that's nothing, really." His face brightened; he rubbed his hands together. "Pocket change, right? But how's that—?"

"Well."

"Well, what?"

"Not exactly pocket change."

Gayle encouraged him to pull up to her desk again. She asked him to take three deep breaths and to let them out slowly. Then take three more. She told him that once he'd done that, she would explain everything.

"Have you ever noticed how I mail everyone's tax forms for them?"

"Yes. I'm the one that carries the boxes to the Post Office."

"Okay, so I do that for a reason."

"And the reason is…"

"For one, it's a nice service. Second, once they sign their return, I make a few changes here and there."

"Oh Jesus God."

"I punch up a deduction here and an expense there; a few donations here, some credits there. Nothing radical. I'm not stupid. Like I said, I change the refund by about two-three hundred dollars. I never go much higher than that; sometimes a little lower. So, for instance, let's say my client is supposed to get two thousand dollars back. My changes raise that to twenty-three hundred. You with me?"

Eddy stared.

"The IRS deposits the two thousand in the client's account and sends me a check for three hundred. Like it's my fee."

"But haven't they already paid you."

"Of course."

"So…the three hundred is…"

"Is a little something from the IRS. See it's not a lot."

Eddy thought about it and again convinced himself it wasn't a big deal. He thought about the millionaires and billionaires who out and out cheat the government each year. What's three hundred dollars. A grain of sand. A ripple. A penny.

"Okay, I get it. Still sounds like pocket change."

"Well…"

"It's not like you're doing this to everyone, right?"

Gayle was suddenly busy with the papers in front of her.

"Gayle? It's not like you do this to everyone."

She grimaced and then fell back in her swivel chair. "Not at first."

"Oh my God, you're doing this to everyone. You're right. We won't have to worry about money in the future because we'll be living at the Hotel Attica. Jesus!"

"Come on, don't be ridiculous. I've been doing this for a long time—"

"A long time. What's 'a long time'?"

"Maybe twenty-five years. Give or take."

"Oh, just twenty-five years. Let me see…so that's basically from the goddam beginning."

"Not exactly the beginning. A little while after."

Eddy leaned over and banged his head methodically on Gayle's desk top.

"Eddy!"

"My God, Gayle. Everyone. Twenty-five years." He squinted until his eyes were slits. "How much money are we talking about?"

Gayle opened her desk drawer and pulled out her calculator. "Let's see. Three hundred dollars…roughly three hundred…twenty-five…" She was quiet for a minute as she redid the numbers several times. She leaned back in her chair, her hands entwined in front of her face. "About two point five, give or take."

"Two point five what?"

"Million. Two point five million. Give or take."

"Give or take." Eddy laid his head between his limp arms on Gayle's desk. "What in the world got into you? Have we ever been desolate, poverty stricken, homeless, for chrissake?" He lifted his head. "What made you do this?"

Gayle was ready for this question although she'd hoped Eddy wouldn't ask.

"Honey, you remember the past differently than I do. At times it was harder than you ever realized. I kept things from you and maybe I shouldn't have."

Eddy's face was a puzzle piece.

"After the first time you were laid off, it was, well, let's say it was a struggle. The kids were young. My business was small. I started it for something to do, that was all. I started doing more taxes and picked up some bookkeeping. And we made it through. I figured that was that. I didn't try hard to grow the business once you were back working. But a couple of years later, you were laid off again. For even longer. And it scared me. Was this going to be the way it goes? We were going backwards instead of forwards."

Eddy hung his head.

"Don't get me wrong. When you were working, everything was good. But every time the business was sold and you were laid off, we went back to square one. So, I got an idea." She shrugged as if to say, 'And that was that'.

Eddy's face got cloudy. "I'm sorry."

"This is why I hoped I'd never have to tell you. I knew you'd think you did something wrong. You didn't. I worry, that's all. And I'm glad I do. Who would have thought we'd be in the predicament we're in? Right?" Gayle got up from her chair and went to Eddy, putting her arms around him, kissing his cheek.

Eddy couldn't escape the fact that Gayle was right. He lived squarely in the moment. She was always out-front doing reconnaissance work on what was coming. He turned his head and kissed her cheek. "Thank you." He kissed her cheek again.

Gayle pulled up another chair. She sat and leaned forward so she could put her hands on his knees. "There's more."

"Jesus."

In the beginning she opened several accounts in local banks, trying to keep the sums small so they wouldn't attract undue attention. But as the flow of money became a river, she needed a more discrete way to handle things. She researched Swiss banks and found one that, how should she put it, specialized in protecting its clients' identities.

"Do you want to know how this works?"

"I guess."

"Do you want the movie length version or the tweet."

"Tweet."

"Okay, mainly the goal is to keep the money invisible. So, it's always on the move, place to place, bank to bank, Switzerland to the Bahamas to the Caymans. Final destination is New York. It comes in drips and drabs, nothing suspicious. No one ever sees more than the tip of the iceberg."

'Tip of the iceberg', thought Eddy, 'what kind of talk is this?'

"This is a joke, right? I mean, you sound like a Grisham novel or something. How could you have done this without me knowing?"

"You had enough to deal with."

"We're going to get caught. This stuff never works out. Plus, it's wrong, right?"

"Well, it depends on how you look at it. I look at it as putting my family first."

"How did you ever…"

"Very DIY, believe me."

Eddy's head slumped again. He wrung his hands. 'I shouldn't have told him,' thought Gayle. It would probably have been enough to say she'd worked something out. He never wanted to know the details. On the other hand, why should she carry the load alone?

"Look, Eddy, I need you…I need you to work with me. We have to be a team. The future depends on us being able to do this." She sounded like a kindergarten teacher explaining why a five-year-old should use the potty.

Eddy blinked repeatedly as he tried to revamp his understanding of Gayle. How could he have not recognized this part of her? It was as if he'd just found out there were fifty-seven states. How could that be possible? How could he have missed something so obvious, so large?

"Is my name on any of these accounts?"

"When I was diagnosed, I had your name put on the accounts with mine."

"How is that possible? Don't you have to sign something to do that? I mean, I didn't sign anything."

"Yes, you did. You signed them all."

"I did?"

"Yes."

"How?"

"I gave you forms and you signed them. Not all at once."

"Did you tell me what they were for?"

"I told you they were 'paper work'."

"'Paper work'. That was all it took. What if we get caught?"

"I've been doing this for a long time. If we're cautious and don't do anything out of the ordinary, we'll be fine."

"And if you're wrong."

"Then we won't be fine."

Eddy gulped but swallowed nothing. "Bonnie and Clyde, huh."

"No bank robberies. No guns."

•   •   •

After meeting with their parents about the lawsuit idea, Sandy and Rich met up at Tim Horton's. They stirred creamer into their coffees. They took bites of their crullers. They wiped their mouths. They looked at each other with raised eyebrows.

"What the hell was that all about?"

"I have no idea," said Sandy.

"You ever heard about them getting an inheritance before?"

"Never."

"I mean, what the fuck. Grandma Kimes was a secretary and Grandpa was a traveling salesman. I don't remember them having money."

"And what was that rigmarole about keeping it a secret, saving it for a rainy day, hoping we would be the ones to get the money, apologizing for needing to use it now?"

"They can't lie for shit. I don't know what the whole performance was about. They were pretty insistent that they had money, though, that they didn't need our help, that they had everything under control."

More cruller. Sips of coffee. Shifting in their plastic chairs.

"You know, Dad's never been the money person," said Sandy. "It's just not who he is. He's a work-hard kind of guy. Not a planner."

"What are you saying?"

"If something's going on, it's got to be Mom."

"Like?"

"I don't know. Her tax business, I mean, do you know anything about it?"

"Not really."

"Me neither. And why is that? It's like, she's been doing it for as long as I can remember, but I don't know anything about what she does, really."

"What's the mystery? She does taxes. She must be doing okay."

"Yeah. You're probably right. Who knows?"

CHAPTER 37

When nothing untoward happened during the ensuing eight months, Eddy started breathing sighs of relief. Maybe their house of cards was stronger than he thought. From time to time, he'd ask Gayle how everything was going and she'd say things like, "They're going." It had been months since Gayle had given him any 'paper work' to sign, so he assumed everything was quiet.

As for the mountainous medical bills, they'd worked out a payment plan that was manageable. It amounted to a second mortgage. On a much larger house.

•   •   •

Peter was an unanticipated causality of the statue disaster. Members of the congregation were trickling away, unable to make peace with what had happened and how it reflected on the church. Eventually, the Ruling Elders asked him to seek a calling elsewhere.

"This is ridiculous," Eddy had said when they met in the garden one last time. The statue's debris was still piled in a corner near the bushes, covered by a gray tarp, a shovel on top to prevent the wind from blowing the tarp away. Jesus the Consoler was less magnificent now, his one arm sticking out like he was signaling to make a turn at a traffic light. Eddy still saw something in his face, though. An everlasting something that he couldn't define. His brokenness made him somehow more sacred, like he'd made it through a crucible and, though permanently damaged, he'd survived, his determined, graceful gaze intact.

"It's fine, really. Time runs out. You move on."

"Where will you go?"

Peter was moving to New Jersey where he'd accepted a chaplaincy at a cancer center.

"Something different. A challenge. Trying to bring comfort, meaning, to people whose lives…well, you know what I mean. You've been through it all."

Peter's face was drawn, the lines deeper, his words unconvincing. He was a man in retreat.

"I'm sorry." Eddy took a long, slow breath, holding back his tears. "You know, Peter, I'm a different person because of you. Thank you. I'll miss you."

They promised to text and email and message, but as Eddy headed back to the car, he knew it was the last time he would hear from his friend.

•   •   •

Eddy's wheelchair sat in a corner of the basement. He hadn't used it at all in recent weeks. Rehab had been a godsend, much to his surprise. It wasn't that he could walk normally. That would never happen again. But his legs were more stalwart now, his good leg sturdy as an oak. He found that if he wore a boot on his "dead foot" and stabilized himself with a cane, he could stand and even walk, if haltingly. Sometimes the pain made him break out in a sweat, but even that had subsided as he'd gotten stronger.

The first time he walked at the rehab center, Gayle had burst into tears. Rich and Sandy came by that evening with a cake that said, "Rise and Shine." He was pleased, especially since the wedding was fast approaching. If he was going to do this thing, he wanted to do it standing.

•   •   •

"I don't want to spend all my time in front of a computer screen." It wasn't that work was going poorly. Everyone at the hospital loved

Rich. They appreciated his expertise and praised his talent. He realized that he was excellent at something that was meaningless to him.

Sandy had tried to convince him otherwise. "You can't possibly be that good at something if you don't get something out of it. I think you're just going through a slump of some kind. Give it some time. You'll pull out of it."

But he didn't. A few months later, he told Sandy that he was planning to leave his position. He'd saved a little money and had quietly picked up a few side gigs to help him if things got lean.

This time Sandy wasn't surprised. He'd been quiet, withdrawn for weeks. Even the quality of his work was beginning to slip. "What are you going to do?"

Rich's cheek began to sputter at the question. His mouth went dry and no matter how much he tried to breathe deep and slow, he couldn't. "Well, I've been accepted into, uh, into a program, a thing...I've been accepted into a social work program."

Sandy skillfully managed the seismic disruption she felt inside. Her face was expressionless for a few short seconds. "My God, Richie, that's, that's so different."

Rich explained that in each of his jobs, the greatest reward came from how well he connected with others. Maybe he could do something with that. The more he thought about it, the more he realized that he wanted to help people, as trite as that sounded. Social work seemed to fit the bill. He punctuated his announcement with a self-effacing shrug of one shoulder.

'This is about Jamie', thought Sandy. He's still working through what happened. He still blames himself. He's trying to redeem himself, even though, in her mind, he didn't need to.

"Richie...I think that's perfect. I think you'd be great at it."

When it became clear that he wasn't going to make enough money doing time-limited consulting, Eddy and Gayle stepped in, gifting him enough money from the "inheritance" to pay for most of his education and some to live on.

•   •   •

"How about over there?" Sandy pointed to a booth.

The hostess escorted them, leaving two menus behind. "Good to see you ladies again," she said.

"Thanks," said Gayle. They took off their coats and piled them in the corner. "I don't even have to open the menu." They laughed as their server arrived with a pot of coffee. They both reached for sweetener and tiny containers of a cream flavored fluid.

"You two look great," she said. "The usual?"

Gayle and Sandy shook their heads.

Sandy watched her mother closely, looking for signs, hints that the cancer was on the move again. Her shoulders relaxed each time her detective work yielded nothing.

It was her mother's idea that they get together for breakfast once a week. "Some girl time" she called it. Sandy loved the feeling of not only being a daughter, but a friend. She wouldn't admit it, but she felt grownup, maybe for the first time.

They talked about the weather, about her work, about her mom's business, about the news, about Rich's school work, about her dad. The conversations were easy flowing. She never tightened up like she used to. She felt comfortable with her mother and comfortable in her own skin.

Sometimes they talked about what had been done to them, what both of them had endured. Along the way, Sandy had even found the courage to talk about Chicago. Most of the time, though, they just talked. It was the sound of their voices together that mattered most. Sandy knew that that was the reason they held fast to this routine. They were healing, not only through words, but through the sacrament of being with each other, through the sacredness of knowing each other deeply.

"I've made up my mind," said Sandy.

"What have you decided?"

"I contacted a lawyer."

"In Chicago?"

"Yes. I'm going to sue Venus's Flytrap."

The server came by and topped off their cups.

"That's good." Gayle reached across the table and took Sandy's hand in hers. "I'll go with you."

· · ·

"Why January?" asked Eddy as he shifted in his wheelchair to ease the pain. Sam leaned on the pharmacy counter.

"Why not January? It's as good a time as any. The darkest season could use a little livening up, right?"

It took barely six weeks before Sam proposed to Rhonda. Her mouth fell open and her eyes widened making her forehead wrinkle like an accordion. "Well," she said.

"I mean this, Rhonda. I love you. Take your time. Think about it."

Both wondered the same thing. Would this precipitate a tailspin, an emotional nosedive? Two weeks later, Rhonda was sitting in her car waiting for the defrost to kick in, when she realized she was still the same; she wasn't changing; she was neither high nor low; she was just right. She called the pharmacy. Nellie told her that Sam couldn't come to the phone. Did she have a message? "Nellie, please right this down....write 'Yes, Rhonda'."

Eddy grinned at his friend. "And liven it up, you will."

Sam didn't smile. "Look, Eddy, you know as well as I do that there's no way to guess what's coming down the track. Looking back on our lives, how many of the most important things that happened, how many of them could we have predicted? Damn few. I still can't believe she said 'yes'. I want to make this happen before something comes along to mess it up. If I've learned anything, it's this: Waiting is for fools."

. . .

The sun had a low, hazy chill to it on Saturday January 18 at noon. Sam had rented the Fireman's Exempt for the ceremony and the reception, which was catered by the Ladies Auxiliary. Rhonda rounded up some of her friends to run streamers across the ceiling and hang clusters of balloons in all the corners. There were twenty round linen-covered tables closely arranged in a three-deep arc, leaving room for the DJ and a modest dance floor.

Rhonda's sister, Patricia, from Peoria, was the maid-of-honor. She paid for the pink rose bouquets and the three-tiered carrot cake. Several retired firefighters arranged standing heaters throughout the hall, anticipating a high of only ten degrees at ceremony time.

Eddy and Sam were quarantined in a meeting room while guests arrived. Sam sat on the edge of a table, his leg dangling. He whistled and looked at the awards hung on the wall. Eddy paced back and forth, if only in his mind. His mouth was dry. He took sip after sip from a bottle of water, then feared he'd have to pee halfway through the ceremony.

Jamie sat in his wheel chair beside his father. He wore a black tux with a red vest and red bow tie. Rhonda had washed his hair and cut it. Sam combed it before they left. "Big day; you ready?" he'd said to Jamie. He'd never seen his son look so much like a man.

Eddy heard the music start. "Okay, that's our cue." He opened the door and with his cane in one hand and a boot on his bad foot, he took a step, then leaned on his pretty good leg, took another step, then leaned, and another and another until he reached the music stand where he placed his notes. Sam followed, pushing his best man into place. He winked at Eddy. Eddy looked at Gayle who finally exhaled. Rich and Sandy gave him thumbs up.

Everyone stood as the maid-of-honor, then the bride entered the room. Rhonda was beautiful in a tea length, diamond white dress adorned with delicate lace. It had a modest V-neck and a deep-cut back. "Whoa," breathed Sam.

Eddy's notes shook in his cold, clammy hands. He said things to Sam, then he said things to Rhonda. He asked them questions. They spoke vows to each other. Rhonda got the ring from Patricia, who pretended at first not to have it. Most of the people laughed. Sam took the ring from Jamie's thumb and placed it on Rhonda's finger. Most of the people sighed.

"I now pronounce you husband and wife. You may kiss." Sam kissed Rhonda, and held her so long that people began to titter. Rhonda and Sam then kneeled by Jamie and embraced him. Everyone reached for tissues.

•　　•　　•

"Did Sam say where they were going for their honeymoon, Eddy?" Gayle was still in her robe and slippers as they settled in for a relaxing breakfast.

"Italy."

"Wow, that sounds great."

"Yeah, he said they were flying into Rome, staying there for several days; then they're taking a train to Florence for several days, including an overnight at a vineyard in Tuscany."

"My goodness."

"Then onto Venice."

"I've always wanted to go to Italy."

Eddy balled his napkin and dropped it on the table. "There's no reason we can't go."

"It's just a dream, Eddy."

"Look, I can work it out. I can. We'll get those private guides or whatever. I know that other 'handicapped' (he said this with air quotes) people travel. I'm sure of it."

Gayle took a bite of her melon. "Okay."

"I'm not kidding."

The morning sun shone on Gayle's face as she reached for the newspaper. She opened it to shield herself from the glare. Eddy buttered his wheat toast, slipped some scrambled eggs onto one corner and took a bite. Quiet filled the room for several minutes.

"So, what's in the news today?" said Eddy.

"The fires in Australia are still out of control." Gayle's face was scrunched with concern. "Just awful."

"I can't imagine."

Gayle looked up. "Bunch of stories about the impeachment. Want me to—"

"No thanks. What else?"

"Shooting in the city...someone drove the wrong direction on 490...Cuomo and the budget...snow storm coming...two new restaurants opening on Park Ave..."

Eddy picked at a tooth with his fingernail. "Hm. Maybe we could try them out."

Gayle turned the page and folded it in half. "Conference championships tomorrow."

"Doesn't matter. The Bills are long gone."

"Next year, right?"

Eddy held up two pairs of crossed fingers.

Gayle scanned the news briefs across the bottom of the page. "Says here that there's a new flu outbreak…"

"Where?"

"Let me see…someplace in China. Wu-something."

"Never heard of it." He balanced more egg on his toast and took another bite. "Did we get our flu shots already?"

"Yeah, at Walgreen's, remember? Last fall."

Eddy shook his head. "If you say so."

Gayle put down the paper and sipped her lukewarm coffee. Eddy chuckled and took another bite of his toast and eggs.

"What?"

"Just so there's nothing in there about an IRS investigation of some kind, you know?"

"Come on, Eddy. There's nothing to worry about."

"Okay, okay."

Gayle rolled her eyes and slid the paper across the table.

"No thanks. I'm good," said Eddy.

ABOUT THE AUTHOR

Broken Pieces of God is David B. Seaburn's eighth novel. He was a Finalist for the National Indie Excellence Award in General Fiction (2011), placed second in the TAZ Awards for Fiction (2017), was short listed for the Somerset Award (2018), was an American Book Fest Finalist for "Best Book" in General Fiction (2019), and a Semi-Finalist in Literary, Contemporary and Satire Fiction for the Somerset Award (2019). Seaburn lives with his wife near Rochester, NY. They have two married daughters and four wonderful grandchildren.

Note from the Author

Word-of-mouth is crucial for any author to succeed. If you enjoyed *Broken Pieces of God*, please leave a review online—anywhere you are able. Even if it's just a sentence or two. It would make all the difference and would be very much appreciated.

Thanks!
David B. Seaburn

Thank you so much for reading one of David B. Seaburn's novels. If you enjoyed the experience, please check out our recommended title for your next great read!

Gavin Goode

"[Seaburn] does a good job of tracking the myriad ways that the different players react to the tragedy."

–KIRKUS REVIEWS

CPSIA information can be obtained
at www.ICGtesting.com
Printed in the USA
BVHW071453140921
616731BV00001B/32

9 781684 337644